PRINCESS OF ZAMIBIA

DELANEY DIAMOND

GARDEN AVENUE PRESS

Princess of Zamibia by Delaney Diamond

Copyright © 2018, Delaney Diamond

Garden Avenue Press

Atlanta, Georgia

ISBN: 978-1-940636-59-7 (Ebook edition)

ISBN: 978-1-940636-66-5 (Paperback edition)

1

Crown Prince Kofi Francois Karunzika, Conquering Lion of the tribe of Mbutu, heir to the throne of the West African nation of Zamibia, descended the royal plane onto the tarmac. He buttoned his coat, eyes narrowing against the cold weather as his four-man security detail marched with him to the waiting SUV.

He climbed into the back of the vehicle, while one member of his security climbed in the front and the others took a car that would follow. His assistant had arrived a day early and was sitting in the back seat.

"Where is she now?" he asked Kemal, a tall man with skin the color of licorice. A strip of blue-dyed hair ran down the middle of his head. Many of the Ndenga people—a tribe that lived on the coast of Zamibia—wore the decorative flourish as a sense of pride and a symbol of their affinity to the ocean.

"She's still at work. She should be leaving soon to pick up the child and go home." Kemal handed over the most recent photo of Dahlia leaving her apartment building that morning, holding a toddler's hand. Noel Sommers, his son.

The air in the vehicle constricted. Kofi's flesh and blood unfortunately carried his mother's last name instead of his—a name that went back for centuries and for many years struck fear in the hearts of their enemies. A name that meant Noel had access to untold wealth and his veins contained royal blood.

He stared at the photo, trying to get a better view of the boy's face, but he looked down as he walked. The image of Dahlia wasn't much better, but Kofi didn't need better. His vivid memory retained all aspects of her body: a round, striking face, full breasts, and a fantastic ass.

"How long before she gets home?"

"Over an hour. She rode the bus today. We should arrive at her address before she does."

Kofi handed back the photo. "I'm going over there alone. Go to the hotel and I'll meet you there later."

"Are you sure you don't want me to come with you?"

Kofi shot a grateful smile in Kemal's direction. For five years he'd been a loyal companion, someone Kofi trusted implicitly and received honest feedback from. Kemal thought reaching out to Dahlia, an ex, and claiming his secret son was a mistake, but he'd come fully onboard once the trip was underway, and Kofi had made it clear this child would be the one to ascend the throne after him.

As soon as he learned about Noel's existence, protecting the future king of Zamibia became a top priority. He hired a team to keep an eye on the boy and his mother at all times, professionals who blended into the background, but would be quick to defend should danger arise.

"I can handle Dahlia myself. I need you to make sure the penthouse is set and ready for my son's arrival."

"I'll get to work." Kemal climbed out of the SUV.

Kofi issued the order to drive to Dahlia Sommers's address, and then he settled in for the ride.

～

"I'M TELLING YOU, she wants to steal your child."

Dahlia pulled the collar of her coat higher around her neck as she stepped into the frigid weather. She'd clocked out and was going to the daycare on foot to pick up her son.

She chuckled into the phone at her best friend Angela's ridiculous comment. "Would you stop? She's being nice."

One of her co-workers at the substance abuse center gave her a cute outfit for Noel. Before leaving, she'd thanked her co-worker profusely and tucked the gift into the satchel across her chest.

"Mhmm. Keep an eye on that woman. Ever since you told me she said, 'He belongs to all of us,' I've been worried. Next thing you know, she'll show up at your apartment and snatch Noel right out of your arms. Because, you know, he's her kid, too."

"Have you never heard the expression 'it takes a village'? She meant that in the nicest way possible, and you know how Noel is. Kid never meets a stranger."

She was lucky to have a son with such an outgoing personality. Ever since he'd been born, she regularly shared photos and short videos of him with her co-workers. By the time she brought him in for the Christmas party a few months ago, the staff not only felt like they already knew him, they'd fallen in love with him. They showered him with affection and gifts, and her son ate up the attention like the little attention whore he was.

"Besides, you don't know me very well if you think I'd let her get two feet with my kid before I tackle her."

"Yeah, yeah, Superwoman. I would believe you, except I've known you since college and you wouldn't hurt a fly."

"My kid is different. I'd go to blows for him."

Angela cursed under her breath and lowered her voice. "My boss just walked into the office."

"You're still at work?"

"Yes, unfortunately. I'm finishing up a report for these slave drivers."

Angela always complained about her job, but she loved the challenge of being a senior consultant. It didn't hurt that she made a hefty six-figure salary and traveled all over the country and the world.

"In that case, I'm gonna to let you go. Talk to you later."

"Good idea. Much as I hate these people, I need this job. Kiss Noel for me."

"Don't I always?"

Dahlia hung up and kept a brisk pace to the daycare, less than ten minutes away. She trudged along the roadway with her head bent low against the wind, cursing herself for not paying attention to the weather report.

The already cold March temperature dropped lower during the day, dousing Atlanta in unusually wintry conditions for this time of the year. Had she known, she would have driven her car instead of taking the bus. She'd lived in New York for years and didn't mind using public transportation. In fact, she welcomed the option, which gave her a chance to listen to audiobooks and incorporate exercise into her daily routine by walking. But on a night like tonight, the cold whipped like fire against her skin and made her eyes water.

When she arrived at the daycare, one of the older attendants, Miss Martha, a plump woman with rosy cheeks and a ready smile for all the children, greeted her at the door.

Dahlia breathed easier in the warm entryway. "How was he today?"

"An angel, as always. I think he wore himself out, though. Don't be surprised if he falls asleep before you get home. His eyes appeared a little droopy when I checked on him a few minutes ago."

"I wouldn't be so lucky." They both laughed, and soon Dahlia was greeting her son, who scampered over with the biggest smile on his face.

He had her wrapped around his finger. It was the best feeling walking into the daycare and seeing his face—that sweet grin and animated brown eyes which never failed to bring a smile to her own face. Her heart swelled. God, how she hated to leave him every day.

"How's my big boy!" Dahlia scooped him up in her arms and gave him a big, loud kiss.

He giggled happily and pulled back. "Mommy, can I have some candy?"

"No, no. No candy for you tonight, mister." She'd never get him to settle down if she gave him sugar this late in the day.

Noel pouted, his brow wrinkling with displeasure. He resembled his father so much right then, her breath caught. Kofi's face came to her at odd times, more and more as his little carbon copy aged into a closer likeness of him.

At twenty-seven months, not only did he mimic his father's expressions, they shared similar features, including the same broad nose and the shape of their eyes. And she was as hopelessly in love with the little bundle in her arms as she'd once been with the man who fathered him.

Dahlia's heart contracted painfully, and she shoved all thoughts of the tall African from her mind. She placed her son on the floor. "Let's get you home and warm, okay?"

Crouching before him, she bundled Noel up in his coat, mittens, scarf, and hat to protect against the elements. They had a short walk to the bus stop and standing outside at the uncovered area could become uncomfortable in this weather. Hopefully the bus would be on time tonight and they wouldn't have to wait long.

"Say bye-bye to Miss Martha."

"Bye-bye." Noel waved.

"Bye, Noel. See you tomorrow." Miss Martha blew him a kiss and they were on their way.

2

***

Kofi settled his gaze on Dahlia as she walked slowly down the sidewalk with a toddler in her arms, bundled against the unusually cold night. She wore a green knit cap pulled low on her head to protect her ears. Dark hair styled in two thick braids peeked from beneath the knit cap to land past her shoulder blades. The child was wrapped just as warmly as she, his head resting on her shoulder as he appeared to sleep.

As she neared, Kofi's stomach tightened and his nostrils flared —an instinctive response to seeing the woman at whose feet he'd once planned to place the world. He couldn't quite see her lush lips from this distance, but he remembered their taste and how she'd trembled beneath him—his harsh breaths melting with her soft pants. His body tightened, every muscle tense. He could almost hear her breathless cries, feel her undulating hips as he drove into her with frenzied thrusts.

Against his volition, his heart rate accelerated, pumping hot blood through his veins. After three years he still couldn't control his body's immediate reaction to seeing her. He clenched his fists to fight the involuntary acknowledgment and swallowed the bitter taste of betrayal. He'd never wanted a woman the way he had wanted Dahlia Sommers. Never needed one as much. And that had been his mistake.

His gaze shifted to the child, and he leaned forward, anxious to get a good look as they came into the light spilling from the front door of the building, but the child's face was hidden from view. He'd hoped to catch an in-person glimpse of the son he found out existed only days ago. Once the private investigator told him and sent the damning photos of a toddler who looked almost identical to him at the same age, he dropped everything as quickly as he could and traveled to the United States.

His eyes narrowed on the mother of his child as her feet hesitated at the bottom of the steps. She looked up the street. For a moment he thought she saw him in the SUV, but then she turned and hurried into the building, clutching the child protectively in her arms. Almost as if she sensed his presence and knew why he came.

Kofi's jaw firmed as he sat back in the leather seat and rested a wrist on his knee. He would wait until she was settled in her apartment, and then he would go up. No rush. He'd found her and knew the truth. And with the truth came the only option for action available.

He would take his son, next in line to the throne of Zamibia. He would not leave the country without him.

~

TONIGHT, the sense that she was being watched was particularly strong. Unable to shake the feeling, Dahlia darted into the apartment building. The disturbing sensation started a week ago. At first she thought it was her imagination, but on quite a few occasions—once at the grocery store, several times on her way to work, and twice walking home with her son—the hairs on the back of her neck stood on end. The feeling unnerved her, but she thought she was being silly. Who would be following her and why? Yet with a son to care for, she couldn't be too careful.

The empty lobby didn't do much to alleviate her feeling of unease with its unpleasant, musty odor and discarded junk mail littering the dirty floor. She found some solace in the security camera mounted overhead, but not for the first time she wondered whether the contraption actually worked.

Dahlia turned the key in the mailbox and removed the envelopes resting inside. As usual, mostly junk mail, but also the gas bill had arrived. With the unusually cold and long winter, she expected a high invoice. She sighed heavily and Noel stirred against her chest, prompting an automatic smile to her lips. She planted a kiss on his covered head.

Poor baby. He must really be exhausted. Normally he babbled incessantly on the trip home from daycare, but he'd slept the entire way. Shifting him in her arms, Dahlia marched down the hall on the first floor, where she let herself into the apartment. She tossed the mail onto a side table and flicked on the floor lamp.

The space outside may be dreary, but inside these walls, she had created a cheerful, homey environment. With the landlord's permission, she'd painted the walls mustard-yellow. The living room contained mismatched furniture she purchased at garage sales, but she used beige furniture covers and brightly colored pillows to create a cohesive color scheme. On a table next to the loveseat was a black-and-white photo of her and Noel. The walls were covered with other framed black and white photos of buildings and must-see sights around the city she'd taken as a photography hobbyist.

She entered the only bedroom, which wasn't very large, but allowed for a double bed fitted with a brightly colored bedspread and a crib for Noel in a corner. Compared to how she'd lived before, her little place wasn't much, but it was comfortable, and it was home.

Dahlia undressed her son, laughing to herself at how he remained deep in sleep as she removed his clothes and put on his pajamas. She placed him in the crib and stroked one plump cheek with her finger.

She named her son Noel, the French word for Christmas. Born a few days early, he arrived into the world at three o'clock on Christmas morning. A healthy baby boy was the best Christmas gift she'd ever received.

"Good night, my little prince," she whispered affectionately.

After changing into sweatpants and an *I love Atlanta* T-shirt, Dahlia went into the bathroom, unraveled her hair from the thick braids, and using her fingertips rubbed oil into her scalp. Next, a trip to the compact galley kitchen, where she made a cup of chamomile tea. She sat down at the table and flipped through her mail. She wrote checks for the water and electric bills since their due dates were the most pressing, but put off paying the gas bill until her next paycheck in two weeks.

Satisfied, she sipped the warm tea and shuffled back out to the living room and was about to turn on the television when a loud knock sounded on the door. She jumped at the sudden, loud boom, and a little bit of tea sloshed over the brim of the cup and trickled onto the carpet.

What in the world?

She'd moved to Atlanta the summer before Noel was born and didn't know a lot of people, didn't get much company, and no one she knew would show up without calling first. Carefully, she set down the teacup and padded across the carpet. Before she covered the short distance, another knock sounded—harder this time and more peremptory.

Dahlia stopped in her tracks, heart racing. She knew in her soul this couldn't be good. She crept to the door on tiptoe and peered through the peephole but couldn't see well since most of the lights in the hall were out. The landlord failed to replace the fluorescent bulbs, though she'd reminded him several times already. A tall bulky man, so tall she couldn't see his face, stood off to the side with his massive arms folded before him. The other man, standing in the center of her view, stood with his face in shadow, his features indiscernible. Yet he was very, very familiar. Achingly familiar.

No. Could it be?

Her mouth fell open and her heart kick-started a frantic tempo against her sternum. Surely she was wrong.

"Dahlia, open the door. I know you're in there."

Her eyes widened and she staggered back. She wasn't wrong. There was no mistaking that voice. She would recognize the accent and timbre anywhere. But it couldn't be Kofi. What was he doing here at her door? What did he want?

Panic gripped her heart and forced it to pause for several seconds before restarting at a manic pace.

"Dahlia." He pounded again, the loud thump echoing in the apartment like a bass drum. "It's Kofi Francois Karunzika. Must I force my way in?"

He would do it, too. He would simply stand back and let his bodyguard kick the door in.

"No," she called out. "Give me a moment." She hoped he didn't hear the tremor in her voice.

Hurrying to eliminate any evidence of Noel, she slipped the photo of them into a drawer and then swept her eyes furtively around the room for any more signs of her son's existence. She grabbed a few stray blocks from the floor and his purple stuffed wiggle worm from the armchair, dumped the items on the bed, and pulled the bedroom door closed so Noel wouldn't be disturbed.

Hand pressed to her chest, Dahlia made her way back to the front door and took a deep breath to calm her pounding heart. She was already falling apart and hadn't seen his face yet. Her palms were sweaty, and she swiped at the beads of perspiration accumulated on her upper lip. She needed to pull herself together.

With slightly trembling fingers, she undid the safety latch and opened the door.

3

"Hello, Kofi." Surprisingly, she sounded absolutely normal though completely unsettled by his sudden appearance.

"Hello, Dahlia. May I come in?" As if she had a choice.

Dahlia stepped aside and allowed him entry. His bodyguard, a big man of at least six feet six, dressed in a dark coat and leather gloves, remained in the hall, his eyes staring straight ahead as if she didn't exist. Now she had a better look, she recognized him. Abdalla was a former decorated soldier in the Zamibian national military. She came to know him during her brief affair with Kofi. Abdalla had served the royal family as a bodyguard for ten years at this point, most of those under specific appointment to protect the prince.

Dahlia closed the door, her eyes zeroing in on Kofi, the picture of perfection in a navy blue coat and black gloves. Tall, dark, and handsome, he wore confidence like a cloak, proud of his ancestry and heritage.

Her chest hurt with the pain of being near him and not able to touch the way she did before. She'd laid with him on many occasions and watched the play of sunlight across his skin as it came through the large windows of his penthouse apartment. Her fingers twitched with the need to stroke across his brow and caress the soft skin of his face, and her mind flashed back to intimate moments they'd shared when she would sprinkle kisses over his circle beard and along his firm jaw, listening to him draw a sharp breath as she flicked her tongue inside his ear.

Kofi gave the room a slow inspection, gaze flicking over the minimal decorations of a sofa, loveseat, and the rocking chair she normally sat in when she rocked Noel to sleep. His eyes were expressionless, so she didn't know if he found her home adequate or not. Based on what he was used to, the eclectic mix of furnishings was assuredly inadequate.

Dahlia glanced quickly at the door behind which her son slept, and the ball of nerves in her stomach tightened. "I would offer you a seat, but I'm sure whatever you couldn't wait until morning to tell me will be brief and to the point." She was exhibiting poor manners, but after three years, he arrived at her home uninvited, and she didn't feel the need to be polite. The sooner he left, the better.

"Yes, thank you, I would love to sit down." Kofi pointedly ignored her not-too-subtle attempt to get him out of there quickly and removed his coat and gloves, placing them on the arm of the loveseat.

She didn't doubt the suit he wore was custom made to fit his muscular frame—a body any athlete would envy. A dark-colored silk tie, gold cuff links, and the gold watch on his wrist completed the look of elegance.

Kofi sank into the loveseat, his dark eyes, similar to Noel's, regarding her with interest. Unable to stand the quiet inspection, Dahlia took a seat on the sofa across from him and laced her fingers together in her lap.

"What are you doing here, Kofi?"

He flashed a smile full of even white teeth, but the smile didn't reach his eyes. He appeared completely relaxed with one arm draped along the back of the loveseat. "I came to see you."

His voice was earthy and deep and caused shivers to run down her spine. The melodious concoction contained influences from his tribal tongue and the other languages he spoke, English and French.

"Why would you come to see me? We both said all we needed to say to each other when we split three years ago."

A thoughtful look entered his charcoal-colored eyes, as if he hadn't remembered that day until now. "Yes, you were very clear, and you had some choice words for me. I believe you called me a dumbass." A phony smile curved his lips.

Dahlia swallowed uncomfortably. She'd been angry and disillusioned, hurt that after the intimacy and close moments they'd shared, he'd believed the worst—that she'd stolen from him.

"I was angry. You know that."

"Yes, I do." Another phony smile.

Deciding it was best not to argue with him so she could get him out of the apartment as quickly as possible, Dahlia asked, "What do you want? I'm sure you didn't find me just to talk about our last argument."

He continued to study her with the same penetrating stare. As he tapped his fingers along the top of the sofa, the gold and diamond ring on his pinky finger glinted under the light. "I've thought about you often since you left me, Dahlia."

His softly spoken words caught her off guard. The way he spoke her name, in his accented voice, swept across her heart like a soft caress.

"I didn't leave you. You accused me of stealing from you."

"And then left."

"What was the point in staying? You didn't trust me and accused me of a crime." He said she'd distracted him, slept with him to keep him in the dark about the almost one million dollars the management company she'd co-owned embezzled from his family's properties. She'd been ashamed but had nothing to do with the theft. Not that he believed her.

"Have you not missed me, even a little?" he continued.

Oh, he was good, but she wouldn't fall for any of his seductive words this time. The words he tried to coax from her hovered on the edge of her lips, but she wouldn't give him the satisfaction. For way too long she'd allowed emotions to rule her head, but she wouldn't allow that to happen anymore. She was stronger, and she had her son to think about.

"I've hardly thought about you. I've been very busy with my life here."

His fingers stopped tapping.

Being cold to him was her only defense against his charms. So what if she spoke an untruth? So what if she'd thought about him every day and wished she could share her son's milestones with him?

"Please tell me, Dahlia, what has kept you so busy these past few years?" All the warmth disappeared from his voice. It held more of an edge. He had changed tactic.

Dahlia smoothed stray strands of dark hair from her brow, and his gaze followed the movement before returning to her face. "I moved from New York to Atlanta after you forced us to shut down Wane Property Management. I found a job here and I've kept busy with work. And you? How has your life been?"

"You're satisfied with your position? Your job pays the bills?"

"How has your life been, Kofi?" Anger slowly misted up inside of her because of his refusal to answer. "What has kept you busy the past few years?"

He stared at her, his face tightening.

"No answer?" Dahlia straightened her back, reminding herself she no longer loved the cold-hearted man before her. He'd accused her of deception when he'd been the deceiver all along.

"There's nothing you wish to tell me?" he probed quietly.

Why was he asking that?

"Is there something *you* want to tell *me*?" Did he know? Her heart raced unsteadily. Was that why she had felt so uneasy recently? Did he have someone watching her? She stood abruptly, a shiver rippling through her body. "I want you to leave."

"Our conversation isn't finished." What did he know?

"I'm done talking to you. I told you everything I had to say three years ago. No, scratch that. I need to add something else to the dumbass comment. You're a liar. A liar and a cheat."

Emotion threatened to overtake her as the hurt came back full force. She'd loved him so much. Given him everything, all of herself, and what had she received in return? Lies. Humiliation.

His brows snapped together. "I never lied to you."

"Yes, you did! How dare you come into my home and question me. Get out."

"Dahlia." Her name was a low warning.

"How dare you! After three years? Who do you think you are?"

"Sit down."

"And not even a word of apology. You know I never stole from you. You had to know. But no, you would never apologize. You're the mighty Prince Kofi Francois Karunzika. Go back to Africa and leave me the hell alone." Dahlia marched over to the door and yanked it open. "Get out!"

In the hallway, Abdalla remained as immovable as a block of stone.

Kofi came to his feet in a swift, lithe movement. "Do you think you can just throw me out like a piece of rubbish?"

"This is not Zamibia. You don't have any power in this country. Your word is not law. If you don't leave now, I'll call the police and have you escorted from the building."

"Is that so?" A slow smile spread across his handsome face. "Close the door, Dahlia. I'm not going anywhere."

"I mean it, if you don't leave—"

"You. Will. Do. Nothing."

His dark eyes glittered at her from across the room, and trepidation skittered down her spine. He was way too confident, even for Kofi.

"You know," he said, using a conversational tone, "I had no idea you moved from New York. Imagine my surprise when the investigator told me he found you here, in Atlanta."

"Why were you looking for me?" Dahlia asked hoarsely, a tightness in her chest she couldn't explain.

"Never mind why. I had my reasons," Kofi replied, voice as hard as steel. "Why did you leave New York?"

"I wanted a fresh start."

"Is that the only reason?" He was enjoying playing his little game, not giving anything away until he was ready. The Conquering Lion of the tribe of Mbutu. Like a lion, he toyed with his defenseless prey, circling, not striking, until he was ready to devour it.

"Y-yes." The lie constricted her throat so tightly it hurt to speak. The cost of living was cheaper in Atlanta than New York, and though she no longer worked in property management, at least here she could pay the bills and take care of her son.

"I've given you ample opportunity to tell me the truth. If I am a liar, so are you, *olufeh mi.*" The endearment didn't hold the same appeal as before. Not when he used it to punctuate a veiled threat.

Dahlia's fingers tightened on the door she had yet to release. He'd known all along. That's why he was here. "No," she said quietly, shaking her head slowly, denying the inevitable.

"Yes, Dahlia. I know your secret. I know you carried my first-born inside you when you left New York. Close the door and sit down. I'm not leaving. Not without my son."

4

Kofi leveled a stare at Dahlia, tension twisted into every fiber of his being.

Slowly, she closed the door, and they stood across the room from each other like enemy combatants, waiting for one or the other to make the next move.

He hated to notice anything about her, but that was impossible. From the first time he saw her she'd snagged his attention, and tonight was no different. She'd let out her hair, and the long tresses fell around her shoulders and down her back in a waterfall of shiny black waves. He recalled the soft texture and how he used to grab handfuls and tug just enough to force her into an arch, exposing more of her throat to his ravenous mouth.

His gaze swept her body and catalogued the fullness of it. Her heavy breasts were highlighted in the snug-fitting T-shirt stretched across her chest, and the loose-fitting sweatpants did nothing to hide the curves of her flared hips and thick thighs he'd spent many nights sliding between.

Dahlia twisted her hands together, and even such an innocent movement made him flash back to her whispering naughty things in his ear in the back of his SUV and slipping a hand down his pants. Those hands were soft and skilled and used to have him so strung out he'd wanted her with him every waking moment.

Dahlia broke the silence first. "Can we talk about this?"

"There's nothing to talk about," Kofi said, his temper flaring much hotter than necessary because he wanted nothing to do with this woman yet couldn't stop thinking about kissing her full lips and forcing her onto her back to relieve the stress of arousal created by simply being in the same room with her.

"I won't let you take him. I won't let you do this to me."

"Do this to you?" Kofi thundered. "And what about me? I've been a father for two years and never knew. I've only seen photos of my own son and never laid eyes on him until today because of your petty revenge." He laughed softly. "Do you for one minute think you have a choice? He is my *flesh*. He is my *blood*." With each emphasized word, he thumped his chest. "I will not be excluded from his life any longer."

"He doesn't know you."

"And whose fault is that?" Kofi demanded. "Do you think he doesn't need me, too?" He ignored her watery eyes and hardened his heart. This situation was much bigger than the two of them. He couldn't go back to his country without his heir.

Her eyes pleaded with him. "Kofi, you have to listen to reason. I tried to tell you, but—"

"Tried, but didn't."

Her hands fisted at her sides as she fought an emotional response. "I promise I won't keep you away from him. You can see him whenever you want. We can work this out."

"Oh, how generous of you," he said sarcastically. "Now you want to work something out, but working something out didn't matter to you before, when I was robbed of the knowledge of my own child's existence. He is my firstborn and must claim his birthright." He moved closer, around the coffee table and toward her. "I won't make appointments to see my own child. He'll have my name, and he'll go to bed and wake up in the palace where he belongs, under the protection of his father and armed guards. He will no longer be left in the care of strangers all day. He'll be educated and reared in the country of his ancestors. And when the time comes, he'll take his rightful place on the throne."

"You have such big plans," Dahlia said bitterly.

"Yes, I do."

"And what about your wife?" she spat. Her words startled him into silence, and he didn't miss the gleam of satisfaction that flashed in her eyes. "Yes, I know you're married now. Did you discuss your decision with her? Wouldn't she have a problem with you bringing a child into her home? And we both know my son can't be the heir because he's illegitimate."

A muscle in his jaw tightened. "My wife committed suicide almost three years ago."

She inhaled sharply and her eyes widened fractionally. "I didn't know."

Marrying Azireh, the daughter of an Ndenga councilman, had been his duty. Originally, she was supposed to marry his brother, Jafari, but after his death, the responsibility to marry her fell to Kofi—as well as all the responsibilities that came with being next in line to the throne. Her suicide had been sudden and unexpected, causing the entire country to mourn not only her passing, but the children they'd hoped would come from the marriage.

"My people need this bit of good news after what they've gone through in recent years. First my brother and mother died. Then my wife died, and we didn't have any children. And my father is an old man who performs less and less of his duties. He and my people need to see our lineage will continue uninterrupted."

His older brother had been next in line to the throne, but that burden passed to Kofi when the plane containing his brother and their mother crashed. He clenched his fist against the pain that always came when he thought of them in the mangled remains of the wreckage.

"I'm sorry about your father, and I'm sorry about your loss, but I can't give my consent for you to take Noel to another country."

"And how do you propose to stop me? The royal plane is at my disposal. I only have to make a phone call, and we'll be in the air and on our way to Zamibia. Do you think your government will stop me? They would laugh at you."

Her eyes widened. "That's kidnapping!"

"Kidnapping?" Kofi scoffed. "It's not kidnapping if I take my son with me. Your government would find your claims preposterous and ignore you."

He was a highly respected head of state visiting from an allied country to the United States. By the time she convinced anyone to take her seriously, he would be long gone with Noel. Without money or influence, there was little she could do.

"You don't have any kindness in your heart. What happened to you?"

You, he wanted to say. Instead, he replied, "I lost my ability to show kindness when I discovered you'd kept my son from me. You could have told me, instead of hiding the truth."

"As soon as I confirmed my pregnancy, I tried. I called. Didn't Kemal tell you?"

He paused. "You told him you were pregnant?"

She opened her mouth and closed it. Her shoulders sagged. "No. I called and he told me you were married and on your honeymoon. With the woman you'd been engaged to the entire time you were here."

Her accusatory stare lanced his conscience, but he refused to feel remorse. His time with Dahlia had been a temporary reprieve from his responsibilities. He'd considered marrying her and making her his second wife, until their relationship fell apart and he learned the truth about the stolen funds.

"We don't have anything else to discuss. My son will return to Zamibia with me. There's no negotiation on this point." Kofi picked up his coat and gloves.

She was right that Noel was not a legitimate heir, but he'd already talked to his father about signing a proclamation accepting Noel as next in line. This type of edict had been made once before, over two centuries ago.

"We have to negotiate, Kofi."

"Negotiate? I can do whatever I damn well please."

"There has to be another way! You can't take him away from me. He's my son, too."

Kofi paused. A wayward thought entered his mind, and his scalp tingled. "Maybe there is another way."

Her eyes narrowed suspiciously. "What is it?"

He weighed the offer for a few more seconds before finally saying, "Marry me. Come back to Zamibia as my fiancée."

Dahlia shuffled two steps back. "What? No! That's preposterous."

"It's the only other option I would agree to."

"Why?"

"Noel is my son, but he was born outside of marriage. If you and I are married, it will make the approval from The Most High Council easier, ensuring they accept him as the legitimate heir."

"You want to take him back and install him as next in line, but your council has the power to veto your decision." Dahlia laughed softly and crossed her arms over her chest. "You need me."

He remained silent.

"We hate each other, Kofi. And would this even work? Don't I need to have royal blood?"

"I can marry whoever I please, and as the mother of my first-born, you'll be accepted, I assure you."

Dahlia shook her head to clear it. "I don't know anything about being a princess. I don't know what to do or say, or..." Her hands flapped in confusion.

"You'll learn. You'll have tutors and coaches available to aid you."

"And how are you going to spin the story about us?"

"No one knows about your theft." Once he'd discovered the missing funds, he'd only shared the embezzlement with the people closest to him and replaced the money from his own bank account. "Pretend we're long lost lovers who reunited," he said, voice dripping with sarcasm.

She swallowed. "And if I say no?"

Kofi clenched his fist. "Then I'll take my son, and you'll have to make appointments around my schedule to see him," he snarled.

Time ticked by in silent, slow motion.

"I can't believe how cruel you are." She swallowed.

"He's coming back with me, and it's better if you come, too. He shouldn't be without you."

"How considerate of you. Don't tell me there's potentially a heart underneath all the ice?"

"No matter what you think, I'm not completely heartless, but Noel isn't an ordinary child. He must be allowed to live the life he was destined to live."

She opened her mouth to speak, but a child's wail pierced the silence. The sound captured their attention at the same time, and as Kofi tossed aside his coat and gloves and moved toward the bedroom door, Dahlia stepped in front of him and blocked his entry.

His face tightened in fury and he stepped closer. Through clenched teeth he said, "Step aside, Dahlia. You will no longer deny me my rights as a father."

"Let me go in ahead of you or you'll scare him. You may be his father, but you're a stranger."

Kofi opened his mouth to argue, but then thought better of it. He didn't want to frighten his son. Noel's first impression of him should be pleasant and calm. With a sharp inclination of his head, he gave his consent to handle the introduction her way.

Dahlia opened the door to the bedroom. In the soft glow of the night light, Noel stood on wobbly legs, chubby little fingers clinging to the bars of the crib, fat tears streaming down his cheeks. When he saw his mother, his cries became louder, as if relieved she was there and he hadn't been left alone. After switching on a small lamp, Dahlia hurried over to him.

"Oh, precious, don't cry. Mommy's here," she cooed. She lifted him from the crib and laid his head on her shoulder. "Shh," she said soothingly, rubbing his back.

Kofi ached to run his fingers over his son's tight curls and brush away his tears. But he remained in position, jealously watching their interaction like an outsider, his heart heavy, his chest tight.

Eventually, Noel quieted down. Then he stopped crying completely and stared at Kofi.

Unable to resist any longer, Kofi gently caressed the soft black curls atop his son's head. "My son," he said huskily. "You have the face of an angel." With a large thumb, he stroked the tears from Noel's cheek. "I want to hold him."

Carefully, Dahlia relinquished Noel into his arms. The little boy didn't utter a sound and continued to look into Kofi's face. Kofi held him aloft, gazing at him in wonder and examining him from head to toe. When he kissed his son's little fist, Noel squealed and laughed, revealing teeth that had come in. Kofi kissed his fist again, and Noel laughed again, this time reaching for his father's mouth and slapping his palm over his father's jaw and bearded chin.

Kofi laughed. "Yes, explore. I'm your baba, Noel."

"Baba."

"Yes, Baba." Kofi lowered to the edge of the bed and cradled his son in his arms, gently rocking him back and forth. Eventually, Noel's eyes fluttered and drooped, and Kofi couldn't take his eyes off him. He lost track of how long he sat there, staring at him.

Finally, he stirred, rising from the bed and placing Noel back in the crib. The child sighed quietly, and soon his gentle breathing whispered through the room as he fell back into a fitful sleep.

After taking a few minutes longer to stare at his son, Kofi returned his attention to Dahlia, who stood quietly nearby, watching.

"We need to talk," he said.

∼

DAHLIA CLOSED the door and watched Kofi run a hand over his

close-cropped hair. When he faced her, his full lips were set in a grim line.

"I need to know your decision. Are you coming back to Zamibia with me and Noel?"

She almost saw the wheels turning in his head. Now that he'd seen Noel and held him, it was clear he was even more determined to take him back.

"I do want to come, but-but I've never been out of the country before and need time to think. You're practically blackmailing me."

"Blackmail?" He laughed without humor. "I'm not forcing you to come back with me."

"You are forcing me. If I don't do what you say, you'll take my son."

"Your decision to come with us has no bearing on whether I take Noel or not," Kofi said evenly.

This wasn't the man she'd fallen in love with. This cold, unfeeling person emerged after the discovery of the theft. She couldn't blame him for his anger, but she wished he'd trusted her more and believed she didn't have anything to do with stealing his money. She hadn't used her 'feminine wiles'—as he'd accused her—to distract him from the truth.

"Does it make you feel better to carry out your vengeance on me?"

"Vengeance? Count yourself lucky I haven't resorted to vengeance." He lanced her with an icy stare. "What's your decision? Will you return to Zamibia with me or not?" His voice took on an imperial, demanding tone.

If she allowed Kofi to take Noel, she could stay behind and fight him in court, but in the interim, years could pass before she saw Noel again as she fought for her rights. And what if she lost? With Kofi's limitless power and wealth, he would very likely be the victor in such a mismatched battle.

Dahlia sighed heavily, tired of his badgering and physically exhausted from her long day. "Can I have a little time to think about your tempting offer?"

"Certainly. I'm a reasonable man. How much time do you need?"

"A week would be nice."

"We don't have that much time. We leave next Friday."

"That only gives me eight days," she exclaimed, eyes wide.

"Too much time has passed already." He was immoveable in his resolve. His eyes narrowed on her pinched face. "You have forty-eight hours. Not a second more."

5

Buildings and street lights streamed by as Kofi stared out the side window in the backseat of the SUV taking him to the hotel. Abdalla sat up front with the driver, leaving him to reflect in solitude during the drive.

He'd wanted to whisk Dahlia and Noel away from their average little apartment building tonight and bring them back with him to the suite he occupied at Presidential Commons, a swanky building downtown where some of the richest people in the city resided. Instead, he left her alone to digest their conversation. He didn't bother to tell her he'd left two men outside the door of her apartment as a means of protection. She would see them soon enough.

His fingers stroked his beard, eyes unseeing as tumultuous feelings raged throughout his body. He'd felt possessive love, fierce protectiveness, and intense pride when he'd looked at his son's cherubic face. Nothing could have prepared him for the intensity of emotions that coursed through him. When he considered all the time he'd lost and milestones he'd missed, a huge crater of emptiness opened in his soul.

The vehicle pulled in front of the hotel and his driver quickly disembarked and opened the door. Without a word, Kofi swept through the front doors with Abdalla leading the way and a second guard a respectful distance behind Kofi. In the elevator, he maintained his silence.

He wished his mother and Jafari were alive to meet Noel. Kofi swallowed the lump in his throat. The pain of losing them never seemed to go away.

"Good night," he said to Abdalla, leaving the big man at the door.

Kemal rose from the sofa in the spacious living room. "How did it go?"

Kofi couldn't help the grin that came over his face and sat on the arm of a chair, in awe the little boy he'd met was part of him. "He's amazing, with bright, intelligent eyes. And he took to me right away."

"So are we on the same schedule?"

"Yes. We leave in a week. Tomorrow I go back, and I'll take Aofa with me," Kofi said, referring to the nanny. He rose from the chair. "I plan to spend the day with my son."

"And Dahlia's okay with your decision to take Noel back to Zamibia?" Kemal asked, one eyebrow arched.

"Not exactly, but she doesn't have a choice. I know about him now. She can't keep us apart any longer." He removed his gloves. "I asked her to come back with me and be my wife."

"Your wife? I don't understand. When was this decision made?"

When they discussed coming here, Kofi only mentioned taking Noel back, but seeing Dahlia again had a profound effect on him. For three years he'd felt nothing, driven only to perform his duties as the prince of his country. Being near her, even briefly, filled the cold parts of him with a fiery warmth that consumed him in a way that threw him off balance.

From the beginning, he'd reacted to her in the same way. When they met a few years ago, he'd managed to rein in his attraction and keep their relationship purely professional for only a short period. As the days passed, their conversations became longer and extended into areas that didn't include real estate. He regaled her with stories of his homeland, and she revealed her love of art and interest in photography.

Over coffee, they engaged in spirited debates on education, how to curtail crime, and in her opinion, the barbarism of capital punishment. *Are we really any better if we kill our citizens and call that justice?* she'd asked. And while he disagreed with her stance on drug use, he respected the compassion she displayed for those caught in the grip of addiction. She considered them victims instead of criminals and thought they should be treated and counseled instead of punished.

Dahlia was the perfect blend of sweet and tart, exuding charm when it suited the situation, but ready to argue with him in a way no other woman dared do. Her openness and free-spirited nature made him laugh. During his stay in New York, he'd thought about her constantly when they were apart and had always created the flimsiest reasons to call.

"It was a spur of the moment decision."

"Forgive me for saying so, but is marrying her a good idea? I know you have carried a torch for this woman for some time—"

"Whatever feelings I have or don't have for Dahlia Sommers are irrelevant," Kofi said in an icy tone. "She's my son's mother, and I don't think they should be apart."

Kemal tempered his voice. "Very well, I understand, but why not take her back to simply care for the child? You don't have to marry her."

Rather than admit Kemal was correct, Kofi walked away. "My decision is made. I gave her forty-eight hours to accept my offer of marriage."

"And if she declines?" Kemal called after him.

Kofi ignored the question. As far as he was concerned, there was no way Dahlia would say no, therefore entertaining the thought of a refusal was a waste of time.

He climbed the stairs and entered the spacious bedroom,

tossing his coat and gloves on a chair against the wall. He went into the bathroom to get ready for bed, anticipating the phone call he'd make tomorrow. His father would be pleased when he told him he'd soon be able to hold his grandson. Particularly since when Azireh passed away, the country learned that she was pregnant.

~

DAHLIA TURNED RESTLESSLY in the bed, unable to sleep. She repositioned the pillow and turned onto her side. Her weary mind couldn't settle after the confrontation with Kofi.

Frustrated, she left the bed and peeped at Noel before padding quietly to the kitchen to make a cup of tea. With only the light above the stove on, she sat at the table, reflecting on how she'd come to this uneasy place in her life.

Melanie Wane, her old partner, was the kind of woman who smiled often and would give you the clothes off her back. Except Dahlia learned the hard way that the clothes might not actually be hers and might have been stolen off someone else's back.

Wane Property Management had managed the New York portfolio of properties purchased by the king and queen of Zamibia, Kofi's parents. The portfolio of buildings hadn't simply been purchased to establish wealth. They financed university scholarships for deserving Zamibian students who wanted to study in the U.S.

For the first couple of years, the Karunzikas worked through an intermediary with Melanie Wane and covered the costs of tuition, lodging, and fees for fifty-five students and hoped to do the same for many more. But with the maintenance and repair expenses increasing, King Babatunde sent his son to inspect the properties and approve any necessary renovations to ensure the investment generated adequate revenue for many years to come.

Dahlia had worked with Kofi from the first day he arrived. She couldn't pinpoint exactly when things changed between them, but from the beginning she'd been attracted to the prince and noticed everything about him, from his elegant way of speaking, to the immaculate way he dressed, to his well-formed features. Their affair only lasted a few months but did have a profound effect on her.

Dahlia closed her eyes, tightened her fingers around the warm cup of tea, and shuddered when she recalled how he'd taken her against the wall in her office. She never considered saying no to him—not then, nor when he'd invited her back to his hotel suite.

Dahlia tossed the rest of the tea in the sink and rinsed out the cup. She turned out the light and crept to the front door. The guards were still in the hall, neither as tall as Abdalla, but with the same stoic, hard-jawed expressions. These men were the best of the best Zamibia had to offer. They wouldn't move. They would give their lives to protect their prince and now had been charged with protecting his heir. If Kofi instructed them to stand there unmoving for a week, they would.

Dahlia trudged back to the room, her heart heavy when she recalled the dramatic way she and Kofi ended their affair three years ago. Melanie had been stealing money from the Karunzikas for quite some time. She created fake companies and prepared bogus invoices to bill the Karunzikas for work that was never done —to the tune of almost a million dollars.

She'd been sickened when she learned about the theft and alarmed when Kofi accused her of being a party to it. She understood his initial distrust. After all, she was Melanie's partner, but she concentrated on growing the business through PR and marketing, and naively let Melanie manage the finances. To this day, she kicked herself for not paying closer attention. Unfortunately, nothing she said dissuaded Kofi from his train of thought.

Dahlia looked down at Noel, sleeping peacefully, unaware of how important he was and how much his life would change in a little more than a week.

She never saw Kofi after the night he accused her of the theft. Through his intermediary, he demanded they shut down the business. She learned later that he replenished the stolen funds himself, but he'd been furious, and she never understood why he didn't turn them in to the police.

When Dahlia found out she was pregnant, she took a leap of faith and called, only to learn that he was married—a mere two months after she'd last seen him. According to Kemal, he'd been engaged for a couple of years.

Not once did she suspect a woman waited at home for him. It destroyed her. What little hope she'd carried of a reconciliation died that day.

Dahlia bit her bottom lip and refused to let the tears resurface. She'd cried plenty three years ago.

Kofi was wrong about her. She hadn't kept their son a secret out of some need to exact revenge. She simply thought he wouldn't want Noel.

The way he no longer wanted her.

6

K ofi always traveled with a group of aides—assistants, bodyguards, and anyone else he deemed necessary for the trip, and the next morning proved nothing had changed. He arrived early with an entourage in tow. Abdalla came with him, along with two guards to replace the ones standing outside Dahlia's apartment.

The last member of the group was a buxom woman with caramel-toned skin and a wide, friendly smile.

"Hello. I am Aofa," she said, extending a hand. She sported a blue stripe down the middle of her braids.

"Aofa will spend the day with me and help take care of Noel while you're at work," Kofi explained. Today he wore more casual clothes, a blue turtleneck under a black sweater and jeans that molded to his narrow hips and emphasized his long legs. Though he wasn't dressed as formally as the night before, he was still just as impressive.

Noel had one arm wrapped around Dahlia's leg, staring up at the strangers.

Kofi crouched before the little boy. "Hello, son." He smiled in greeting.

Dahlia's heart tightened at the tender way he spoke to their son.

"Hello." Noel reached for his father's face and elicited a throaty chuckle from Kofi. He held the toddler's face in his hands and kissed him on the forehead.

Dahlia turned away from the sight of the two of them together, father and son, their faces close together and their smiles identical.

"I'll see you later, then," she said.

"Does he have any allergies I need to be aware of?" Kofi asked, coming to a stand.

"No."

"We'll see you this evening." Kofi took Noel's hand, and Dahlia watched them walk out of the apartment, her son grinning and waving to her over his shoulder. She waved back.

He has no loyalty, she thought wryly.

After the door closed, the first thing she did was call in to work. Kofi gave her forty-eight hours, and she planned to make full use of her time.

Next, she called Angela and gave her a quick summary of the events that took place the night before and this morning.

"He can't just take Noel," Angela said when she heard the whole story.

"I don't know that he can't." Dahlia pinched the bridge of her nose as she paced the living room floor. In less than twenty-four hours, she'd gone from living an ordinary life in Atlanta to considering a move to a small kingdom in West Africa.

"So you're just going to pack up and leave?"

"Not quite," Dahlia whispered. Nervous the men outside the door might hear her, she walked into the bedroom and shut the door.

"You have a plan," Angela said, dropping her voice to a conspiratorial tone, as well.

"I took the day off. I'm going to make some calls and see if I can find an attorney to help me—one with experience in international child custody disputes."

"Good idea. What Kofi's doing can't possibly be legal."

"That's what I hope. Wish me luck."

"Good luck. How about we meet up later? This damn job is sending me to California in a couple of days, and I want to see my best friend before she flies thousands of miles away to a foreign country and I never see her again."

Dahlia buried her face in her hand. "Don't say that. I'm hoping that doesn't have to happen."

"I'm sorry, honey." Angela heaved a sigh. "I want to see my godson, too, but I guess that's not going to happen since he's with his father. Let's meet at the Starbucks in the Target shopping plaza at say, one o'clock?"

Dahlia glanced at the digital clock on the dresser. That gave her several hours. "I'll see you then."

~

THE CONVERSATION with the attorney didn't go well at all. Dahlia would not have good news to share with her friend when they met for coffee.

She tamed her hair into a bun, buttoned her coat, and slung her satchel across her chest. She exited the apartment and, giving a tight smile to the guards posted outside, walked down the hallway.

After a few steps, she realized she was being followed and stopped. Turning around, she eyed the man following her. He appeared to be of Middle Eastern descent, good-looking, with the same stoic expression as the other guards.

She attached a disarming smile to her face. "What are you doing?"

"I am coming with you." He spoke in heavily accented English.

"I'm going to meet a friend, er, what's your name?"

"Yasir." He gave a slight bow.

"Yasir, it's not necessary for you to follow me around. It's perfectly safe, and I'll only be gone for a couple of hours or so."

"I will come with you."

"I'd rather go alone," Dahlia said in a firmer voice.

He shook his head. "That is not possible. I cannot let you drive."

"Excuse me?"

"It is my job to protect you."

She laughed and stared at him. "Yasir, I've been driving since I was sixteen. Yes, the traffic in Atlanta can be a bit crazy, but you're being ridiculous."

"I've been given strict instructions not to leave your side or let you drive."

"Strict instructions by whom? Kofi?"

"Yes."

Dahlia gritted her teeth. Now that she thought about it, she'd never seen Kofi drive. The no-driving policy must be royal protocol, guidelines she now fell under. No one in this country knew who the hell the prince of Zamibia was and certainly had no idea she was the mother of his heir, but her life was already going through changes and she hadn't left the country yet. First bodyguards, now she couldn't drive. Fabulous.

She tossed the keys to Yasir. "Fine. Let's go."

～

WHEN THEY ARRIVED AT STARBUCKS, Yasir went and sat in a corner, inconspicuously drinking coffee while she waited for Angela to arrive.

"Hey, honey!" Angela swept in, arms wide. She was immaculate as always, her tawny skin graced with the right amount of makeup to highlight her features. She wore a scarf around her neck, her hair parted in the middle, and dark glasses perched on her nose. They'd been friends since college, clicking right away because of their shared sense of humor.

Dahlia stood and pulled her friend into a tight squeeze. She didn't realize how much she'd needed a hug until then. "Ordered your favorite, a caramel brûlée frappuccino." She extended the cup across the table as Angela sat down, and took a sip of her own caramel frappuccino with extra caramel drizzle.

"Thank you." Angela took a long draw on the straw. "Ooh, that's good. After my morning with those lunatics, I needed this." She huffed out a satisfied breath and studied Dahlia. "Did you get a chance to talk to an attorney?"

Lips pursed, Dahlia nodded.

"Bad news?"

She cradled the cup in both hands and leaned across the table, which caused Angela to lean forward, too. She kept her voice low. "According to him, this wouldn't be your normal custody battle. Kofi could take my son without my permission, and there's nothing I could do about it. He's protected by functional immunity."

Angela's brow furrowed. "Is that the same as diplomatic immunity?"

"Very similar," Dahlia answered. "As a head of state, functional immunity protects him and his actions while on U.S. soil. Kidnapping is nothing. He could literally murder someone and not be charged, although he might have to face the consequences in his home country. Except, he's the prince of Zamibia, and the chances of him facing prosecution..."

"Are nil."

"Exactly."

"Damn." Angela sat back in the chair, her distraught face reflecting Dahlia's turbulent emotions. "You don't have any choice, do you?"

"Doesn't appear so." Dahlia sipped her drink.

"Well, you look great. Not like someone being forced to move to another country."

"I'm holding it together, but barely. I keep thinking about Noel and what the change would mean for him. I mean, my goodness, my son is a prince. I can't begin to understand the type of responsibility he'll have to bear later in life. And if I go, where do I fit in? It's all so overwhelming." She pressed a hand to her temple.

"You could leave and not tell him. Just sneak away."

"Sneaking away is not an option. Ever since yesterday, I've had company outside the apartment, and today I have an escort." Dahlia glanced at the table where Yasir sat, and Angela followed her gaze.

"Shit, he's fine. Who is he?"

"My guard. Or my tail, depending on how you view his presence. Privacy is a thing of the past, and apparently I'm no longer allowed to drive. He chauffeured me here." When she'd first met Kofi, she commented on the people always surrounding him, a phenomenon he seemed well-adjusted to after years of living under a microscope in his country. She hated the thought of having to live under those conditions.

"Did Kofi say anything about how he treated you when he left? Did he look you up because he finally came to his senses and wanted to apologize for doubting your innocence?"

"No. I don't know why he looked me up. Probably some sixth sense he had a kid out in the world. One thing for sure, he's furious."

Angela frowned. "If anyone should be angry, it's you. He never told you he was engaged."

"His wife passed away."

"Oh."

Dahlia plucked at a paper napkin. "He's different. Harder. Colder. Not the man I knew three years ago. I think her death deeply affected him. He said she killed herself."

"Damn."

"I can't imagine thinking you'd spend the rest of your life with someone and then losing them suddenly," Dahlia said. Actually, she could. She'd fallen too fast and too hard for Kofi and imagined what life would be like if they spent the rest of theirs together. So despite her anger and sense of betrayal, she felt sorry for him. It must have been devastating to have to bury his wife so soon after they married.

"Hey." Angela touched her fingers. "You're crying."

"Am I?" Dahlia swiped away the tear from her cheek and laughed. "My emotions are all over the place. I don't know what to think or feel. I don't want to uproot my son and move to a country I don't know anything about, but I feel as if I can't stop Kofi. I don't have the money or the power he does, and immunity basically gives him carte blanche to do whatever he wants."

"If anybody can stop him, you can," Angela said with way too much confidence.

Dahlia smiled weakly. "No, I can't. You're nice, but I can't think of any other options, and I don't have it in me to fight."

"*You* don't have any fight? You lost both your parents in an accident when your father fell asleep at the wheel. The same accident put you in a coma for five days. You were fourteen and you recovered."

The accident took place in Arizona. While Dahlia dozed in the backseat, her father swerved into oncoming traffic. Both of her parents died at the scene.

"That's different."

"How?" Angela pursed her lips.

"I didn't have a choice, Angie. I was literally fighting for my life."

Her parents had traveled all over the country doing odd jobs, and she'd been along for the ride. Her life had been interesting. She'd visited almost every state. Her parents didn't earn a lot of money, but the three of them had fun. Her life had been one big adventure.

Their deaths had had a profound effect on her. When she came out of the coma, she'd resolved to live life to the fullest. When her grandparents died, who'd taken care of her after her parents' death, she didn't miss a beat. She'd lived her life fearlessly, and when she met Kofi, abided by the same belief.

"Live in the moment with me."

She remembered the softly spoken words as he'd looked into her eyes. She'd done it. Fearlessly, recklessly, and without reservation. She may have ended up with a broken heart, but she'd also wound up with the joy of motherhood. She didn't regret having Noel for one minute.

"Five years ago, you weren't fighting for your life when you joined Melanie's business. You were only twenty-three. I took the safe route and went to work for a bunch of assholes who suck the life out of me every week, but you joined Melanie's company as a partner."

"And ended up with a partner who embezzled money from our biggest client," Dahlia reminded her.

"You did it, though. You're way braver than I am."

"But what if I'm not brave?" Dahlia asked softly. "What if I'm scared? Really scared this time. And I'm not completely sure of all the reasons why I'm so terrified."

Angela moved to the chair beside her. "Listen to me. You've been raising a kid on your own with no help, and Noel is a great kid. You're going to be the best damn princess Zamibia has ever seen."

"I guess."

"You don't have a lot of choices, or a lot of time to decide. You go with Kofi, or you leave, on your own terms." She dropped her voice. "Run. He can't take Noel if he can't find him."

Dahlia's gaze flicked to her. "What are you suggesting?" she whispered.

"You know what I'm suggesting."

Dahlia glanced at Yasir. He appeared to be reading the paper. His position gave him a sweeping view of the entire restaurant, and she suspected he was well aware of every movement of every person in the place—the people in line, the couple quietly arguing, the folks sitting by themselves with headphones, tapping away on their computers. It was his job to notice the details, and she was almost afraid he'd sense her thought about running and tip off Kofi.

"How do you feel about Kofi now?" Angela asked.

"I don't feel much of anything." That wasn't completely true. He evoked a strong, emotional response from her that she tried her best to tamp down.

"You sure?"

"I don't love him anymore, if that's what you mean. He and I barely knew each other, and we were only together for a few months. Realistically, people don't fall in love that easily or that fast."

"You were pretty broken up when you found out he was married."

Angela held her through the crying sessions when she realized she'd been nothing but an interlude for him. That his heart belonged to someone else.

"I was hurt. I admit I got my feelings tangled up in him. It's easy to do when you meet a man who says all the right things, pays attention to your needs, and basically sweeps you off your feet. He was charming and promised me the world."

She swallowed the lump in her throat. She'd actually thought they had a relationship built on mutual attraction and admiration. Not to mention he could be extremely funny when he let his guard down. And tender. So tender. And protective. She'd always felt safe with him, like nothing could harm her. Not only because of the guards, but because he himself was a trained soldier with centuries of warrior blood running through his veins. The way he walked and talked, he commanded respect and always seemed in control.

She emptied her lungs with a soft huff. "Our relationship wasn't real. This is real. Moving to Zamibia is real. Noel is real. My relationship with Kofi wasn't. It was an illusion, and the man I had feelings for doesn't exist." She stared at her hands as a bite of pain nicked her chest.

"What if he does still exist?" Angela prodded softly.

The old Kofi was hard to resist. If he reappeared, she would have to fight hard to keep from falling for him, and remember he'd deceived her and could do the same again.

"He doesn't," Dahlia said firmly. "The Kofi I thought I loved— I'm not sure he ever existed at all."

7

S he decided to run.

Thank goodness for Angela. Today, Dahlia accepted her best friend's offer to escape to her parents' cabin in the mountains. Angela made the offer the day before yesterday, before they left Starbucks. Tonight, before she caught an evening flight to California, Dahlia told her to leave the keys under the flower pot in her back yard.

She would not let Kofi control her life and that of their child without fighting back. She didn't know anything about Zamibia and had no connection to the country. It was small and never made the news like the much larger countries that surrounded it. Besides, she couldn't risk going there, where Kofi's word was law. Anything could happen if she didn't abide by his rules. Who knew what he'd do? She couldn't take the risk. Once she was in the mountains, she would get a message to him and let him know they were safe. At that point, she would be able to negotiate from a more equitable position.

"We're going on a little adventure," Dahlia told Noel, keeping her voice light and upbeat.

"Abencha," he said, eyes bright as he danced on stubby legs

around the room, oblivious to the seriousness of the situation. He giggled almost nonstop, clearly thinking the way she rushed around, stuffing clothes and other items into bags was some kind of game.

Dahlia swept her gaze over the room, hoping she hadn't forgotten anything. If she did, she couldn't turn back. She'd packed only what she absolutely needed, but after enough time passed, she'd let Angela come back to the apartment and get more items.

She crouched before her son and buttoned his coat. Handing him his purple wiggle worm, she asked, "You ready?" She grinned to maintain levity.

He clutched the toy to his chest. "Yes!"

"Okay. Let me check something real quick, and then we're going on our adventure!"

"Abencha!" he repeated with the same level of enthusiasm.

"Sit still, okay?" She hoisted him onto the bed and then turned out the light.

Peering through the slats in the blinds, she watched for movement on the sidewalk or in any of the cars. One vehicle drove by, and a piece of paper blew down the street, propelled by a light breeze. Nothing out of the ordinary, but she was still nervous. Two of Kofi's guards remained outside the door, which meant she had to be careful.

Dahlia grabbed the backpack and duffel bag and tossed them out the bedroom window onto the grass at the side of the building. She lifted Noel out and lowered him to the ground. He watched with curious eyes as she gingerly climbed out after him.

"Mommy—"

"Shh." Dahlia put a finger to her lips and he fell quietly immediately.

Heart racing, she eased the window closed and paused to listen while scanning the area. Only night sounds could be heard. Nothing indicated they'd been discovered. With the backpack on her back and Noel resting on her hip, she picked up the duffel bag and walked quickly to the back parking lot where she'd parked her car.

After she'd tossed the luggage in the trunk, Dahlia strapped Noel into the car seat. All the while, her eyes darted to and fro, searching for any unusual movement in the dimly lit parking lot. In the car, she gripped the steering wheel and sat absolutely still as a wave of fear washed over her. Her stomach was pained and queasy.

Was she crazy to run? Selfish? No, she was doing the right thing. Kofi was the one in the wrong.

Dahlia started the car.

"Mommy."

She turned to look at Noel. "Yes, precious."

"I love you." He grinned.

The first time he'd said those words had been after a tickle-fest when the two of them lay sprawled on the bed. He'd sat up and given her a kiss and told her he loved her. A pure and sweet act, and so needed after a long day, tears had come to her eyes. She'd needed those words then, and he must have sensed she needed them now.

Dahlia grinned back and squeezed his foot. "I love you, too. More than anything else in the whole wide world." She'd do anything she needed to do to protect him and keep him in her life, on her terms.

She turned around and switched on the headlights.

Abdalla stood directly in front of the car.

Dahlia screamed. Two more men approached on either side, all of them dressed in dark coats. She immediately recognized Yasir.

Ohmigod. Ohmigod.

Her fingers tightened on the wheel. Did they have guns? Would they hurt her?

A glance in the rearview mirror revealed Noel's wide eyes as he tightened the hold on his stuffed animal, and yet another guard stood behind the small sedan. They had them surrounded. Abdalla alone appeared big and strong enough to keep the car in place by simply gripping the front bumper.

Yasir bent to eye level and tapped the window with one finger. "Miss Sommers, please exit the vehicle."

Dahlia stared at him for a moment, trying to catch her breath. Then she rolled down the window two inches. "No," she said, voice shaking.

"Please, ma'am." He remained polite, but there was no missing the determination in his voice, like when he'd insisted on going with her to Starbucks.

"Or what?" Her voice went up several octaves in panic. "You'll break in and pull me out of the car? You'll hurt me in front of my child?"

"No, ma'am." His voice remained calm but firm. "We have strict instructions not to hurt you. But we also have strict instructions not to let our prince leave."

Our prince. They were already referring to him as theirs, as if he was no longer her son. He already belonged to them.

Tears of frustration burned her eyes. Dare she try running them over? The thought of hurting another human being made her nauseous. She didn't even believe in the death penalty. She couldn't run over these men for doing their job, and they would never betray Kofi. They had pledged their allegiance to him, but that didn't mean she couldn't try to change their minds or throw herself at their mercy.

"Tell him you didn't see me."

"Please get out of the vehicle, ma'am."

"Listen to me, please, I—"

Dahlia heard the most pitiful sound. A long whine came from the backseat. She turned to see her son, Noel, clutching his wiggle worm with tears running down his cheeks. Her heart broke. He was scared, and she was adding to his fear.

She glared at Yasir. "Look what you've done."

Yasir didn't reply.

"This is America. Kofi can't do this."

Yasir straightened and spoke boldly. "He is Prince Kofi Francois Karunzika, the Conquering Lion of the tribe of Mbutu. He can do whatever he wants."

Dahlia inhaled a deep, shaky breath and let her shoulders slump in defeat. "Fine," she murmured. "I'll go back in."

"No, Miss Sommers. You're coming with us."

8

Dahlia sat in the back seat of a black SUV with Noel and Abdalla, while Yasir sat up front with the driver. They made the ride to Kofi's penthouse in silence, the only words spoken had been when they'd initially settled into the vehicle. Abdalla made a call, said a few words in Mbutu, and hung up.

Noel fell asleep on the ride, so she held him in her arms as they walked down the hallway to Kofi's penthouse, one of two on the top floor. Like a prisoner, she walked in the middle of the men, Yasir to the back, and Abdalla carrying her two bags in the front.

When they entered, Kofi turned away from the view outside the window. "Take the bags upstairs to the room at the end of the hall," he said. He kept his gaze on Dahlia, who stared back at him with as much venom as she could.

"Aofa," he called. The nanny came out immediately from a side door. "Please take my son upstairs to his room."

Dahlia didn't fight as the older woman lifted the toddler from her arms and then silently climbed the stairs.

A staring contest and silence continued until Abdalla returned.

"Thank you for your excellent assistance tonight. Your work is done," Kofi told both men. They gave slight bows and exited the apartment.

"Drink?" Kofi walked over to the bar.

"No."

He poured her one anyway—Brandy on the rocks with a twist of lime, a drink he'd persuaded her to try and she now enjoyed. He handed her the glass and she took it, making sure their fingers didn't touch. If he noticed, he didn't react, and went back to the bar.

Dahlia took a sip. The burn in her throat woke her up a little bit. She watched as Kofi poured himself the same drink.

Even if he hadn't been a prince, he'd be an arresting man. He moved with quiet grace and wore his clothes well. In the comfort of his own home, he wore loose-fitting pants and a dashiki, exposing the ropey thickness of his muscular arms. She'd never seen him in traditional dress before.

His neat facial hair hinted he was a man who took care of himself, and his strong profile suggested inbred confidence that came from years of being told he was special and different.

"How did you know I would try to leave?" Dahlia cradled the glass in both hands.

Smiling slightly, he replied, "I considered what a reasonable, trustworthy woman would do, and assumed you'd do the opposite."

Ass.

"You didn't trust me."

"Not even a little bit."

Kofi sipped his drink, eyeing her over the rim.

"I didn't betray you three years ago."

"And yet here we are, and your actions once again prove you can't be trusted."

She scanned the room, which gave her time to think. "What happens now?"

"What happens now depends on you, Dahlia. You've made it

very clear to me, painfully clear, I cannot let my son out of my sight, or you'll try to steal him from me."

"Steal him? Are you serious?"

"Do you prefer the word kidnap?"

"I needed a little time to adjust to the idea—"

"Enough!" He slammed the glass on the metal bar top. "I have been more than patient with you on numerous occasions. Apparently my generosity wasn't enough. Did you forget I didn't have you thrown in jail for the crime you committed against my kingdom?"

"I never stole that money. Melanie stole from your family."

"Even if I could have believed you, your actions since then have proven to me you're capable of theft. You're willing to steal the heir to the throne, so why would I doubt that you stole money from us?"

"Unbelievable." Dahlia shook her head. "I can't get through to you. Nothing gets through to you."

"I'm smart enough not to fall for your deceptive ways." He walked slowly over to her. "The game ends now. You want to come back to Zamibia? I will grant you the opportunity to do that. But this time, you do as I say. Everything I say."

She didn't like the sound of that. "What do you want me to do? No one would believe in this farce of an engagement."

"They will if we get our story straight. We'll simply say we separated, but loved each other all along."

"Did you forget you were married before?"

"In my country, a man can have as many wives as he can afford."

"Oh, right. How lovely to live in a society where a man's appetite for multiple women is ingrained in society as the accepted norm."

"Based on the rate of divorce in your country, I'd say the men have the same appetite. But I guess the norm of extra-marital affairs and broken homes is better." He smirked when she didn't respond.

"As I was saying, we were in love, and I found out about my son after you contacted me. Believe me, it would be better to say you contacted me than for my people to know I was the one who tracked you down. You'll act like a loving fiancée. You'll pretend we're reunited lovers. You play the game, or this doesn't work."

She fortified her nerves with another sip of Brandy. Tense silence vibrated between them.

"I don't have much choice, do I? First, you threaten to take Noel and now, you force me to marry you and pretend we're in love."

"You needn't make my proposal sound like a death sentence. I assure you, you'll be the envy of many women, as you'll have a life of wealth and privilege."

"I only have to lie through my teeth." Dahlia smoothed her fingers over the long plait on her right shoulder. "I'll do what you say on two conditions."

Kofi chuckled. "You're in no position to make demands."

"They're small requests. You can grant me two small requests, can't you?"

He eyed her suspiciously. "That depends on what they are."

"I want my best friend Angela to be at the wedding." Dahlia took a deep breath, averting her eyes to the sofa. "My last request is—I'm sure you'll have other women in your life. After all, I was the other woman." She swallowed the shaft of pain that came out of nowhere. "I just ask that you...you're discreet with your liaisons. I would rather not go through the humiliation of having you flaunt your affairs in my face."

The room became so quiet she heard the clock ticking on the wall.

"There's no problem with having your friend attend the ceremony. As for the other...I'm always discreet. I've never brought any of my mistresses into my palace apartment, and that won't change."

Dahlia nodded numbly. Mistresses. How many were there?

She'd half hoped he would deny the need for those types of

liaisons and offer to treat their marriage as a real one. How foolish could she be? "Thank you," she whispered through wooden lips.

"You'll remain in the penthouse until we leave." A statement. Not a request.

"Yes, Your Highness." She lifted her head to glare at him, as if that would do any good. He held all the power, and all the control.

He walked slowly toward her, and her body tensed on his approach.

"Don't get any silly ideas of running off, Dahlia." He caught her chin in his hand.

The firm pressure filled her body with heat. She froze, hypnotized by the intensity of his stare. She knew this man. She knew his touch, his kisses, and his husky, knowing laugh as he joined their bodies and she begged for more. But sex and sweat-damp skin was the last thing on his mind.

"Don't you dare run from me again. If you run, I'll follow you. If you hide, I'll find you. Nothing will keep me from my son ever again."

~

KOFI KEPT his eyes trained on Dahlia as she rushed up the stairs.

His suspicions had been correct. He'd suspected she'd try to leave, and a sixth sense made him send reinforcements to her apartment and instruct the men to pay extra close attention to her tonight.

He poured what was left of her drink into his glass and took a swallow.

His life was rigid and boxed in by protocol and traditions he'd adhered to since childhood. Even his marriage to Azireh had been arranged for him. Kofi accepted he should marry her—until he met Dahlia. She'd been a beacon of light in the darkness of duty and obligation his life had become.

A smile came to his lips when he remembered their pillow

fights and wrestling in bed like children. She became his escape for a short while, away from the restrictions of his life.

He thought of all the things that had attracted him to her. Not only her beauty but her empathy. She couldn't stand to see anyone in pain. Three years ago he'd decided he would marry her, making her his second wife. He'd only needed to convince her. Then he uncovered the theft.

Kofi strolled over to the window, barely acknowledging the buildings illuminated by lights. He swirled the drink, frowning down into the glass.

Despite what she'd done, he couldn't turn her into the police. He made her and her partner dissolve the company instead. To this day she continued to claim her innocence, and he wanted to believe her, but how could he? She'd hidden his son, another deception he found hard to overlook.

He stopped moving and stared down at the amber liquid.

Was he making a mistake? The question gnawed at him more times than he could count.

No, he thought for the umpteenth time with grim determination. He drained the glass.

He had a right to claim his son. Why not claim his son's mother, too?

9

Monday morning, Dahlia woke to Noel's arm across her throat and his knee in her ribs. She eased from under him and rolled to the side of the bed.

Much as she liked sleeping with her little man, she wondered how she didn't wake up with bruises after a night in the same bed. She went into the adjoining bathroom and got ready for the day. After a refreshing shower, she put on a robe and went back into the bedroom, to find Aofa seated on the side of the bed, playing with Noel.

"Good morning." Aofa's voice boomed with cheer. "I knocked, but there was no answer. I came to see if you'd like me to get the prince ready for the day."

"What's going on today?" Dahlia asked.

"Prince Kofi is taking him to the zoo and then the park."

Noel bounced on the bed. "I love the zoo!" he exclaimed. She'd taken him there twice in the fall.

"What is your favorite animal?" Aofa asked.

"Snake."

"Snake?" Aofa said.

"What sound does the snake make?" Dahlia asked Noel.

"Ssssss." Proud of himself, he grinned.

"What about the lion? He's the king of the beasts," Aofa said.

"Lion is big and scary." Noel held his hands up like claws and made the cutest little roar.

Dahlia and Aofa laughed.

"Would you like me to get him ready, ma'am? That way you and Kemal can work on your affairs this morning."

"My affairs?"

"Yes. I'm sure he can explain the details, but you're moving abroad. You'll need to close accounts and put an end to all your financial obligations in America."

"Oh, right." She hadn't thought that far ahead because she thought she'd be long gone from here.

Dahlia took a good look at Aofa. She didn't doubt the woman's ability, but Dahlia was used to just her and Noel. When they moved to Zamibia, Aofa would be responsible for taking care of him, and Dahlia needed reassurance she could be trusted with her son.

"What kind of experience do you have as a nanny?" she asked in a conversational tone.

Aofa stood and clasped her hands in front of her ample hips. "Ms. Sommers, it is an honor to serve as the nanny for our young prince, and I'm sure you trust Prince Kofi would not have chosen me if I were not qualified. I worked for his uncle, Prince Kehinde, for many years, taking care of two of his grandchildren. They are off to college in London now. Afterward, the Nigerian ambassador hired me to care for his children. As you can see from the blue dye in my hair, Kemal and I are from the Ndenga tribe. He told me Prince Kofi was looking for a nanny right away. I submitted my CV, and with a recommendation from Prince Kehinde, he hired me. I know this is your first child, and I understand. But please do not worry. I am a grandmother, and I love children. Your son is safe with me." She glanced at Noel, who started jumping on the bed again.

"Even though he has all this energy? Noel, stop jumping on the bed."

He ignored her and continued jumping and giggling.

"Even with this much energy." Aofa chuckled.

Satisfied with the answer, Dahlia asked, "How many grandchildren do you have?"

"Four. Two boys and two girls. They live in Cape Ndugu, a small fishing village on the coast. Do you know it?"

Dahlia shook her head.

"Many Ndenga live there. I don't get to see my grandchildren much now that I work in the palace again, but when I have time off, I go straight to the Cape to see them." She smiled in a matronly way. "The palace is ready for your son. He has his own room, already filled with toys and books. His room is right next to yours, and you can make any changes to the decorations you wish. He will be happy there."

"Thank you." Dahlia breathed a little easier. Knowing she'd have Aofa on her side, assisting as she adjusted to her new life, helped put her mind at ease.

"I will get him ready in the bathroom next door." Aofa lifted Noel off the bed.

"Bye-bye, Mommy." He waved.

Dahlia waved back as he disappeared through the door.

She dressed quickly and went downstairs, wondering about breakfast, and followed the scent of bacon into the kitchen. At the entrance, she stopped. Kemal was at the counter pouring himself a cup of coffee.

He paused when he saw her, and the chill of unease trickled down her spine.

Dahlia couldn't quite put her finger on why, but from the first time she met him three years ago, she'd had the distinct impression he didn't like her. Nothing had changed. He didn't crack even the smallest of smiles.

He was extremely efficient and invaluable to Kofi. While he was Kofi's personal assistant, he was also treated as a close friend and confidante. For that reason, she'd never mentioned her unease about his suspected dislike of her.

"Good morning, Miss Sommers," he said in an even tone.

"Good morning, Kemal."

"Breakfast is on the counter. There is plenty of food, but if you'd rather have something else, you simply have to let me know, and I'll ask the cook to prepare it for you."

"That won't be necessary," Dahlia said. "Um, where is Kofi?"

"Prince Kofi is in his office, working. Would you like me to get him for you?"

"No, that won't be necessary."

"Very well." She could almost swear he turned up his lip. "In that case, Prince Kofi asked me to help you close out any accounts you have and take care of any other matters you need to handle before you leave for Zamibia. When you're done eating, we can get started."

He stalked off to the dining table and computer already set up there.

Although hungry, Dahlia decided not to eat. She didn't think she'd have much of an appetite sitting at the table with him, facing his judgment as she ate. Instead, she poured a cup of coffee and sat down with him, and they went over all her bills and financial obligations.

Once he'd gleaned all the information he needed, Kemal went to work with the phone to his ear. All her expenses were to be paid off, including outstanding credit card bills she hadn't been able to put much of a dent in. It felt good to have all those financial obligations immediately taken care of, but strange. She'd been on her own for such a long time, having someone else making the calls and paying the bills felt odd. Like she was a cheat or someone getting off easy.

While Kemal occupied himself with terminating the lease, utilities, and the like, she submitted a letter of resignation to the center where she worked, effective immediately. She made phone calls to say her goodbyes, but saying goodbye to Angela was the hardest because her friend was still in California and they wouldn't see each other before she left.

By the end of the day, she was much closer to severing her ties to the U.S., in preparation for starting a new life in Zamibia.

10

Aofa told Dahlia that Kofi needed to see her, and she went downstairs and found him in the kitchen, spooning a rich-looking dark sauce onto a plate. The aroma of cloves, garlic, and peppers wafted over to where she stood.

"Have you eaten?" he asked, without looking up.

He continued working, shirt sleeves rolled up to reveal mahogany arms sprinkled with hair. Seeing him in a domestic setting created heat low in her belly that spread to her loins. How many times had she trailed her fingers along those same arms, or melted into the warmth of his body when they held her tight against him?

Dahlia snapped out of her reverie. What was wrong with her? Kofi practically held her against her will, and all she could think about was how hot he looked.

"Not yet." She entered the kitchen. "No one to serve you tonight?"

"There's no need for staff to wait on me hand and foot every minute of every day."

"That's not how it was before." She moved around him. He used to always have a servant or valet nearby at all times.

"I've become a bit more independent since then. Plates are in the cabinet over there."

Dahlia retrieved one of the dishes. Kofi took it from her and spooned a piece of chicken and sauce on it. "You're actually preparing my plate?" She cocked an eyebrow.

"Don't look so shocked."

"I can't help but be surprised you're serving and being nice."

He added rice and beans and then vegetables to the dish, drizzling the spicy sauce over everything. "It's easier to be nice when I get what I want. Winning mellows me out."

She wanted to smack the smirk off his face. "You're gloating, and it's not a good look."

Dahlia proceeded to the dining area, already set with water glasses, and where a bottle of wine chilled in a bucket of ice on the table. She sat down.

Seconds later, Kofi placed the plate in front of her before sitting across the table.

He spread a napkin across his lap. "Are you still doing photography?" he asked, before uncorking the wine.

"I take pictures, but not as often as before. Renting dark room space isn't affordable anymore."

He hesitated, his gaze meeting hers before pouring wine in her glass and then doing the same in his. An uncomfortable silence settled over the room.

She couldn't afford to pursue her hobby after Kofi forced her and Melanie to close the property management business. Disposable income became a thing of the past, especially after having Noel. The same as her mother, she took tons of pictures but preferred a film camera to digital. There was nothing like the excitement of developing film in a dark room and uncovering the gem of a perfectly taken photo.

"What did you want to talk to me about?" Dahlia purposely shifted the conversation. Shoulders tight, she braced for more demands.

Kofi tore off a piece of bread and used it to sop up some of the sauce from the plate. He popped the chunk into his mouth and chewed. "You have a lot to learn when we arrive in Zamibia, and I'm sure you have questions."

"I do. I've accepted a position I don't know anything about."

"The duties of the princess are general in nature, focused on building goodwill and PR. You'll host dinners for visiting dignitaries, attend state functions, and become a patron for the charitable organizations of your choice."

"Sounds like a lot of work."

Kofi cut into a piece of chicken. "You'll have a full staff to help you, people who consider working in the palace a privilege and an honor. Before you arrive, Kemal will make sure you learn the basics to get you past the press when we land. There are a few details about protocol you'll need to learn, and after that, you'll basically be in school, learning our history and culture. You'll be expected to learn at least a few words and phrases in French and in Mbutu."

No surprise there. Zamibia had three official languages—French, English, and Mbutu, spoken by the Mbutu people, the largest tribe in the country.

"Anything you want to ask me?" Kofi said.

Dahlia pushed the rice and beans around on her plate. Glancing up, she asked, "Can I get out of marrying you?"

He chewed slowly and took a sip of wine. Her nerves stretched taut as she waited for a reply.

"Of course. Let me take Noel and you can stay here."

"You know that's not an option."

"Then why ask the question?"

She ate some of the chicken and took a swig of water to wash away the spiciness. "One of us should ask questions."

"What does that mean?" He rested his wrists on the table and waited.

"You never asked if I was seeing anyone."

"You're not."

"How do you know?"

"I found you, remember? My investigator gave me a full report of all your activities. I'm certain you moved to Georgia not only because of the lower cost of living, but because your best friend, Angela, lives here, and you've worked at the substance abuse center since you left New York. You go to work, pick up Noel, and go home. Some days you run errands."

Her life sounded terribly boring when summarized in that fashion.

They ate in silence for a few minutes, and the only sounds were of the utensils hitting the porcelain plates. Dahlia observed him from across the table, taking stock of the majestic beauty of his face and each measured, controlled movement. Her insides twisted with nostalgia or regret, she couldn't be sure. He seemed so aloof.

"You never told me why you came looking for me." After the way they parted, she never thought she'd hear from him again.

Kofi kept his gaze on the plate, and she had the distinct feeling he didn't want her to read his expression.

"I hadn't been back to the United States in the three years since...since you and I were involved. I was curious about what you were up to."

"What would you have done if you'd found me and there was no Noel?" She held her breath, anxious to hear his response.

"And you hadn't kept my son from me?"

"Yes. If you found me and Noel didn't exist at all."

He picked up his glass of wine and studied it before looking at her again. "We'll never know the answer to that question."

Disappointed, Dahlia lowered her lashes and continued to eat.

～

DINNER ENDED, and Dahlia helped Kofi load the dishwasher, something she never thought she'd see him do. He really had relaxed since the last visit.

She dried her hands on a towel and edged past him. "Good night."

"Before you go, there's something I need to give you."

She stopped her progress across the floor and turned to face him.

"Follow me."

She followed him into the living room, where he opened the locked drawer of a desk and took out a red velvet pouch with a gold drawstring. He opened the little bag and removed a gold ring with the largest diamond Dahlia had ever seen.

She gasped.

Two trapezoid diamonds sandwiched a larger emerald cut stone, all of them shining with such brilliance she almost needed shades.

"It's beautiful." Dahlia said softly. It was the most exquisite piece of jewelry she'd ever laid her eyes on. Her throat locked up, and for a fleeting second she wished this could be a real engagement and he'd come to find her because he missed her.

Kofi set the pouch on the desk and extended his hand. Dahlia laid her palm over his, her fingers trembling slightly, an awkward tension in the air as he slid the ring onto her finger. A perfect fit.

"Now our engagement is official," he said. A possessive gleam entered his eyes.

The warmth from his hand crept past her palm, moving steadily upward.

Dahlia laughed shakily. "Someone will probably cut off my hand to get this ring. I better be careful."

His face hardened. "No one would dare harm you, or my son."

He spoke with such conviction, she didn't doubt his words for a minute. No one would want to have to deal with his wrath.

Kofi pressed his mouth against the back of her fingers. The act shocked and thrilled her, taking her back to the first time they met. She'd been charmed by him then, high on the idea that this man was paying so much attention to her, and the feeling never went away, only intensified over time.

Torn between wanting to maintain contact but heartsick over the memories, she tried to pull away.

His fingers tightened around hers. "Where would you like to go on our honeymoon?"

"Honeymoon?" Dahlia repeated. Her pulse skipped a beat.

"We'll be married. It's expected."

"And what do you expect us to do on the honeymoon?"

"What do newlyweds do on a honeymoon?" Kofi asked.

Dahlia successfully tugged away her hand and distanced herself from him. Wrapping her arms around her waist, she said, "Are—are you saying you expect me to sleep with you? Because if you're talking about sex, that's not what we agreed to. This isn't supposed to be a real marriage." Her heart rate accelerated.

"You do realize that as my wife, you'll be expected to bear me more heirs?"

"Bear you more...*heirs*?" He couldn't be serious. Their marriage was to be in name only, to legitimize their son. Had she misunderstood?

"Of course. Sex between a husband and his wife is the most natural thing in the world," he drawled. "I have a right to touch my own wife, don't I?"

Dahlia's breath caught in her throat as she remembered quite clearly being touched by him, the unbridled passion they'd shared etched in her memory as sure as a sculptor's design in stone. Kofi may be composed and cultured in his day to day life, but in the bedroom, he was intense and demanding. His kisses were divine and his stroke damn near earth-shattering.

She couldn't open herself up to that kind of intimacy and feeling again. Not when they almost destroyed her before, and not when she knew she would be competing with other women for his attention.

"You'll have mistresses. You won't need me."

"On the contrary, I do need you. To conceive the legitimate line for the monarchy. That's your duty."

This was a nightmare. "Are you telling me you're going to breed me like some kind of cow?"

"Don't be crass."

"Don't be crass?" Her voice grew louder in dismay. "That's exactly what you're saying. Talk to the council, because I won't do it. I'm going to Zamibia for my son, that's the deal. Get yourself a mistress. Or another wife."

His eyes flashed angrily at her. "The more you talk, the better I like those ideas."

Her heart hollowed out. Enraged, Dahlia grabbed a pillow from the sofa and flung it at him.

11

K ofi caught the pillow and panic flared in her eyes. He tossed it aside, and for two heart-pounding moments they stared at each other. Then he charged across the room at her and she ran for the exit, but he grabbed her around the waist and lifted her off the floor. She let out a soft cry and kicked her feet in the air, tugging on his arms, to no avail.

Kofi tossed her onto the sofa and fell on top of her back, fingers curling around her wrists with the force of steel bands. "Still feisty, I see."

"Go to hell. I'm not going on a honeymoon with you, and I'm definitely not sleeping with you."

"We need to have more children."

"Have them with your mistress!" she choked out.

"Once you're the princess, only the children you and I have will be next in line for the throne," Kofi growled.

"Have the council make an exception the way they did for Noel." Dahlia tried to wiggle free, but he only tightened his hold as she struggled. Her floral print dress rode higher on her thighs as she rubbed her cushy ass against his crotch. His flesh hardened from the electrifying contact.

"That's not the way this works," Kofi said huskily in her ear. "We must have more children. An heir and a spare is the norm."

"My god, are you saying what I think you're saying? That it's your *job* to get me pregnant?"

"Dahlia—"

"That it's my *job* to have another child?" She glowered at him over her shoulder.

He closed his eyes, counting backward from ten.

"Answer me! Sleeping with me is your job? Thank you so much, Your Highness. How flattering."

"It will be your duty and mine to continue the line," Kofi said grimly. With difficulty, he flipped Dahlia onto her back and using one hand, kept her hands joined above her head. Lips pressed together in a mutinous line, she fought him the whole time, but the end result of her stretched beneath him meant her breasts arched upward in a temptingly delicious way.

Her eyes spat fire at him. "You think I'm a thief and a liar. Do you really want another child to be associated with someone like me?"

"Not that again."

"Yes, that again. Get off!"

She thrashed around, trying to break free, bucking hard, but he refused to let her go. Meanwhile, the organ between his legs thickened and hardened, his senses becoming aware of every move her soft body made.

She froze. No doubt feeling him against her thigh, hard and ready. He saw the exact moment anger transformed into lust. Kofi shifted, slid a leg between her thighs, and moved a hand to her hip. She let out a soft moan and bit down on her lip, eyes shuttering closed. Definitely not a sound of rejection.

He hadn't been able to think straight since he saw her again, and right now he didn't give a damn about heirs or duty. He wanted to lose himself inside of her.

Her heightened breathing sent warm breath brushing his bearded chin right before he mashed his mouth over hers. He pushed his hands under the folds of the dress and tore off her underwear with the ease of tearing tissue. When he penetrated her mouth with his tongue, she opened willingly, mouth clinging to his as he took his fill, sucking her lower lip and nipping the tender flesh with his teeth.

He broke the kiss and moved lower, kissing her chin until she tilted her head higher and allowed his tongue to trace the erratically beating pulse at the base of her neck. She groaned and curved her back at an acute angle, and he covered her incredible breasts with his hands. Soft and full, they filled his palms.

"Kofi..."

"I love the way you say my name," he whispered. "Do you have any idea what it does to me when you say my name in your American accent?"

A shudder lanced through her and found an answering tremor in his body. As he sucked her neck, his hands caressed her soft thighs under the folds of the dress. His hips tilted toward hers three times in quick succession, simulating intercourse, and she answered the call by lifting upward to enjoy each provocative thrust.

He kissed her ear and sprinkled tender pecks of affection down her jaw to her rounded chin and went lower. His mouth skimmed her breast through the dress, while a hand squeezed her bare ass. When he cupped between her legs, she drew a sharp breath. She was so wet and warm, he wanted a taste. Sliding down her body, he kissed her through the clothes and finally pressed his face into the wet arc of her legs. He inhaled her sweet feminine scent and flicked the tip of his tongue along her clit.

She shuddered again and inhaled sharply, letting out desperate little noises, trying to stifle the sounds so no one else heard. He stayed there for a while, slicing his tongue along her core and filling his mouth with her flesh. She squirmed about the sofa, knees bent and legs spread, hand at the back of his head.

"Taste so sweet," he breathed.

Damn, this woman.

He knew her. Knew her scent and what every type of moan meant—more, less, or right there. He hadn't forgotten a single signal nor forgotten how good she felt in his arms. Everything about her was achingly familiar.

He moved higher again, licking his lips, and dropped a kiss on her mouth, the tip of his tongue moving on the inside boundary of her lips. Dahlia whimpered and rubbed against him like a lioness in heat. Her arms fastened around his neck and her fingers strolled through the soft coils on his head.

Anger had transformed into blinding hunger, no longer hiding beneath the veneer of civilized discourse. A need so great he could hardly think. All he could do was seek relief.

"Unzip me." He wanted to feel her hands on his hard flesh—cupping, stroking, twisting him inside out.

"Kofi..."

"Please." He guided her hand to his crotch. He'd never begged for anything in his life, but every man had his weakness, and she was his.

The first time they had made love, the pulsing attraction between them had erupted into a volcanic heat and he'd lifted her against the wall. Completely out of control, he'd buried his face in her neck and gripped her thighs as he plunged into her wet, willing body with a ferocity he'd never before experienced. He wanted to lose himself like that again.

He sucked the side of her neck and, shifting a hand beneath her dress again, tried to slip a finger inside her, but she stayed his hand.

"Don't." Her voice trembled.

"Dahlia—"

"Please, Kofi. Stop." She pressed her palms against his chest, and he stilled. Easing back, he looked into her face. She wouldn't look at him.

With a heavy groan, he launched himself off of her and sat in the corner of the sofa, burying his head in his hands. He smelled the musk from between her legs and wanted to go back there again, press his face to her slick heat and eat until he was satisfied.

Dahlia sat at the other end of the furniture and tugged the dress down to cover her nakedness.

Neither of them spoke.

Finally, Kofi stood and went over to the window, and her gaze blurred behind a screen of tears.

"This isn't going to work," she told him.

"Says who?"

"Me. You're asking too much."

She barely managed to stop him. Her body hummed from his hands on her breasts and his tongue stroking between her legs. Her fight or flight instincts were fully engaged, warning that she couldn't sleep with him, but if he'd pushed a little harder, she would have succumbed. Living with him would be torture enough. Intimacy could destroy her.

"I feel so sorry for you, Dahlia, but you're stuck with me. Maybe it's your punishment for stealing from my people."

"I didn't steal that money."

"It no longer matters."

"It matters to me! I can be trusted."

"Yes, you've proven that, haven't you?" He turned to face her.

"I messed up when I tried to take Noel, but don't tell me you wouldn't have done the same if the roles were reversed. He's my child and my closest relative. I have very little family left—people I rarely talk to. He was all I had." *He was all I had of you.* "You were going to take him away from me if I didn't follow you to Zamibia, and I didn't know what to expect once I arrived there." She took a quivering breath and swiped at her damp eyes. "You have to believe me, Kofi."

"People make mistakes."

"I've made mistakes, but I'm not a thief."

He stared at her, hands on his hips. "Why do you want me to believe you?"

"I..." She sniffed. "I don't know." It was too humiliating to admit she wanted their marriage to work. To be real. She couldn't admit she didn't want anger between them all the time and didn't want Noel to see them at each other's throats. She couldn't admit she wanted him to need her as more than a baby-making machine.

"If you don't know, then my trust must not be very important to you. As for whether or not we'll be sleeping together, I promise not to attack you again like a wild boar, but don't pretend there's no longer chemistry between us." His voice grew huskier as he spoke. "That chemistry is all over my mouth and fingers. I can still smell how much you want me."

Heat swamped her face. "Wanting you doesn't change our situation. You don't get it, do you? Three years ago you acted like I was your everything, and then you left and married another woman. I never heard from you again. Now you pop up, threaten to take my child, and oh, by the way, I'm supposed to have more babies with you to continue the Karunzika line."

"What do you want me to say?" he asked sharply. He took two steps forward. "You want the truth, Dahlia? You *were* everything to me. Is that what you want to hear? I wanted to place the world at your feet. Yes, I was getting married, but in name only. I wanted y—"

He heaved a sigh and ran a hand down the back of his head.

"I wanted to marry you," he said in a thick voice. "You really want to know what I would have done if I'd found you here and Noel didn't exist? I would have asked you to marry me and given you the ring you're wearing. The ring I had made especially for you before I learned you'd kept my son a secret." He laughed bitterly. "And do you know why? Because I'm a fool. Because for three months, three years ago, I thought I'd found someone I could trust. Someone different from every other greedy, selfish man and woman I've met in my life and tried to protect myself and my people from."

Sensing what his last words would be, she bent her head. She didn't want to see the disappointment in his eyes. Hearing the words would be difficult enough.

"That's why I came looking for you, Dahlia. I held out hope." His voice dropped lower, became thicker. "But I was wrong. You're the same as everyone else. You can come to Zamibia or you can stay here. But if you come, you abide by the rules of my country, and in my country, I make the rules."

He left the room so quietly, she didn't know he was gone until she lifted her head and saw the empty space where he'd stood. The torn panties on the floor and the dampness between her thighs indicated their lust for each other, but they would never be close again. She saw that now.

Pain scoured her heart.

She told herself she was a fool. She told herself not to cry. She cried anyway.

12

ANNOUNCEMENT FROM THE OFFICE
OF HIS MAJESTY
KING BABATUNDE FRANCOIS KARUNZIKA

HIS MAJESTY KING Babatunde Francois Karunzika, Most Honorable Leader of the Nine Tribes of Zamibia, is pleased to announce the engagement of his son, His Royal Highness Crown Prince Kofi Francois Karunzika to Miss Dahlia Sommers of the United States. The king also welcomes the couple's son and his grandchild, Noel.

The wedding will take place on Saturday, April 14th. The couple and their son will live in the prince's apartment in The Grand Palace of Zamibia.

∼

DAHLIA HELD the English version of the press release, which included the royal seal—an illustrated lion with a full mane and a crown sitting on its head. There were numerous versions—one in each of the tribal languages and one in French.

The wedding was actually happening. She was going to marry Kofi and become a member of the royal family. She'd left her life in the States behind and embarked on a new life, in an unfamiliar culture, and a life made more intimidating by the social norms she'd have to adhere to as a princess. The big knot in her stomach only grew larger and tighter as they sat on the tarmac awaiting word to descend from the airplane.

The royal plane rivaled Air Force One in size and the number of amenities on board. In addition to being able to seat up to eighteen passengers comfortably in fully reclining seats, the jet contained a master suite with adjoining bathroom, guest bedrooms and more baths, offices, a conference room, and a dining room. There was a well-stocked kitchen and pantry, as well as a bar and lounge. One of Kofi's doctors flew with them and oversaw the medical suite, a state-of-the-art facility complete with medical equipment and pharmaceuticals in case of emergency.

The trip had been mostly uneventful, with last minute preparation and advice from Kemal, who'd prepped Dahlia on her new role.

"Remember to smile, always."

"Wave with your fingers close together, never apart."

"You may walk beside Prince Kofi or behind him, but never in front."

"Prince Kofi will carry Prince Noel off the plane. It is important that the people immediately see his close bond with his son."

So many rules, and they were only the beginning. The past two days she received a ton of instructions to prepare her and her son for their new life. She glanced at Noel, blissfully unaware of the changes to come as he played with a magnetic drawing board. He did a horrible job of drawing, but the toy kept him busy now that he was awake. She ran a gentle hand over his curls. He would adjust, and she would have to adjust, too. Somehow.

One of the flight attendants crouched in front of Dahlia's chair. "Are you all right, ma'am?" she asked.

Dahlia didn't know if she sensed her unease. She hadn't seen Kofi for hours, but Kemal told her he was working in one of the offices on board, handling royal business and squaring away the final details for their arrival.

She placed a brave smile on her face. "Yes, I'm fine. Thank you for checking."

"Can I get you something to drink while we wait?"

Dahlia shook her head. "No." If she ate or drank anything she'd bring it back up. "Do you know why there's a delay?"

The other woman nodded. "The crowd is larger than expected. Our citizens are curious to see Prince Kofi's fiancée, and of course, his son."

"Crowd?" Dahlia glanced at Noel, more worried than she was before. "It's not dangerous, is it?"

"Oh no, not at all. But the crowds must be controlled and organized for easy passage to the palace. Please, do not worry. No harm will come to you or our prince." Like the security guards, she referred to him as "our" prince. She'd already claimed him.

"You don't know that for sure."

The flight attendant smiled reassuringly. "Oh, but I do, ma'am." She leaned closer. "You never have to worry about your safety in Zamibia. Only a fool would harm a member of the royal family."

She was either a liar or very naive. "Then why the bodyguards?" Dahlia asked.

"Well, one must be prudent." She laughed. "But I promise, you have nothing to fear. In Zamibia, harming any member of the royal family is the only crime punishable by death." She straightened to a standing position.

Dahlia blinked. "I had no idea."

The young woman placed her hands together in a prayer-like position. "You have nothing to fear."

Dahlia and Noel were left alone for a few minutes, and then the cabin door opened and Kofi entered. She took a silent breath as she absorbed his magnificence, the most recent memory of his fingers and mouth on her body sending her skin into a heated flush. He wore dark shoes polished to a shine, a dark suit, and a vibrant-colored scarf that draped off his shoulder and matched the tie.

"Are you ready?" he asked.

"Yes."

He extended his hand and helped her from the chair. In that split second, her heart ached for the past, back to the time when he looked at her with affection instead of suspicion. Too soon, he released her and lifted Noel from the seat. Their son whined for a few seconds because he had to give up his toy, but soon he settled against his father's torso.

They exited the plane with Kofi leading the way down the stairs and Dahlia a few steps behind. A gust of wind blew across them, and she was glad an assistant on board had secured her hair into a bun at her nape. A cheer went up from the assembled crowd of mostly media. Cameras flashed and journalists yelled questions at them in French, English, and Mbutu.

Dahlia stood beside him on the tarmac, smiling and waving—making sure to keep her fingers together as instructed. Noel viewed the throng with curious eyes and when he was comfortable, waved back. The group erupted into laughter, and then the questions started.

"Prince Kofi, how did you meet?"

"Miss Sommers, how did he propose?"

"Miss Sommers, are you ready for the challenge of being part of the royal family?"

Kofi lifted a hand and the crowd went silent. "We'll answer your questions at a later time, but for now, we're tired after traveling for many hours. Please, give us a few days to relax, and give my fiancée and son time to acclimate to their new home." He lifted Dahlia's hand and, gazing into her eyes, kissed the knuckles.

"Awwww," the crowd said, and camera flashes went off in quick succession.

Dahlia's chest tightened at the tenderness in his eyes and the soft touch. She couldn't handle him like this. Charming, almost back to the man she'd known before. She preferred him angry and cold, which made it easier for her to keep a wall between them and remain justifiably distant.

She bit down on her lip and then remembered that she should smile. With trembling lips, she forced the corners of her mouth into a curve. Kofi didn't let go of her hand, and after a while, her fingers closed around his and she leaned into him, taking strength from his solid presence.

After a few minutes, Kofi allowed them to be led away by Kemal and his bodyguards. Dahlia ducked into a waiting limousine with him, the red, green, and black striped flag of Zamibia whipping around in the wind on the hood.

The limousine was in the middle of a caravan of cars, including police motorcycles at the very front and back. They eased off the tarmac and traveled at a slow crawl through the city streets of Jouba, the capital. Dahlia looked out the window at the mix of old and new evident in the architecture. Skyscrapers towered above colorful buildings made of brick or what appeared to be mud. Signs were written in all three official languages. Entrepreneurs sold street food and hawked knickknacks from carts right in front of a sprawling mall with a parking lot filled with cars.

Because of the tinted windows, Dahlia could see out but no one could see in. As they passed by, young people ran along with the car and waved, others—older and with more deference—dropped to one knee and bowed their heads. The ride to the palace wasn't very long, but about a mile from the destination, police barricades blocked either side of the road to keep back crowds of people who craned their necks to catch a glimpse of their prince and the newcomers. The people were a mix of modern and traditional like the buildings. They wore kente designs and Ankara print clothing as well as Western-style dress.

When they finally turned onto the road that led up to the palace, Dahlia's mouth fell open. Tall, green, cone-shaped trees flanked either side of the roadway, drawing the eye to the palace at the far end. The large, three-story structure sprawled across the landscape on a mound elevated above street level. The entire palace was a sandstone color with a verdant-green roof, and what appeared to be a giant metal door at the front was the same color as the rooftop. Dozens of windows dotted the exterior in the shape of arches and rectangles.

The cars crept forward, bringing them closer to a decorative sandstone-colored wall that lined the front of the mound, with a series of sculptures displayed before it, including the head of a roaring lion at the very top of the wall. The caravan turned right and up an incline to the circular driveway. By the time they stopped in front of the building, a line of employees had emerged. Servants dressed in white shirts and tan pants, and ten guards dressed in crisp blue-on-blue military gear stood on either side of them. The guards held themselves perfectly still with a gun on one hip, a dagger on the other, and one hand on ceremonial spears at their sides, gazes fixed on some object in the far distance.

Kofi climbed out first, holding Noel who'd remained silent as he absorbed his new surroundings. Dahlia followed behind Kofi, and as soon as his foot touched the sidewalk leading up to the palace, the entire line of servants and guards dropped to one knee and bowed their heads in unison.

While Dahlia stared, lips parted in awe at the respect Kofi commanded, he didn't even acknowledge them. She realized with a start that one day, her son would command the same amount of deference.

13

"**K**ofi!" His cousin Imani ran to him and threw her arms around his neck.

Laughing, he squeezed her tight and lifted her off the floor. "What are you doing here?" He held her at arm's length, observing her bright eyes and her hair cut in a bob a few inches off her shoulders. "You cut your hair? Is that what you've been doing in Barrakesch?"

Barrakesch was a Middle Eastern country and a long time ally of Zamibia. Their relationship started when the Arab nation sold the Zamibians guns to help them fight the British over a century ago. His cousin went to graduate school at a top university there and was now ensconced in the Zamibian embassy as an ambassador. Her title was Lioness Abameha, an honorific reserved for female members of the royal family ranked lower than a princess.

Imani thumped him on the arm. "You don't like my hair?"

"It suits you. Short and sassy."

She thumped his arm again, her grin broadening. "I came home because I want to meet your son and future wife."

"Then you'll have dinner with us?"

Imani lived in her father's apartment in the palace, with their own set of chefs and servants to cater to their family.

"I will. Baba and his wives are out of the country, and I don't want to eat alone."

Kofi's father entered the room and cleared his throat.

Grasping his fist, Kofi held it against his chest and bowed his head as a sign of respect. "*Bawoh*, Father, my king."

Imani gave the same sign of respect. "*Bawoh*, Uncle, my king."

King Babatunde nodded and shuffled to the sofa across the room. He settled his wooden staff against a table where the sole item sitting on its surface was a photograph of Kofi's mother, Queen Nahla, in full regalia.

His father was a giant of a man, taller and thicker than Kofi. Most days he wore traditional attire, and today's outfit consisted of a white agbada with bronze embroidery and a matching fila on his head. His skin was a lighter color than Kofi's, closer to the golden brown hue taken on by the baobab trees when sunlight filtered across their trunks at dawn.

The old man moved slower now, much slower than before Jafari and Queen Nahla passed away. But Babatunde was more than twice Kofi's age and a lack of vigor expected. Kofi thanked God and his ancestors for sparing the life of his father, at least.

A servant approached and handed the king a glass of bissap, a drink made from dried hibiscus flowers. His father drank half the maroon beverage before giving a curt nod, indicating he'd like more. The servant filled the glass from the pitcher on the tray and then turned to Kofi. He waved him away, but Imani took a glass and sat beside the king.

"He looks like you when you were a boy," Babatunde said.

"Yes, he does." Kofi smiled.

There was no doubt Noel was his son in appearance, but he inherited his mother's temperament. The little boy was friendly, and Kofi already felt fully bonded to him. Aofa adored him, and the few staff he'd interacted with had fallen under the spell of his inquisitive nature and warm giggles. When Dahlia and Noel left to go to Kofi's apartment in the east wing, the boy marched ahead, as if he knew the way, while everyone else followed behind, watching him turn his head from side to side as he examined his new environment.

Kofi's grandfather commissioned the construction of the palace when King Babatunde was a boy, not long after gold mines were discovered in the mountains. Some rooms were open to the public as a tourist attraction, but for the most part the palace consisted of living quarters and offices for the royal family and staff.

Caramels, varying shades of gold, and rich browns pervaded the decorations. But so did deep blue and purple. The wood floors looked polished enough to glow in the dark. The marble floors were covered with hand-woven rugs, most sent from far-reaching villages in the kingdom by citizens who'd received the honor of having their work accepted and utilized by the royal family.

"How did you ask her to marry you? Did she say yes right away?" Imani's eyes practically glowed with red hearts.

Kofi stroked his beard for a bit before he answered. "I asked her in her apartment, the first night we saw each other again. At first she was unsure and doubted her ability to be an effective princess, but I basically gave her no choice but to accept my proposal."

"Awww, true love. How romantic." Imani sighed.

"There's nothing wrong with arranged marriages," Babatunde said.

"Arranged marriages are the old way. The new way is to find the person you love and make a life with them. That's what I intend to do," Imani said.

"What does your father have to say about your idea?" Babatunde asked.

"He agrees and will let me choose," Imani said, a trace of defiance in her voice.

"Make sure you choose wisely." Babatunde centered his attention on Kofi. "I like Dahlia. She seemed nervous at first, but I can tell she's strong, like your mother." A soft smile crossed his features.

To this day, his father couldn't mention his mother without a wistful smile taking over his face. Strong winds from an impending storm had been to blame for the plane crash that killed her and his brother, but no explanation had been enough to ease the trauma of losing two members of the royal family in one fatal blow. The entire country had mourned.

Sadly, his parents' relationship soured near the end because his mother discovered in the early years of their marriage, Babatunde had taken a lover and gotten her pregnant. Queen Nahla never forgave him for cheating and having an outside child. His father never forgave himself for hurting her and lived with the guilt of knowing he'd never won her forgiveness before she passed.

The king took another swig from the glass and then set it on the mahogany table. "She needs to be strong because she'll have a lot to learn and get used to."

Kofi remained silent, suspecting his father wanted to say more.

"You should talk to the council right away."

His ears perked up. "Why?"

"They expected you to choose another bride from one of the tribes. They feel shut out that you chose an American."

Kofi went to the open window behind his father's sofa. As far as the eye could see there were orchards and gardens that supplied much of the food for the palace, a testament to the country's origins as an agrarian society, before their warlike instincts developed as a means of self-preservation. The voices of the workers carried on the wind, and he heard them laughing and yelling at each other as the day came to a close.

"I can marry whomever I please."

"And they will accept her because you chose her, but I suggest we throw an engagement party to introduce her to members of the council. I know we're short on time, but that should take care of any offense to their delicate sensibilities."

For once, his father suggested a metered approached. Usually, Babatunde did whatever he wanted with little thought to diplomacy.

"All right," Kofi agreed.

Babatunde sighed heavily. "I know how you feel about this woman. Do you think you can trust her?"

Kofi remained silent. His father knew about the embezzlement, and he didn't want to lie to him or reveal his remaining reservations about Dahlia.

"You need to be wise, Kofi. Lead with your head, not your heart. Make sure she's ready to face them. If you don't, the press will not be kind."

Kofi laughed bitterly. "I know all about the press."

Eleven years ago at the young age of nineteen, he'd made the terrible mistake of sharing his private thoughts with a fellow student in London, a young woman he cared about and thought cared about him. Instead, she'd simply been milking him for information to sell to the tabloids. Acknowledgment of the advantages he received as royalty, as well as offhand comments about the pressures and limitations of being a young prince, had been printed out of context and made him appear simultaneously arrogant and ungrateful. A PR nightmare and a harsh lesson to learn. He'd spent years performing public service, anxious to change the narrative about himself.

"And then there is the issue of the oil. The representative from Titanium Oil came back while you were gone." A few months ago, oil had been discovered off the coast of Zamibia, and the company set up an office to offer their services as a partner to the government.

"Alistair Davies? What did he want?"

Kofi walked around to face his father.

"More of the same. To convince us we need them to help us with drilling the oil. I put him off, but he asked for a meeting."

Imani snorted. "They want to rob us."

"They've been very persistent," Babatunde told Kofi. "We may need the help, but I don't trust them. I worry they'll find a way to stir up conflict through bribes or some other means and threaten our way of life."

The royal family benefited from extraordinary wealth, but unlike the royals of other countries, the Karunzikas were generous. By keeping the businesses that mined the gold state-owned, they kept the majority of the money in the country, only hiring consultants as needed. They built hospitals, schools, and other public facilities for the benefit of their citizens. Roads had been improved and public transportation upgraded. Jobs created around the mining industry were not only service positions, but executive and management roles mostly filled by qualified Zamibians.

Thirty years ago, they instituted universal healthcare and funded education from elementary school through college. This made the Zamibians very loyal. Loyalty meant physically and mentally able young men and women who finished high school often chose to give a year of military service. As an alternative, others volunteered to work for eighteen months in the government or a local non-profit in their region before attending college or a trade school.

"Can't we kick them out?" Imani asked.

"It's not that simple, and they might be able to help us," Kofi muttered.

They needed to handle the delicate nature of rebuffing the outsiders with diplomacy before escalating to more aggressive measures. For years they'd had a tenuous relationship with the British because they'd failed twice in their attempts to take over Zamibia. The Mbutu were the fiercest and most warlike of the Zamibian tribes. With them leading the way, the country fought a valiant first war against colonization. But after seeing neighboring countries come under European rule, they knew it would only be a matter of time before the British turned their attention to them again. That's when they reached out to Barrakesch, purchased more guns, and trained and armed every member of the country willing to fight.

The second time, the British attacked by sea, but they were ready. They defeated the invaders, making Zamibia one of only a few African countries—Liberia and Ethiopia being the other two— that had never been taken over by a European power.

Babatunde grasped his staff and rose from the chair with a groan. "I'm an old man. I no longer have the patience to deal with these foreigners. You know what your job is. Keep our people safe and happy, govern fairly, and continue our line. You're not successful if you don't do all three." His father spoke with a firmness that demanded a response. He spoke to Kofi not only as a father, but as his king.

"I understand," Kofi said.

"I know you have to go to a meeting in the north country for a couple of days, but when you get back, take care of the council and set up a meeting with Davies. See what he wants, and make a decision about what we should do." Babatunde then left the room.

14

A t the sound of men's voices, loud and strong, Dahlia left the rack of clothes she was sorting through and went over to the window.

Downstairs, Kofi and Abdalla practiced hand to hand combat with a long stick in each of their hands. Today was Kofi's first day back since he left town for a meeting in a region north of Jouba a couple of days ago.

Kofi moved with swift agility, looking as lethal as his leonine title suggested. Abdalla, big as he was, moved fast, as well. Both men were shirtless, their muscular bodies glistening with sweat, but her eyes remained riveted on Kofi. She licked her suddenly dry lips.

The tendons and muscles in his arms grew tight as he circled the bigger man, seeking to strike first. Three lines of tiny, evenly spaced circles stretched across the upper plane of his back. The raised skin, implemented during a scarification ceremony, indicated his warrior status.

She hadn't spent much time alone with Kofi before he left town. They ate dinners with the king, formal affairs at a long table in an ornate dining room in the king's quarters. Afterward, while she and Noel went back to the apartment, Kofi remained with his father. She assumed they talked late into the night. He never knocked on her bedroom door to say good night.

Which was an interesting part of their marriage—separate bedrooms. They were separated by a short hallway, a secret passageway at the back of her bedroom, behind a wall. One day she'd have to get a map to see where all the other passageways and secret rooms were hidden in the palace.

Similar to the rest of the palace, bright colors adorned her room, along with hand-painted textiles and decorative touches such as handmade furniture carved with intricate designs from trees native to the country. The floor near her bed was covered with a plush, camel-colored accent rug she enjoyed losing her toes in, currently occupied by Noel and his toys.

Their living quarters were located on the second floor in the east wing. The entire apartment was the size of a large penthouse, and the palace itself was so huge the first couple of days she'd been tempted to leave a trail of breadcrumbs to find her way back and forth.

And, she was overwhelmed by all her responsibilities, which made her tired and cranky. Every day, someone needed her attention for one task or another. Did she want to change the paint on the walls in her office? Ready to choose the fabrics and furniture for Noel's room? There were also numerous introductions. She met Imani, Kofi's cousin, and other members of the family who lived in the palace or stopped in to meet her and "our young prince," as they called Noel.

Dahlia froze and caught her breath as Abdalla swung low at Kofi's leg. Kofi deftly slid out of harm's way and doubled back, twisted his club and struck Abdalla in the arm.

"You shouldn't worry." Mariama, her maid, came to stand beside her in front of the window. She'd been so engrossed in the performance below, she didn't hear the young woman come in.

"Looks rather dangerous," Dahlia murmured.

"Prince Kofi is a skilled boxer and an expert in the African fighting arts Dambe and stick fighting. He will land as many blows as he takes."

Dahlia turned away from the window because she couldn't stomach watching the men hurt each other.

Tomorrow they took engagement photos, so she sorted through the outfits Lisette, one of the stylists, brought to the palace. Speak of the devil, the petite, dark-haired French woman waltzed into the room with a container filled with scarves.

"I knew I'd left something in the car." She plopped the see-through box on the bench in front of the bed. "What about this?" She held up a red and green scarf and pulled a cream pantsuit from the rack. "And this?"

Dahlia tilted her head to the side. "What do you think?" she asked Mariama, who now sat on the side of the bed.

"I like whatever you like, ma'am."

She was young, with large doe eyes and short-cropped hair, only nineteen, and obviously grateful for the position of working with Dahlia. Her deference at times embarrassed Dahlia, but she worked hard and was clearly trained well.

"You can be honest with me, you know," Dahlia said.

Mariama smiled shyly.

Dahlia sighed. "Maybe the pantsuit. Yes, the pantsuit."

"And what about this, for an evening event?" Lisette pulled another article of clothing from the rack. A black, strapless gown covered in hand-sewn beading.

"It's beautiful," Dahlia said dully. At some point she needed to sit down with the social secretary and schedule events, which included attending functions with Kofi that were already on his calendar. Yet another task on her to-do list.

"It would be perfect for one of the formal dinners. You should try it on."

Unaccustomed to having extra people around all the time, Dahlia took the dress into the dressing room, which was literally the size of her old apartment, but only contained the clothes and shoes she'd brought from the States. Lisette's job was to increase her wardrobe, put matching outfits together, and fill the closet with high fashion clothing, some of which hadn't hit the runway yet.

Dahlia slipped on the dress and stepped into the bedroom. "Well, what do you think?" she asked, doing a quick twirl.

"Pretty, Mommy," Noel said.

Dahlia blew him a kiss.

"Noel has good taste. You look lovely." Lisette knelt in front of her and folded up the hem. "I think we can go a little shorter here, no?"

"I think you're right."

Lisette held the hem in place using pins from the cushion attached to her wrist and then got to her feet. "*Bon*. Let's see what other goodies we can find."

They went through all the clothes, pulling out the must-haves and leaving the discarded choices on the rack. Accessories and shoes were also set aside. By the time they were on the last two dresses, poor Noel had fallen asleep on the rug.

"I'm not sure about this one." Dahlia came out of the dressing room in a blue dress and turned her back to Lisette.

Before the woman could pull up the zipper, Kofi's deep voice said, "I'll take care of that."

Her stomach contracted. Glancing over her shoulder, she saw him approach from across the room. As usual, he exuded power and confidence, this time in a dashiki shirt and matching pants.

Lisette drifted out of his way and Mariama went to stand against the wall, hands clasped in front of her.

"This dress is exquisite," Kofi said quietly. He'd taken a shower, because she smelled the pine-fresh scent of soap, and the unique scent of his cologne—a proprietary blend created just for him. The same one he'd worn years ago.

His hand rested on the zipper at the base of her spine, and Dahlia held her breath, intensely aware of the intimacy of the moment, and kept her hand pressed against the bodice of the expensive gown to keep it in place.

"I think it might be a little too small," she said.

He didn't move right away to zip her up. Instead, he brushed his knuckles along the skin of her lower back.

Dahlia tried to edge away without being too obvious, but Kofi held her fast by tightening his grip on the dress. Lucky thing, too. Her trembling legs might not have taken her far.

"What are you doing?" she murmured in a hushed voice to ensure neither the stylist nor Mariama could hear.

"Zipping your dress," Kofi said calmly.

"Are you sure?"

His knuckles continued moving up her spine, causing the flesh of her back to tingle and every hair on her body to stand on end.

"Be patient," he whispered.

Her body warred within itself, part of her wanting to pull away, the other part wanting to succumb to the sensations he evoked.

Finally, he did as he said he would do. He slowly slid the zipper into place, securing the dress against her body. Hugging her curves, it drew tight around her ass and left nothing to the imagination. Dahlia turned to look at him, smoothing her hands over her hips, when she noted the darkened pupils of his eyes.

"I like this one very much," he said louder, turning to the stylist.

"Me, too. Would you like to see the last one, Your Highness?" Lisette draped a red dress over her forearm. The Grecian-inspired design cinched over one shoulder.

"Yes, I would," Kofi said, his voice lowered to a deeper timbre.

"I can show you later," Dahlia said.

"I'd like to see it now."

They stared at each other, in a sort of standoff.

"I could help you get dressed," Lisette said, her gaze shifting between the two of them with uncertainty.

Dahlia couldn't continue to argue without making a scene. "I'll take it to the dressing room."

Lisette helped her with the zipper and Dahlia slipped back into the dressing room. Taking a deep breath, she put on the dress.

When she stepped back into the room, Kofi was seated on a chair, his right ankle crossed over his knee and speaking into one of his cell phones. When he caught sight of her, he said something quickly in his native tongue and hung up.

Dahlia knew she should twirl around to show off the dress and how it looked on her from all sides, but she couldn't move. His eyes riveted her in place, his gaze smoldering as he regarded the way the fabric molded over her full breasts, cinched below them by the intricate beading, and then fell loosely to her ankles. The red color flattered her exposed shoulders and arms, and when Lisette pulled back and pinned up her hair, she felt regal and elegant.

"*Voila*!" the French woman said excitedly. "Red is her color, no? She looks absolutely ravishing!"

Without taking his eyes from Dahlia, Kofi said, "Leave us."

Without a word, Mariama scooped up the sleeping Noel, and she and Lisette scurried from the room, a knowing smile at the corners of the stylist's lips.

15

D ahlia's stomach tightened into a coil of tension. "I suppose you like this one, too." She filled the silence with the first thing that came to her mind.

"Yes, I do." His smoldering gaze almost seared her from across the room.

Dahlia ran her hands nervously over her hips, unnecessarily smoothing the material. His eyes trailed the movement over her curves. "Well, now you've seen it, I'll go change."

His mouth lifted into a rueful smile. "Don't worry, Dahlia. I intend to keep the promise I made to you." He glanced at his watch and stood. "I spoke to the council today, and they approved the proclamation that Noel should be next in line to the throne."

"That's good news."

"Are you settled in?"

"Working on it," she hedged.

"I spoke to Daisy. She said you haven't talked to her much."

"You contacted my chief of staff behind my back?"

"Only because I haven't seen any movement toward establishing yourself in your new role."

"It's not that easy."

"What exactly makes it so hard?" Kofi crossed his arms over his chest.

"Everything. The language, for one. English is no problem, but only a few people around me speak it. I know two words in French —*au revoir* and *bonjour*. Forget about Mbutu. Then there's the food, it's so...different."

"Have you tried any?'

"One or two dishes," she admitted, a bit embarrassed. "What I did try was so *spicy*. I tried to cook my own meal the other day, and I think I insulted the chef. I'd kill for a burger right now. Or some chicken and waffles."

"You sound miserable."

"Maybe I am, a little," she said, hoping for sympathy.

"And who's fault is that?"

"Not mine. It's not my fault I don't speak the language and the food is unfamiliar to me. This is your life. You're used to living in it."

"You have an entire staff, including a chief of staff to manage everyone for you."

"Forget it. You expect me to be perfect and you haven't given me any help. But why would I expect help or anything else from you?" She was too embarrassed to say she felt lonely and missed her friends, especially Angela. "Funny how you keep telling me what I should be doing, but what about you? We're getting married. You're going to be my husband. Maybe you could start acting more like a husband, unless you have someone to fill that role for you. Or should I just accept I'm in this alone?"

"You're never alone, Dahlia."

"Oh right, because I have a full staff and security guarding the front door."

She felt like a fish out of water, the same way she'd felt when her parents passed away. Alone and lost without anyone to turn to. Living with her grandparents didn't help much. They were loving, but older, and didn't have much time or energy for a child her age. The same way Kofi didn't have time for her.

She should have tried harder to get away. She wished she'd never come and hated everything about this place—the heat, the microscope she already lived under, the ridiculous rules she'd already learned so she could fit in. The demands on her time. Even hearing the other languages got on her nerves, because sometimes people would speak and she didn't have a clue what they were saying. She was an outsider, and being an outsider made her frustrated.

She stared at her hands. "Don't let me pull you away from your own duties."

Kofi studied her. "You're overwhelmed."

"Maybe," she admitted, glancing away.

"Where's your binder?" he asked.

Dahlia stared at him for a moment, wondering where he was going with this, but then she walked over to the nightstand and pulled open the drawer. She removed the thick spiral bound folder Daisy handed her the day after she arrived.

"Sit," Kofi said.

His commanding voice irritated her, but Dahlia did as he instructed. They sat on the bed next to each other, and he flipped to a page that listed a long line of potential organizations for her to work with.

"What do you see?" Kofi asked.

It was hard to concentrate with him sitting so close, smelling so good, and his voice so rich and low.

"My choices are wildlife conservation, building a new soccer stadium, working with orphans, promoting entrepreneurship among women..." She gasped.

"Why did you stop?"

"One of the choices is drug rehabilitation." She underscored the words with a forefinger. She never saw it before because she hadn't paid attention to the list.

"The program is new," Kofi said, his face inscrutable.

"I thought Zamibia didn't do much in the way of rehab."

"We didn't. A couple of years ago I asked law enforcement to steer people toward treatment instead of prison when they arrest them. We're in the early stages yet, but getting positive reports so far."

Did he implement the change because of their conversations? For personal reasons, she'd always volunteered at the substance abuse hotline, even when she lived in New York and worked in property management. She manned the phones to let people know about resources available to them for prevention, treatment, and support. Not only those in the throws of addiction, but their family members, as well. She'd had conversations with Kofi about how Zamibia handled addicts. They locked up people who should be getting treatment, in her opinion.

"You changed your policy?"

"It's evolving," he replied.

"I could help in this area," Dahlia said, getting excited. She'd learned a lot after years of volunteering and from working at the substance abuse center in Atlanta.

"There's something I need to show you. Something I didn't get the chance to because I was out of town."

She followed him out of the apartment and down the hall to another room. Kofi opened the door and let her step inside. Her mouth fell open. A dark room, complete with an enlarger and other photography apparatus.

She swung around to see him standing with his shoulder against the doorjamb. "Why?" she asked softly.

He gave an elegant, one-shoulder shrug. "Maybe I'm not the monster you think I am."

He hadn't been at one time, when lavish gifts had been the norm—dinners in expensive restaurants, fine clothes, and a diamond pendant necklace she'd sold to help with the move to Georgia. Kofi could be quite generous.

"Thank you."

He walked over to where she stood and brushed loose hair that had fallen from the updo from her shoulder. As if he couldn't stop himself from touching her, he let his hand slide down her arm. Goosebumps sprang up in the wake of his touch.

She swayed toward him, her fingertips grazing his hard chest.

They looked into each other's eyes, and then...his phone rang.

Dahlia blinked, and Kofi stepped back. The moment was lost.

He answered the phone. "*Bawoh.*" He listened and said a few more words in Mbutu. Then he hung up. "I need to go."

"Of course. Go."

"You're okay?"

"Yes. I'm fine now."

His gaze lingered on her. "You're not alone," he said. He then turned and left.

She went back into the apartment, skin tingling where he touched her and the scent of his cologne still in her nostrils.

Mind swirling with new possibilities, she changed clothes and retrieved the binder. Holding it to her chest, she exited their residence and took the stairs down to the first floor, nodding a greeting to anyone she met in the hallway.

She entered the suite she'd been told was hers and took stock of the entire space. The outer office contained a desk set up for an administrative assistant and a waiting area with chairs and a coffee table. A small conference room off to the left held a long table and enough chairs to seat twelve. Inside the larger office, which was hers, the walls were stark white and the furniture sleek and modern. She wanted something more feminine but also preferred a traditional style, which meant those pieces would have to go, and the walls definitely needed color.

Taking a deep breath, she set the binder on the desk and walked out and down the hall to her chief of staff's office.

Daisy, a thin woman whose purple head tie matched her skirt and top, stood right away. "Yes, Miss Sommers?"

"Could you..." Her voice wobbled a bit, but Dahlia took a fortifying breath, straightened her shoulders, and walked closer with bolder steps. Daisy was her employee. Dahlia had managed employees before when she co-owned the property management business with Melanie. Nothing on this type of scale, but her work experience included overseeing personnel. She simply needed to apply what she'd learned to a new environment.

"Set up a meeting with my social secretary to review events I'll need to attend after the wedding. I also need you to draft the qualifications for an administrative assistant for my review, and find out how soon palace maintenance can have my office painted."

Daisy looked up from the notepad she'd been writing on. "They can do it right away if you tell them the colors you want."

"In that case, have someone come by my office in about an hour to discuss options."

"Yes, ma'am."

Dahlia walked out but then, remembering her manners, stepped back into the doorway. "Thank you, Daisy."

"You're very welcome, Miss Sommers."

The smile that lit up her chief of staff's face was so bright, one would think Dahlia had paid her a profuse compliment. She thought about Kofi's comment, that people considered it a privilege to serve in the palace. She walked away with a newfound sense of purpose.

Before the meeting with maintenance, she needed to make a quick trip upstairs. Time to have a chat with the chef.

16

Like Nairobi, Johannesburg, and other African cities, Jouba was a modern metropolis. But mixed in among the skyscrapers and other modern buildings were traditional structures representing architecture from centuries past. For the sake of posterity, the monarchy spent millions to preserve a crumbling stone fortress and mud-dried buildings that had survived over the years.

The desire to preserve their history while driving forward with advancements influenced Kofi's daily decision-making. He worked hard to protect their way of life, and the meeting with Alistair Davies was a means to continue in the same vein.

Flanked on either side by security, he strolled through the lobby of the Jouba National Hotel, a glass and steel structure designed to mimic the tall towers of Sahelian architecture. As he passed by, some citizens stopped and respectfully bowed, while others, along with tourists, snapped quick photos.

He took the elevator up to the appointed floor and marched down the hall to the reserved room where one of his guards entered first, and he followed behind.

Although he often wore suits from top designers, Kofi felt most comfortable in traditional West African attire. Today's royal blue agbada included gold embroidery on the front, and he wore a matching fila on his head.

While his security situated themselves inside the door leading to the balcony, Kofi stepped out and joined Kemal and Imani, already seated at the table. He wanted another set of ears, and he trusted them both. Kemal was his right hand, and Imani was intelligent and cared as much as he did about the country and its people.

"Are you prepared to offer them anything?" Kemal asked.

Kofi took his seat at the head of the table. "Today we're here to listen. We're not making or accepting any offers. My father has concerns about doing business with Titanium Oil, and I have my own reservations, but it doesn't hurt to listen."

A few minutes later, Alistair arrived, a man of medium height with light brown hair and a gregarious smile. Right away, he extended his hand. "Thank you for meeting me."

Kofi lifted an eyebrow when he saw Ambassador Stephens from the UK directly behind him. With golden blonde hair pulled back from her face, she also approached with a hand extended. "Prince Kofi, how are you? Congratulations on your engagement."

"Thank you."

"Allow me to add my congratulations, as well," Alistair added. "I just learned that you'll be taken off the market in a few weeks."

They all laughed, and after introductions were made, sat around the table.

"I have to say, ambassador, I didn't expect to see you today," Kofi said.

She crossed her legs. "The head of Titanium Oil asked us to get involved because of our long-standing relationship with the royal family and thought I might be helpful in the negotiations. My goal is to help broker a deal that's beneficial to both parties."

A brilliant smile remained on her face while she talked, which Kofi found intriguing and irritating at the same time.

The conversation started with pleasantries, and while they

chatted, a waiter brought out pitchers of water and bissap and filled their glasses. He immediately followed up with a platter of biltong, a South African import of dried cured meat.

"Today's choices are beef, antelope meat, and sausage," the waiter said.

"That will be all. Thank you," Kofi said.

"I think I'll pass." Alistair eyed the platter suspiciously.

"It's quite good. I've grown to love biltong. Makes a great snack." Ambassador Stephens picked up a piece of meat.

"How about we get to the heart of the matter, as I don't want to waste your time." Alistair folded his hands on the table. "First, I have a question for you. Why do you have a problem with outside investment?"

"We don't have a problem with outside investment. You're staying at a Hilton Hotel a few miles away, if I'm not mistaken," Kofi pointed out.

"Of course, the Americans," Alistair said dryly.

"And the Chinese, the French, and our neighbors in West Africa," Imani interjected.

Kofi heard the irritation in her voice and smiled. "To Imani's point, we're not a closed off society. Trade has been an important part of our lives for centuries. That's why despite the many dialects spoken here, we chose to include English and French among our official languages, allowing us to easily conduct trade with our friends in Senegal, Côte d'Ivoire, Ghana, Nigeria, etcetera."

"If you're unopposed to trade, why not do business with us? Drilling for oil on land is quite an undertaking, can you imagine drilling in the ocean?" Alistair paused, as if waiting for an answer to the rhetorical question. "It's challenging, to say the least. We have a good reputation—excellent, in fact. We have an embassy established here in the capital, and we have experience. There's absolutely no reason why we can't help you with your offshore drilling."

"And what kind of guarantees can you make about protecting the environment?"

"Whatever guarantees you need. We don't want to disrupt the lovely ecosystem we've seen in Zamibia. The water is a beautiful turquoise like I've never seen, and I'm sure the fishing villages along the shore would be most upset if we killed off the plant and animal life they're so dependent on." He laughed.

"We want to see a proposal, of course, and our normal procedure involves getting proposals from different companies. Then, there's the issue of The Most High Council. Before any final decisions are made or documents are signed, they must approve."

Ambassador Stephens cleared her throat. "Allow me to interject. You're insulting me, Your Highness. I've lived here long enough to know the real power lies with the Karunzika royal family. Whatever you say goes, and the council is brought in only as a courtesy."

Kofi chuckled but didn't deny her assessment. He drank some water.

"I know you'll want to look at other options, but I strongly believe that working with Titanium Oil will benefit you and your people. They're the best in the business at this. Imagine the cost of having to acquire all the technology necessary to build the rig and do the drilling, and that says nothing about what money can *not* buy." She tapped the side of her head. "Knowledge. It would take time for you to get to the point where you can do what this company is capable of. We're talking years and almost a billion dollars. Why delay? Every day that passes means you won't be able to exploit the oil that's there, which would allow you to invest in more social programs, and improvements in infrastructure, and anything else you deem important. Why bear the brunt of the investment alone, when you could share the costs and continue funding current projects?"

"I appreciate your consideration of our needs," Kofi drawled. "But since you've lived here for a long time, you know we do things at our own pace. Besides, the oil has been underground for millions of years. Even if it takes us years to start the extraction, a few more years won't make a difference."

"Are you saying I'm wasting my time, Mr. Karunzika?" Alistair asked, his voice sounding decidedly testier.

"*Prince* Karunzika," Imani said.

Alistair glanced at her and straightened his shoulders. "Prince Karunzika."

Kofi laughed internally. His cousin was a little spitfire.

"You're not wasting your time. But I do have to warn you, we're in no hurry to make a decision. We will take our time and evaluate every alternative, and any decision we make will be in the best interest of the Zamibian people, not a multibillion-dollar corporation. My advice to you, is to learn what you can about our country, and then give us a proposal that demonstrates we would be better off working with you instead of someone else, or drilling ourselves."

"We're willing to put in the work, but we've hit stumbling blocks the entire time I've been here," Alistair said.

"Such as?"

"Well, I'd hoped we could deal directly with King Babatunde, but then this meeting was set up with you." He almost sounded offended, as if he'd been brushed off.

"We could have assigned this to one of our ministers, yet you're sitting here with a prince," Kofi said evenly, letting him know he should be honored for the privilege.

Alistair shifted in his chair. "I didn't mean to offend."

"A project of this magnitude is normally handled directly by the king, but my father has asked me to take over the major commercial projects. Speaking to me is the same as speaking to him, and any contract I sign is binding on the kingdom. My advice to you is, do your research. The perfect place to start is with the woman sitting right next to you."

A corner of Ambassador Stephens's mouth drifted into a faint smile. "Don't worry, I'll make sure they do their homework. The next time we approach, we'll be well prepared."

"It's been a pleasure talking to you." Alistair pushed back his chair and got up.

Everyone around the table stood as well. "Have a good day," Kofi said. Silently, he watched them leave. Then he, Imani, and Kemal took their seats. He picked up a piece of antelope biltong and bit into it. Chewing slowly, he mulled over the meeting.

"What are you thinking?" Imani asked.

"What do you think about the conversation?" Kofi countered.

One crossed leg bounced over the other. "I don't know. They made valid points about the cost and the wait. We could use their technology and their knowledge because this is a new area for us."

"Gold mining used to be a new area for us, but we've done quite well."

When they discovered gold in the mountains, the king at the time made the decision to not let outsiders control the mines. He established partnerships but kept a majority stake, and in the decades since then Zamibians learned enough that they no longer needed an outside company. The monarchy employed well-trained men and women to supervise and manage the process. Thus, they kept most of the money in the country and avoided having their government officials bribed in exchange for preferential treatment.

Kemal spoke up. "That was a different time. We live in a world that moves at a faster pace nowadays."

"Have you given up on green energy alternatives?" Imani asked.

"No, but they're a work in progress," Kofi said.

The Office of the Minister of Energy researched harnessing the power of wind and sun to provide energy. They'd achieved modest success in some of the rural areas.

"There is another alternative," Imani said slowly. "Let me look into my contacts in Barrakesch. They're our friends, and they have a lot of experience with oil drilling. Like us, they've set up state-owned companies instead of establishing a joint venture with a foreign corporation."

Frowning, Kemal said, "Is working with them any better? Any partnership runs the risk of getting corrupted."

"The difference is, they've been our ally for a long time. We might be able to make it work." Imani looked expectantly at Kofi.

He stroked his jaw, contemplating the options. "Put out some feelers," he told her. "See what the government is willing to do. I'll also talk to Wasim," he said, referring to one of his best friends and a prince of Barrakesch. "In the meantime, Kemal, have someone keep an eye on Davies and Ambassador Stephens. Especially her."

"Why especially her?" Kemal asked.

"Because we expect the enemy to come from outside, when in reality he—or she—could be right here among us."

17

Three days before the wedding, Dahlia wore the red Grecian-inspired dress to a formal reception hosted in her and Kofi's honor by King Babatunde. She'd gone through quite a makeover. Eyebrows plucked and newly formed, lashes elongated, manicure and pedicure, a hair regimen that left her curly locks shiny and soft in an upward sweep, and her skin buffed so smooth it was now as soft as Noel's. She was a new woman.

The purpose of the event was to introduce Dahlia to the nine council members, their wives, and other guests. A man with a loud bass voice announced the king into the Sun Room first, a room decorated in different shades of yellow and gold. Babatunde wore a crown lined with jewels and heavy robes edged in kente cloth. In lieu of his wooden staff, he held a jeweled scepter in one hand and leaned on a male attendant.

Promptly following his entrance, the speaker announced Kofi and Dahlia. They entered arm-in-arm and paused at the threshold as the guests applauded.

"Relax," Kofi said from the side of his mouth, while managing to keep a smile on his face. He chose not to wear a crown to the formal event, opting instead to demonstrate his sovereignty with the head of a golden lion pinned to the lapel of his tuxedo.

Dahlia had tightened her hold on his arm, completely unaware she was doing it. She took a breath and relaxed her grip.

"You're marrying into the royal family. These people are anxious to meet and impress you. You don't have to impress them."

The words went a long way toward calming her nerves, and when he escorted her forward, her pulse rate slowed to a more normal rhythm, and the smile on her face became more natural.

They separated from each other as the night wore on, as some of the visitors were anxious to speak to Kofi privately about various matters. She overheard one of the council members talking to him about the need for funding a new library, and a chief from the Mbutu tribe asked if a member of the royal family would attend the ritual ceremony of new lion warriors.

Dahlia circulated among the guests, and with each introduction her confidence increased. The social secretary prepared her well, giving a rundown of each guest and one two pertinent facts she could ask about their children, pastimes, or spouses. And, lucky for her, no one laughed at her attempts to speak a few words of greeting in Mbutu and French. The two hours she spent with each instructor had paid off.

Parched after hours of talking and smiling almost nonstop, Dahlia separated from the wife of one of the elders and searched the room for a server.

A good-looking man of Middle Eastern descent stepped into her line of sight. "Miss Sommers, it's a pleasure to finally meet you. I am Prince Wasim ibn Khalid al-Hassan of Barrakesch, and a good friend of Prince Kofi." He wore the traditional flowing robes and headdress of the men from that region of the world.

"Nice to meet you, Prince Wasim."

"Wasim, please."

"Wasim," Dahlia agreed. She extended her hand, and with a graceful bow, he lightly kissed the back of her fingers. With his good looks and the sparkle in his eyes, this man could be quite a charmer.

"It's nice to finally meet you after hearing so much about you. You're more stunning than I was told," Wasim said.

Definitely a charmer.

"Oh dear, please tell me you're not flirting with my cousin's fiancée." Imani, lovely in a strapless dress, sidled up to Wasim's side and gazed up at him with a pout.

Keeping his attention on Dahlia, he asked, "Did you hear that? Like a mosquito or a buzzing fly." He swatted in the general vicinity of his ear.

"Ha, ha. Isn't he funny?" Imani asked, while keeping her gaze on Wasim. "And look, he's playing the role of Middle Eastern sheik tonight. While everyone else is in Western dress, he's wearing a *ghuthrain* and *dishdasha*." She tugged on the sleeve of his robe.

"Wearing the clothes of my culture is not playing a role, *habibti*. No more than you're playing a role wearing your colorful print." His gaze swept her exposed shoulders as he tugged on her dress.

Imani sighed dramatically. "It's called Ankara print. How long have you known Kofi, and me for that matter, and you still don't know that? Maybe it's time for us to sever our ties with Barrakesch."

"You would never do that. You owe us from the time we saved your asses by giving you guns. If not for us, you would have fallen under British rule. You're welcome." His smile was overly sweet.

"We *bought* those guns, thank you very much. By the way, I'm sure you appreciate the massive discounts we give you on all the gold and agricultural products we export to your country. You're welcome."

Dahlia gently cleared her throat. She was pretty sure they'd forgotten she was standing there.

Color tinged Wasim's cheeks.

"Sorry, we got carried away." Imani shifted from one foot to the other and cast her gaze lower in embarrassment.

"That's okay. I'll leave you two alone and circulate a bit."

Dahlia excused herself from the two friends and encountered Kofi, who had just broken away from speaking to one of the elders and approached her. "Drink?" he asked.

She couldn't help but remember the last time he'd offered her a drink with the exact same question, under vastly different circumstances. "Yes, please."

He flagged down a server and handed her a glass of champagne.

"I saw you talking to Wasim. Please tell me he wasn't flirting with you."

"Not much. Imani put a stop to it," Dahlia said.

"Lucky for him, or I might have to tear his heart out." Kofi sipped from his glass.

"That's rather harsh," Dahlia said, although she received a little thrill.

"Why do you think they call me the conquering lion?" With so much heat in his eyes, he looked as if he wanted to conquer her, right there on the marble floor.

Warmth crawled up Dahlia's neck, and she diverted her eyes to Babatunde, seated across the room and talking with one of the council members.

"I developed some photos today."

"Photos of what?"

"Before-and-after pictures of my office, pictures of the roses in the greenhouses. My favorites are of Noel, of course, but there's one of the workers harvesting the strawberries, singing while they work. It's a great shot."

"I'm glad to see you're making good use of the room. Maybe we can make you the official palace photographer." Amusement colored his voice.

"I wouldn't want to put anyone out of a job," she bantered back, edging a little closer. She couldn't help wanting to be nearer. His good mood invited closer contact.

"True. You'll have plenty to do once we're married, including more of these types of events, where we meet with the council members and listen to their concerns."

"Can I ask you a question?"

"Of course."

"Why are all the council members male?"

He didn't answer right away, his gaze encompassing the room. "Old traditions die hard."

"Including the one where only male heirs can take the throne. What if Noel had been a girl? Would you have fought so hard to have her come to Zamibia?"

He turned his head to look at her. "I would want any child who is of my blood to live under my roof and my protection at all times, male or female."

Satisfied with his answer, Dahlia fell quiet.

Kofi placed a hand at the base of her spine, and the warm touch almost made her purr. "Come, there are more people for you to meet."

∾

DAHLIA PEEPED IN ON NOEL, fast asleep with two body pillows on either side of him. He lay sprawled on the bed, his purple wiggle worm peeping out from under his torso, the eyes begging to be rescued from the weight of her son. Aofa slept in a separate bed nearby, and Dahlia could hear her gentle snores from the doorway.

She quietly closed the door and faced Kofi, who'd been looking over her shoulder. They walked down the hall and stopped outside her room.

"I won't see you again before the wedding. I have to take a short trip, and the day before the ceremony, we can't see each other. It's bad luck."

She acknowledged his words with a nod. Both her assistant and the social secretary explained that part of tradition to her. They'd also explained that the night of the wedding, tradition dictated that the new bride wait for her husband to come to her room and seduce her, initiating her into the art of making love.

Dahlia twisted the diamond ring on her finger.

"You did good tonight."

"I did?" She looked up at him, quietly anxious for his approval.

"Well, except when you referred to Chief Ode's wife as Amai instead of Ama."

Dahlia winced and covered her face. "I can't believe I called her by the wrong name, but my social secretary must have given me the wrong information."

"Are you blaming the help, a woman who's lived in this country all her life and knows every member of the council?"

Dahlia laughed. "Do you think Ama was upset?"

"No. It's an easy mistake to make, and I'll smooth things over by sending them more cows or building another well in their town."

"Really?"

"No." He chuckled.

"Kofi!" Dahlia shoved him and encountered his hard chest under the tuxedo. Her eyes lingered where she'd touched, and she breathed in through suddenly parched lips.

"Have a good night," Kofi said. He didn't move.

Dahlia nodded because she couldn't utter a word right then. She thought Kofi might come closer, but instead shook his head slightly, as if he'd talked himself out of some act, and backed away.

"Good night," he said again.

"Good night," Dahlia whispered, watching him walk away.

She entered her bedroom and leaned back against the door. She closed her eyes and pressed a hand to her chest, right over her racing heart.

Disappointment burned through her. She'd wanted him to kiss her or return her touch.

So much had changed between them since her arrival. First he gave her the dark room, then he helped her relax into her role as partner and future princess. She couldn't get enough of seeing him interact with Noel, play-wrestling, feeding him, and teaching him words in Mbutu. He was so patient and gentle with their son, sometimes she found herself staring at them.

Noel was enjoying himself immensely, as if he'd always lived in The Grand Palace. He loved spending time with the animals on the property, but his favorite spot was the stables, where he fed carrots to the horses. He roamed the grounds at will, chatting up the gardeners and "helping" the workers who took care of the fruits and vegetables. No one treated him like a nuisance. He was their prince and future king.

Dahlia sighed, gnawing her bottom lip. Only a few more days and she'd be married. Could it be...she was actually looking forward to it?

18

D ahlia examined her appearance in the gilded oval mirror in her dressing room.

"You look fabulous," Angela said, sitting on a cushioned stool. She'd flown in on Thursday. Her presence had brought a calming effect, as well as put Dahlia in an extra good mood.

"It's hard to look bad in all of this." Dahlia twisted to examine the side view.

The loose-fitting white gown was made entirely of silk and trimmed in gold. It settled on her body in an elegant drape that brushed the floor. The short sleeves and round neckline allowed an inordinate amount of gold to be on display—in her ears, strewn around her neck, and covering her wrists and upper arms. Even her hair, twisted into thick ropes and pulled back from her face, was intertwined with threads of gold throughout.

"You're getting married." Angela rose from the chair and walked over to Dahlia. Taking her hand, she said, "What's going through your mind right now?"

She met her friend's eyes head on. "Make the best of this situation. Besides, how bad could being a princess be, when you have dozens of people at your beck and call?"

"Well, from what you said, you and Kofi are in a better place, right?" In addition to eating and drinking too much, she and Angela spent the past couple of days catching up.

"We're okay with each other."

"Honey, it's me. Are you only okay or better than okay? What's really going on?"

Dahlia smoothed a hand down a long twist. "I sense he's holding back. Or being patient. As if...I don't know. I think he's waiting for a sign from me." Not exactly the arrogant, pushy man she knew.

Angela tilted her head, her gaze thoughtful. "You're falling for him again, aren't you?"

Dahlia opened her mouth, but then promptly shut it. What was the point of denial? She was falling for him again because he was turning into the Kofi she'd fallen in love with three years ago.

"It was bound to happen. Maybe he has feelings for you, too," Angela said gently.

"Maybe. Even if he does, at any time he can get another wife or mistress, and there's not much I can do about it. Hell, at one point, I told him he should." The anger and ugliness of their reunion in the States seemed like a long time ago, but less than two months had passed.

"That was before, when a lot of animosity existed between the two of you. But listen, I didn't ask the question to make you upset. Come here." Angela pulled her into a hug. "Have I told you that I missed you?"

"No. But I know you did. I missed you like crazy, too," Dahlia said, her voice thick. She pulled back and looked at her friend. "I'm glad you came."

"Are you kidding?" Angela's eyes were overly bright with tears. "You're getting married and about to become a princess. Even those damn slave drivers couldn't make me miss this day." She managed a watery smile.

At a soft tap on the doorframe, both women turned their heads. Mariama stood in the doorway.

"It is time," she said in her soft-spoken voice.

Dahlia took a deep breath and straightened her shoulders. She let Mariama add the last piece to the dress, a silk head covering the same white color, trimmed in gold to match her dress. She then applied gold lipstick and added gold dots around her eyes using face paint.

Dahlia took one last look at her transformation and faced her best friend. Angela smiled reassuringly and squeezed her hand, and all three women exited the room.

Golf carts took Dahlia and ten attendants to the other side of the palace, where the ceremony would take place in a large event room. A long, purple rug ran the entire length of the hall. Angela left to claim her seat, and at the appropriate time, the doors opened and the sounds of hands beating softly on drums could be heard.

The ten women, dressed in gold dresses and matching gold head ties, tossed down white rose petals as they made their way down the purple carpet. Dahlia followed behind them, keeping her eyes demurely focused on the floor, according to the custom. When she arrived at the altar, she lifted her gaze. Kofi stood beside her in a flowing robe, also white and trimmed in gold. His face remained expressionless, but his eyes were alive with undisclosed emotion.

Did he feel it, too? Just a little bit. The gravity of this momentous occasion. That no matter their reason for standing before these people today, they would soon embark on a road where their lives would be inextricably bound together for years to come.

The priest spoke in both English and Mbutu, in a confident, loud voice. The ceremony included acknowledging the ancestors, repeating pledges to each other, and praying over the couple. At the end, the officiant tied their wrists together to represent they were now one unit. He used a strand of cowrie shells, to symbolize fertility and prosperity. After one last prayer, he introduced the couple to those in attendance.

Because her coronation would take place in a private ceremony later, the officiant made the introduction by saying, "I now present to you, Prince Kofi Karunzika and his wife, our future princess, Dahlia Karunzika!"

Cheers and loud claps went up from the group, and the drummers beat a faster rhythm, joined by the sound of ivory horns as they made their way down the long carpet to another room, empty except for more servants waiting for them. After the makeup artist retouched Dahlia's makeup, she and Kofi took a myriad of photos —together, with their male and female attendants, and with Noel. The photos with the king saddened her a bit because her own parents were missing, but Dahlia didn't dwell on the sentiment too long.

The final step involved walking out into the sunlight to introduce the new family to the thousands gathered on the grounds. When they stepped out onto the balcony—Dahlia, Kofi with Noel in his arms, and King Babatunde—some of the people dropped to one knee and bowed their heads, but many others let out a loud cheer and waved Zamibian flags in joyous unison. Dancers in traditional garb and face paint high-stepped and twisted their bodies in a flurry of movement. Drummers, whose instrument in times past were used to relay messages across miles, beat a frantic rhythm that joined with the chorus of voices.

Overcome with emotion, tears filled Dahlia's eyes. Then she remembered the rules and fixed a smile on her face and waved with her fingers close together.

Her gaze slid to Kofi. Noel, excited by the crowd, laughed and waved his hands vigorously from the perch on his father's arm, and the crowd cheered louder. Kofi smiled and waved, too. His profile was so lit up, he seemed like a new person. Nothing compared to this man's smile. She wanted to climb on top of his face, he looked so sexy.

Tomorrow they left for their honeymoon, one week in Tofo, Mozambique on the Indian Ocean. But tonight, they consummated their marriage. Heart racing at the prospect of a night in his arms, Dahlia returned her gaze to the people below.

A section of the group shouted louder than the rest. *"Eyeh-kabo! Eyeh-kabo!"* they chanted.

"Do you know what they're saying?" King Babatunde murmured from the side of his mouth.

Dahlia listened closely. "No," she admitted, though she was certain they were speaking Mbutu.

"That is Mbutu," the king confirmed. "It means *Welcome.*"

Emotion clogged her throat. Her smile broadened, and she privately vowed to do her best so that she was worthy of such enthusiastic acceptance.

∼

FROM THE BALCONY in the Great Hall, Kofi took stock of all the wedding guests.

Despite the short notice, hundreds of dignitaries, heads of state, and ambassadors attended the ceremony. They brought lavish gifts from their homelands—exquisite diamonds culled from the mines of South Africa and rich tapestries from Ethiopia. The Moroccan delegation brought belly dancers to entertain the couple and their guests, while Ghanaians sang and performed the Nmane dance to the beat of drums in honor of the bride.

Goats, sheep, and cows had been slaughtered, and fruits and vegetables harvested from the palace grounds for the three-day celebration. News cameras and journalists from all over Africa captured the events on video and in print.

Wasim and another friend from his university days approached and came to stand on either side of him. Wasim extended a platter of grilled goat meat, and Kofi popped a hunk of the flavorful meat in his mouth.

"What's the real story between you and Dahlia?" Andres asked, a prince from a small European principality. He ran his fingers through his dark hair and rested his back against a column, arms folded over his chest.

Kofi braced his hands on the stone railing, his gaze drifting to where Dahlia sat on a cushioned chair edged with an intricate gold design. She was deep in conversation with her best friend, Angela. In a short while, they'd leave their guests and the celebratory atmosphere to enter the coronation room, where his father would give Dahlia her new title.

His stomach and chest tightened, but the choking sensation from his first marriage, like a noose around his neck, didn't surface this time. He felt surprisingly free.

"There's no real story."

"He's lying to us now," Wasim said.

These men were his best friends, as close as brothers, and knew him better than his older brother ever did. Jafari had been consumed with his role as the crown prince and the rigid constraints he'd been forced to live within. Kofi had lived a more exciting life with these men by his side.

Wasim peered around Kofi to look at Andres. "Do you remember him telling us how much he despised her but wouldn't tell us why? And how he never wanted anything to do with her again because she'd betrayed him, but never told us how?"

"Then two minutes later proclaimed she was the love of his life," Andres pointed out with a chuckle.

"Remind me never to get drunk around the two of you ever again," Kofi said drily. "All you need to know is that she's the mother of my child, the heir to the throne."

They fell silent because *that* they understood. They carried the same burden of responsibility he did. That's why they'd been close at school. The three socialized with some of the wealthiest young people in the world, but wealth and privilege were among the few things they had in common with the children of government officials and business owners. None of those young men and women understood the added strain that came from having to create a legacy an entire country depended on.

"Thanks for helping set up the meeting with the head of the Ministry of Oil. Hopefully, our two countries can work together on this project," Kofi said to Wasim.

Nothing had been finalized, but Barrakesch and Zamibia had entered into an exploratory agreement, and Kofi's office had already notified the ambassador and Alistair Davies. Neither was pleased by the news.

"Don't thank me. Thank Imani. She was quite persistent."

"Who's Dahlia's friend?" Wasim asked, shifting his gaze to Angela.

"Hey, I had my eye on her," Andres said.

Kofi shot both men a warning look. "Down boys. Reserve your charm for someone else. Angela leaves tomorrow."

"Tomorrow? Too bad," Wasim said.

"Angela. Nice name," Andres murmured.

"Time for a toast." Wasim called over a waiter and gave him instructions. After a few minutes, he returned with two champagne-filled flutes and juice in a glass for Wasim.

"I'll start," Andres said. "I wish you the best, my friend. You deserve some happiness."

Andres, like Wasim, attended Kofi's first wedding and the funerals of his mother, brother, and wife.

Andres raised his glass. "May you both live a long and happy life together."

"And through the grace of Allah, may your house be filled with love and the sound of children's laughter," Wasim added.

They clinked their glasses together.

Kofi tossed back the champagne and then settled his gaze on Dahlia. He fully intended to have everything they wished for him with her by his side.

19

Mariama entered the room. "Your bath is ready, Your Highness."

Your Highness.

Hearing others refer to her as "Your Highness" instead of simply "Miss Sommers" or "ma'am" would take some getting used to. The private coronation ceremony had taken place that very night in the coronation room where she received a gold crown bedecked with diamonds. It was one of five differently adorned crowns, and she learned each one served a special purpose and were only worn during formal events, ceremonies, or when officials came for state visits. King Babatunde had given her the title of Great Wife, an honorific which meant she was the one through which the royal succession would pass.

"Thank you, Mariama."

Mariama helped her remove her jewelry, and Dahlia removed the shoes and dress she'd worn during the coronation. Although Mariama hovered nearby, she undressed without embarrassment. She'd gotten used to having her maid in the room with her and understood this was part of Mariama's responsibility, to ensure even the most mundane of tasks–a bath–would be pleasurable and carefree.

She sank into the tub, filled with warm water and red and white rose petals. Leaning back against the pillow, she let the warm, rose-scented water relax her body and mind as it flowed over her skin. The soft petals tickled away the remnants of stress from the long day. She was in heaven.

Dahlia dozed a bit and woke to Mariama tapping her on the shoulder and holding a large towel.

"Thank you."

In the bedroom, she dressed in a white nightgown, and Mariama let down her hair until all the chunky twists fell around her shoulders. An artist came and covered her hands and wrists in intricate henna designs and after completion, they both left her alone to wait for Kofi.

Dahlia sat on the side of the bed, waiting. She'd seen the way Kofi looked at her earlier and knew he'd arrive any minute. She hoped he'd be pleased. The anticipation made her heart flutter.

She sat there and waited, and waited, the silence in the room seeming loud as time stretched on. Swallowing hard, she glanced at the clock. Had she misunderstood the marital custom? Was she supposed to go to him?

No, she didn't misunderstand. He was supposed to come to her. According to custom, the groom came to the bride on their wedding night.

She checked the time again. Two more minutes elapsed, but it felt like two hours.

She finally realized he wouldn't come, because he thought she didn't want him. She'd sensed him holding back, containing the 'wild boar.' If he wouldn't come to her, then she would go to him. She would have to be the one to take the next step—to bridge the gap.

Rising from the bed, Dahlia took a deep breath and went to the panel in the wall. She opened the door and slipped into the hallway, which was illuminated by small lights that lined the floor on either side. Moving quietly on bare feet, she turned the knob at the other end and pushed open the door.

Bare-chested, Kofi lay on his back in the bed, staring up at the ceiling. He sat up immediately when she entered, looking at her like he'd seen a ghost.

Dahlia let the door close quietly behind her and drifted closer, hands clasped together to keep them from shaking.

"Tonight is our wedding night. I'm your wife."

"Yes, you are."

"You didn't come to me."

"So you came to me." A few seconds ticked by. "Come here, wife."

She crossed the rest of the way and stood in front of him. Their eyes locked on each other as Kofi snaked his hands under her nightgown and tugged her lacy underwear down to her ankles. She stepped out of them, never letting her gaze leave his.

Slowly, he lifted the hem of the filmy nightclothes past her hips, and she finished undressing by tugging it over her head and discarding it to the floor.

His breathing pattern changed when he looked at her naked body, and he muttered something in his tribal tongue, licking his lips as he stared at her breasts. One finger traced the henna design on the back of her hand up to her wrist, and that mild touch sparked heat in her veins and made her step closer to stand between his open legs. Big hands cupped her hips and smoothed up the curve of her waist, riding higher to either side of her breasts.

"My wife," he said softly, nostrils flaring, eyes hooded as he looked at her.

Her pulse quickened and her loins throbbed at the softly spoken words. "My husband."

He kissed her belly, and his tongue left a moist trail from her navel to the middle of her chest. The familiar touch of his lips and facial hair triggered a sizzle against her skin, making her press closer. As if a switch suddenly turned on, Kofi stood and lifted her off the floor and placed her on the bed.

Their lips fused together in a hot, fierce kiss that tangled their tongues. He pressed hard against her, kissing deeply, thoroughly. The edge of his teeth nicked the inside of her mouth, and she plunged in, too, delving deep to taste him. He filled her mouth and kissed her with brutal, uncontrolled desire. Her lips clung to his as he crushed her to him, his tongue stroking throughout the warm, damp cavern of her mouth. She whimpered with need as he simultaneously kissed and sucked her lips, taking what she'd come to willingly offer.

For far too long she'd been without this type of intimacy. Alone, fighting, struggling. But the rush of Kofi's touch made the wait worthwhile.

Her nipples hardened into painful points against the hard warmth of his bare chest and the drag of the hairs sprinkled on his torso. Smoothing her hands over his back, she explored the hard muscles and the scarred tissue on the upper portion that warned he was a formidable fighter.

He pulled her on top of him, and she slid along this body. Soft against hard. Smooth against rough. She felt his hands cradling her hips as he thrust up against her.

With fumbling, hurried fingers, she undid the knot of twine holding his pants around his waist and helped him maneuver the article of clothing from his firm body. He was a gorgeous specimen of a man. Broad-shouldered and lean-waisted, coupled with a beautiful landscape of tight abs and muscular arms. She licked those abs and filled her mouth with the sweet taste of his skin.

Snaking a hand lower, she slid her finger into the tuft of hairs at his groin and teasingly massaged all around his shaft, watching his face contort into what could only be described as an expression of agonizing pleasure.

"Dahlia..." Unintelligible murmurings climbed up his throat.

She sucked his flat nipples and nipped his hard pecs. "You're beautiful," she said, her voice husky and low. Her body pulsed with need for him. Familiar, natural need that simmered beneath the surface whenever he was near.

She clasped his erect shaft, smoothing moisture from the tip up and down his hard length.

With a deep-chested groan, Kofi filled his hand with her hair and used the twists as leverage to tug her onto her back in the middle of the bed. The other hand grabbed her bare bottom and squeezed, and she lifted her body close to his.

She flicked her tongue into his ear, and like a heat-seeking missile, his probing fingers found the desire that hammered between her thighs. Her thighs parted willingly, opening around his hips and affording him unrestricted ease to cup and slide one finger into the slick warmth. She whimpered as his finger strummed within her, but it wasn't enough. This was agony.

She ground her hips against his hand, panting and hungry and desperate to relieve the intense pressure below the waist, wound so tight she could hardly wait for him to enter her. She would only be satisfied when his body claimed hers.

"Dahlia," he groaned on a ragged breath. "You're ready for your husband, yes?" He slapped her ass and then curled his fingers into the flesh, grabbing in a firm squeeze. The stinging blow echoed into a pounding heat at her core, so intense she almost came.

"Yes, Kofi, yes," she breathed.

He tugged at a nipple with his teeth, torturing the dusky-colored flesh into a more turgid peak. The soothing lave of his tongue followed each nip of his teeth. He rained little bites over the soft crests until she couldn't take anymore teasing and grabbed his head, arching her back and forcing his face into the valley of her breasts.

The suckling pull of his mouth forced her eyes closed, and her head fell back against the pillows. Kofi's hands and mouth continued to travel across her body, and he continued to press kisses all over—her palms, elbows, waist, and inner thighs.

Dahlia stretched her arms above her head, giving herself up to the heat that coursed through her veins. Lovingly, he smoothed a slow-moving hand against the flat plane of her abdomen, gradually moving upward to her aching breasts, and she squirmed, finding it more and more difficult to breathe.

"Kofi..."

"I'm here, *olufeh mi.*"

Taking his erection in hand, Kofi guided it to the wet folds between her legs. She opened, allowing his powerful body to lead her down the familiar path to the heights of sensual bliss. He grunted when he sank into her, and she gripped his shoulders as his hands eased up her outer thighs, shifting her into the position he desired.

He looped one leg over the arm that supported him on the mattress and twisted her other to curve around his waist like a belt. She lay open to him as he slowly slid in and out of her body over and over again, creating a sensory overload.

Dahlia wound her arms around his neck to hold herself in place as he tightened his hold and plunged his hot shaft faster into her. A shudder of satisfaction and relief rolled under her skin and echoed in his masculine frame. At the same time, his mouth stroked over hers in an urgent kiss—hot, drugging, so intense she lost all sense of where she was. Their merged bodies slapped together in perfect harmony.

As passion built between them, he gritted his teeth and pummeled her body harder, the intense pleasure forcing him to bury his face in her neck. In and out, as deep as he could go, he pumped his hips and forced her hoarse moans to fill the air while she kept pace.

When they came, they came together, their bodies perfectly in tune with each other, welcoming the flash of heat that spiraled into unimaginable ecstasy. Her entire body shook with the strength of gale winds sweeping through the plains. His breath stuttered against her collarbone as he thrust with a savagery that forced her to sink her nails into his skin to hold on.

When it was over, he let out a long exhale and his full weight collapsed on top of her before he rolled onto his side and pulled her with him. She turned her face into his shoulder, breathing in the unique scent of his skin combined with the bewitching smell of sweat and sex.

Dahlia couldn't deny the truth anymore. A dull ache filled her chest. Her intense feelings for Kofi had never died. She loved him just as much, more, than before. She didn't know where their relationship was headed, but in a short time, he'd become a vital part of her life, and she didn't want to lose this feeling with him.

∽

KOFI WALKED NAKED from the adjoining bathroom back to bed. He eased under the sheets, careful not to create too much movement and wake Dahlia, who lay on her side with her back to him.

When he finally settled into a comfortable position, she pressed her bottom against his hip. He glanced at her. Was she asleep or awake?

Moments later, she inched farther back and pressed her bottom more insistently against him.

Definitely awake.

Kofi turned and spooned her. "Dahlia?"

"Hmm?"

"What are you doing?"

He traced a line down the middle of her back and she moved with a snakelike shimmy. He dragged his finger all the way down along the crack of her ass, and she moaned, lifting into his hand.

"Don't tell me you need more," he murmured. He was already getting hard at the thought of taking her again.

"Maybe. It's our wedding night, isn't it?"

"Yes, it is." He couldn't believe she'd come to him. "What did you have in mind next, *binriya mi*?" He whipped the sheet away from her body and trailed a hand up the curves of her dark brown skin, stopping right below her breast.

"What does that mean?" She turned onto her back and faced him.

Gorgeous. She looked like a goddess with the gold threads running through her hair and her lips swollen from his kisses.

"My princess."

"How do you say my prince?" she asked.

"*Aremoh mi.*"

She said the words, but her pronunciation was off. He repeated them, slower this time.

"*Aremoh mi,*" she said with more confidence.

Two simple words, and he felt as if a new world opened up, an understanding between them.

"I want you to touch me, *aremoh mi,*" Dahlia whispered.

"Where?"

She took his hand and covered a breast. The dark nipple hardened under his palm, becoming a tight little berry. He squeezed the soft flesh and she arched into his hand.

"You're so sexy," he muttered, plucking the berry into his mouth. His tongue traced the outer edge and sucked.

Dahlia gasped and cupped the back of his head, smoothing a hand down his neck and across the markings that covered his upper back. He loved her hands on his body, the delicious things she did with barely any effort ignited his skin and made his stiff flesh harder.

For so long he tried to forget her. Forget her laugh and the sweep of her hair across his chest. Forget the way she hid her giggles behind her hand. Her openness and optimism had all been relegated to the past. But in reality, he hadn't forgotten a thing. Every nuance, every feeling, every sensation remained in his subconscious the entire time, waiting for the perfect opportunity to resurface.

Now there was no more hiding, no more stifling his feelings to protect him from the living, breathing manifestation of all his love and desire. Yes, love. He'd accepted his feelings when the officiant tied their hands together to signify their union as husband and wife. He'd never experienced such heart-racing euphoria with any other woman.

Her thighs fell apart as he settled between them and pressed his mouth against the curve of her throat, inhaling her rose-scented skin. He listened to her soft moans and desperate pleas and laughed softly, knowingly, as his hard flesh sliced between her legs. With each thrust of his hips, she tightened her grip, sinking her fingers into his shoulders as her body clamped around him like a vise.

When he was almost at the end of his rope, he withdrew. Frustrated, she sucked air between her teeth in a huff.

"Over," Kofi muttered. She turned face down and lifted her bottom in the air. He almost couldn't bear the sight of her in that position. "This is how I want you. I want to see this lovely behind." He smoothed a hand from her lower back down over the soft globes of her bottom.

When he pushed the head of his length to her entrance, she pushed back into him. His hard flesh drove into hers, sliding with ease into the snug fit. He reached around and played with one breast. Soft and lush, it filled his hand. Her back arched deeper, and each time his hips slapped against her ass, she cried out. Her head dipped lower and the twists tumbled forward in a display of black ropes and glinting gold. Gathering a fistful he tugged, taking control, until her fingers grappled for purchase in the pillows.

Before too long, she came apart, screaming down the walls. She shook uncontrollably as he emptied inside her, gripping her hips as spasms of pleasure wrenched through him like a burst dam.

When they returned to some semblance of normal breathing, he pulled her close and she pressed her face into his neck.

He lay like that for a long time, holding her close, hand fisted in the cottony softness of her hair, quietly overwhelmed.

20

Dahlia and Kofi arrived at Inhambane Airport in Mozambique at ten o'clock at night after a long, twelve-hour flight. From the airport, a caravan of hired cars, which included a full entourage of attendants, drove almost twenty miles to the lazy seaside town of Tofo. Though known around the world for its dive sites that offered glimpses of manta rays, dolphins, and whale sharks, the location still managed to maintain a sense of seclusion. Kofi had rented an entire guest house, which meant they had a large strip of the beach entirely to themselves.

After eating a three-course meal on the royal plane, Dahlia was far from hungry, but she pinched a bite of the coconut muffin she found in her room on a tray filled with other baked goods. She sauntered over to the huge sliding glass door and pulled it open. The sound of the ocean washed into her ears, and in the distance she saw the dark sea lapping against the white sands of the shore.

Angela flew back to the States before Dahlia and Kofi left Zamibia. Their bittersweet goodbye consisted of an early breakfast before Dahlia instructed a driver to take her friend to the airport.

She missed her already. In her gut, she felt a long time would pass before they saw each other again, and that filled her with sadness.

Kofi came up behind her and looped an arm around her waist. "It's late."

Dahlia nodded.

"What's wrong?" He made her face him and tilted her head up until he saw her eyes.

"I'm being silly."

He frowned. "Tell me."

"I miss Angie." She shrugged.

"That's not silly. It's understandable. You've known each other since college, and I'm sure she was there for you when Noel was born."

Dahlia nodded, emotion clogging her throat. No friend was as reliable as Angela. She'd thrown her a baby shower and held her hand in the delivery room when Dahlia had no one else.

"I should go check on Noel," she said.

"He's asleep, and Aofa is with him. We'll get him in the morning."

He closed the sliding glass door and led the way to the bed, where Mariama had scattered red rose petals on the sheets. They undressed and slid beneath the cool linens, wrapping their arms around each other. Kofi rubbed her back with gentle up and down strokes. He knew what she needed and gave it to her. There'd be no sex tonight. Tonight she'd only be held.

~

THE FAINT LIGHT of dawn cast a dim glow through the mosquito netting around the bed, allowing Kofi to get a good look at his wife lying curled against him, fast asleep. One arm was thrown across his chest, her steady breathing ticking his collarbone while her soft cheek used his shoulder as a pillow.

Kofi lifted one of her twists and carefully wound the hair around his forefinger. He stilled as she moved in her sleep, rubbing her soft body against his and settling more comfortably. He wanted to spend the rest of his life the same way—waking up with her pressed to him, her sweet smell clinging to his skin and the sheets. He hadn't brought her to the continent in the best way, he admitted with a rueful smile, but they were together now. They could make their marriage work.

Kofi folded an arm behind his head and contemplated the days ahead, balancing his new family and palace affairs.

Sensing Dahlia's gaze on him, he turned and saw her eyes opened.

"You're awake. Good morning." He squeezed her closer in greeting. Shifting his hand beneath her mass of hair, he stroked her upper back.

"Good morning." She smiled and stretched like a satisfied cat, letting out a low moan. She lifted onto one elbow and looked down at him, her hair falling to the side. She bit her lip in an almost shy manner. It was adorable. "Is something wrong? You seemed deep in thought for a moment."

"Thinking about palace business and all the work I left behind."

"You shouldn't be thinking of palace business right now. Turn off that part of your brain and tell me what's on the agenda today."

Kofi held up a crushed rose petal. "First, finding out where all of these went. I think I have one in my ass."

Covering her mouth, Dahlia let out a pure, unfiltered laugh that filled the room and vibrated throughout his entire body. "I thought the roses were a nice touch. Mariama brought them all the way from Zamibia."

"They were a nice touch," he conceded.

"But seriously, Your Highness, what do you have planned after breakfast? A walk on beach and swim, maybe? Or spend the day relaxing in the hammock?"

"Relaxing? No, no. We're going to do something much more fun."

"What did you have in mind?"

"These waters are renowned for their marine life. We're going snorkeling."

Her eyes narrowed. "You mean *you're* going snorkeling?'

"I said *we're* going snorkeling."

"I've never been snorkeling in my life."

"Can you swim?" They had so much to learn about each other.

"Yes."

"Then between me and one of the instructors from the dive center, you'll be fine. There's plenty of marine life around here—manta rays, whale sharks—"

"Whoa." Holding the sheet to her chest, Dahlia sat all the way up and her eyes widened. "Did you say sharks?"

He chuckled. She was such an expressive woman. Noel definitely inherited his outgoing personality from her. "I said whale sharks."

"What's the difference?"

Kofi sat up, too and spoke calmly to ease her fears. "They're not interested in humans. They're filter feeders. Their throats are the size of U.S. quarters, and because of that, they eat small organisms called plankton."

She frowned, looking askance at him. "We're not taking Noel with us." Neither of them had wanted to leave him behind, so they brought him on the trip, and Aofa as well to help care for him.

"No, he's too little. Only you and I are going."

Dahlia gnawed on her lip.

"Do you really think I would endanger your life?"

She shifted her mouth into a thoughtful moue that made him want to kiss her lips.

"I've just never gone snorkeling before."

"What better time to learn? I'll be with you the entire time." He slid a hand under her hair and cradled the back of her neck and give her a soft kiss.

"If I die, I'm coming back as a ghost to haunt you."

"Trust me. I would never let anything happen to you."

~

THEY ATE breakfast on the private balcony outside the room, over-looking the ocean. A feast covered the table and was much too much for only two people. Dahlia had never tasted mangoes so sweet, though Kofi swore the ones in Zamibia were more delicious.

"You have to try this," she said, picking up a piece of pineapple with her fingertips and feeding it to him across the table.

He licked her finger and a tingle of pleasure shot up her arm. She giggled, shaking her head at him.

"Good, but not as good as the ones—"

"Yeah, yeah. Not as good as Zamibian pineapples."

He grinned and speared a poached egg with his fork.

The old Kofi was back—almost. She sensed a reservation in him, as if he were holding something in. A quiet thought she wished he'd share. Perhaps he continued to hold doubts about her, about them. She'd have to do her best to eliminate whatever distrust remained because she liked this unspoken truce between them, where they were allowed to relax and enjoy each other's company.

He quirked a brow at her.

"What?" she said.

"I was about to ask you the same question. You're staring at me."

"Am I?"

"Mhmm." Then his mouth lifted into a sexy smile, and her private parts went berserk.

Her breasts especially had grown accustomed to the suck of his mouth. She regretted not taking the time to make love this morning. She wished she knew what the stubble on his face felt like on her skin. The thought left her breasts wanting and achy.

"I was not staring." She slathered sweet potato jam on her toast and pretended to ignore him.

Kofi folded his arms across his bare chest. "You know what I think? I think—"

"Excuse me, Your Highnesses. Prince Noel was asking for you." Aofa approached with Noel walking beside her with his hand in hers.

"Mommy!" he squealed, and making a mad dash, pulled Aofa along with him.

"Good morning, precious." Dahlia swooped him up onto her lap and showered him with kisses. "Did you sleep okay?"

"Yes. Did you sleep okay, too, Mommy?" Noel asked.

"Yes, I did."

"I will leave you alone," Aofa said.

As she turned away, Kofi called her back. "We're going snorkeling later today. We'll need you to watch Noel while we're gone. Come back in about forty-five minutes."

Dahlia watched her son steal a piece of mango off her plate.

"I would love to spend more time with him. He reminds me of my youngest grandson." Aofa's expression widened into a happy grin. She talked about her grandchildren a lot. Working in the palace was an honor, but Dahlia could tell she hated being away from them.

Noel shoved the fruit in his mouth. "Mmm," he murmured, chomping away.

"Isn't that the best mango you've ever tasted?" Dahlia asked.

Noel nodded, licking at the juice running down his chin.

"See, I told you," Dahlia said to Kofi.

"You coached him," he accused.

Dahlia laughed and pulled her son in close.

Kofi leaned across the table. "Son, we're going to have to work on your loyalty."

Noel stared at him for a minute and then burst into giggles.

Dahlia kissed the back of his head and looked across the table at Kofi.

Today was going to be a good day.

21

After her initial bout of nervousness subsided, Dahlia adhered to the snorkeling instructions, relaxed and enjoyed the grandness of nature out in the vast ocean. She, Kofi, the instructor, and a helper saw not only whale sharks and manta rays, but encountered dolphins, too. As instructed, they stayed the appropriate distance away from the whale sharks to keep from accidentally getting bumped. The giant creatures lazily swam by, mostly uninterested in her and Kofi as they swam around them.

The manta ray circled with the same lazy elegance, their wing-like fins gently carrying them smoothly through the water. In the end, she and Kofi fed fish to the dolphins and were treated to their acrobatics as they slipped in and out of the waves, performing for food.

Hours later, they returned to the guesthouse to find Aofa snoozing in a hammock on the beach. Noel napped on top of her.

Dahlia tapped Aofa's shoulder and the woman jerked awake.

"I didn't mean to scare you." Dahlia kept her voice low so as not to wake up Noel. "I wanted you to know we were back from snorkeling."

Aofa stifled a yawn. "How was it?"

"Exhilarating. Unbelievable. Better than I imagined." Beside her, Kofi chuckled. "Well, it's true. I can't believe I've never gone snorkeling with whale sharks and dolphins before."

Kofi squeezed her shoulder. "And to think, you didn't want to go."

"I was wrong." She couldn't stop smiling. They were acting like...a couple.

"I'm so happy for you." Aofa swung her legs onto the sand, and Dahlia held the hammock steady so she could get out, impressed the entire time that the nanny kept Noel safely cradled in her arms.

"How long has he been asleep?" Dahlia asked.

"I'm not sure, since I fell asleep myself," Aofa said sheepishly. "What time is it?"

"A little after two o'clock," Kofi answered.

"When I last checked, it was a little after twelve o'clock, so not very long. No more than a couple of hours."

Dahlia rubbed her knuckle across her son's cheek. "Tomorrow I'm giving him my undivided attention. We're going to play in the ocean."

"What do you have planned for the rest of the day?" Aofa asked.

"Eat and then do something with my hair." Dahlia smoothed a hand over the damp twists. "We're going out tonight. Apparently, there's a fairly lively nightlife in town, and the owners of the guesthouse suggested we visit a couple of the beach bars, get a few beers, and dance."

"I think that's a lovely idea. May I say, Your Highnesses, you both look very happy and relaxed."

Kofi took her hand, his eyes filled with affection. "That's because we are."

"Good. I'm happy to hear that. And don't worry, I'll keep an eye on Noel."

Dahlia clasped Aofa's free hand in her own. "I haven't said this before, but I appreciate all your help with him. You've made the transition much easier for me, and he adores you."

"The honor is mine." Aofa bowed briefly.

~

A FEW HOURS LATER, Dahlia sat at the foot of the bed slipping on sandals, and Kofi appeared in the doorway. She'd already dismissed Mariama, so he and she were alone in the room. He didn't say a word.

"Are you just going to stand there?" Dahlia asked.

"Maybe."

She slipped on the second shoe and then walked over to him. "What do you think?" She placed both hands on her hips.

"Beautiful, as always." He weaved his fingertips through the riot of loose curls that trailed down her back. "Do you still have regrets about coming to Africa?"

"None." She answered without thought, without hesitation. That's what love did. It obliterated doubt. She always wanted to be near Kofi. Touching him. Hearing his voice. It was crazy, and dangerous, and painful—and the best feeling in the world, all at once.

"No regrets?" he asked again.

"None." What a difference from only a few weeks ago, when she'd regretted getting on the plane and wished she'd put up a stronger fight to resist coming to the continent.

Kofi kissed her, softly, his mouth little more than a whisper against hers. She indulged in the taste of him, wrapping her arms around his torso and pressing her breasts against his hard chest.

He smiled against her lips, and a seductive, flirty quality entered his eyes and heated her skin. "I promised you dancing. Though I would much rather do something else, I'm going to keep my promise. Let's go."

The driver took them into town, and the beach bar was jumping when they arrived. Music poured from mounted speakers as a surprising number of people, many of them in their early twenties, danced in the sand.

The owners of the guesthouse had said a lot of backpackers came to Tofo and stayed at some of the less expensive accommodations. Most of the people were Africans, Europeans, and Americans. Abdalla and Yasir were already stationed near the bar, dressed inconspicuously in T-shirts and jeans, each holding a beer she knew they'd never drink because they were on duty.

She and Kofi squeezed between the people at the bar, ordered two local beers, and drank them while watching the dancers get down on the sand.

"Care to join them?" Kofi asked.

"Do you have moves like that?" Dahlia asked teasingly.

"Considering you've seen a lot of my moves, I can't believe you asked that question."

He set their beers on the bar and took her by the hand, leading her into the middle of the group. Sliding an arm around her waist, he pulled her close and swayed their bodies together in a rhythmic movement where they ground their hips against each other.

Dahlia tilted her lips up to his ear, and he bent his head. "This is less like dancing and more like making love," she said.

"Making love is a type of dance."

She pressed her face into his neck and inhaled him, his fragrance, and the scent of his skin. A scent she would never get tired of.

Hooking her arm around his neck she whispered, "I never want to leave here."

He kissed her temple and then rested his forehead against hers.

Her heart filled with emotion, and she wanted to be reckless tonight. Live in the moment. To tell him how much she loved him, how much she had never stopped loving him, though she tried her damndest. How much she would love him, even after the end of eternity.

In the middle of the music and the barely audible sound of the ocean nearby, Kofi locked eyes with her. His hips rubbed against hers, the sexy rhythm of the music making them move to the beat. "I missed you." His kissed her cheek, the underside of her jaw, and her neck. "I missed you every day of the three years we were apart."

"You did?" She wasn't sure she heard him correctly over the sounds of music and people talking.

"I never stopped thinking about you." He let out a heavy breath, and his eyes darkened with regret. "I should have never left you in America."

Dahlia stroked his jaw. She'd longed to hear words like this come from his mouth, and now that she did, she was speechless knowing he'd experienced some of the same heartache that had tormented her day after day.

"I was a fool. A dumbass."

She laughed. Finding humor in their argument showed how far they'd come.

Kofi stopped moving, and his gaze intensified. "I love you, Dahlia. I should have told you a long time ago, but I couldn't admit it even to myself."

Closing her eyes, she willed herself to be brave enough to whisper the words that trembled on her lips. "Kofi..." She clasped her hands at the back of his neck. Their faces were close together, as if no one else was around. "I feel like I've waited my whole life to hear you say that. I love you, too. My heart broke when you left. I died that day."

Looking deeply into her eyes, he said, "I died, too. God, I wish I'd never left you."

Her bottom lip quivered. "I'm sorry about Noel. I wish..."

"Shh."

She shook her head to cut off the interruption. She had to tell him. She needed him to know. "I didn't keep him a secret out of spite. I did try to reach you. I swear, I did. You were on your honeymoon, and when I found out you were married, I...I didn't think you'd care. You have to believe me."

His eyes locked onto hers as if trying to see into the innermost part of her being. "I believe you." He kissed her softly. "And I don't believe you were an accomplice in embezzling the funds from our accounts, either. I should have trusted you from the beginning when you told me you had nothing to do with the theft. I'm sorry, *olufeh mi*."

Finally! Dahlia grinned as he pressed his face into the crook of her neck. His beard tickled her skin. She turned her lips to his cheek and squeezed him tight as his hands slid down and grabbed her ass. They stayed right there, and she didn't care who saw. They held on to each other and started slow dancing even though the music had a rapid tempo.

Her heart filled to the brim with her love for him, and she wanted to show him how much, skin to skin. She didn't care about dancing anymore. She wanted to be alone with him. "Kofi, let's—"

"Your Highness."

Reluctantly, they pulled apart. Abdalla stood behind Kofi. From the grave expression on his face, she knew something was wrong.

"What is it?" Kofi asked. His body went very still, and the husky timbre of his voice was replaced with a firm, authoritative tone.

"We received a call from the palace. There's been an accident."

22

Whenever members of the royal family traveled, assistants packed what amounted to a small wardrobe, which included mourning attire. That way, should a death occur while they were abroad, they would be appropriately attired when they descended from the plane.

Such was the case when Kofi, Dahlia, and Noel arrived. They flew all night and slept on the plane. When they disembarked, they all wore long black robes. Dahlia wore a black scarf over her head, edged with gold because of her status as a princess. Kofi wore a black and gold fila.

They walked onto the tarmac with solemn faces. Noel, walking beside his mother, took cues from his parents and didn't wave and grin like the last time.

"Your Highness, do you know what caused the collapse?" a reporter asked from behind the barricade.

One of the mines had collapsed, trapping the miners. Officials were unsure of the death toll, but rescue efforts through the night resulted in several dead being pulled from the rubble.

Kofi paused to briefly address the assembled journalists. "As soon as we know the cause, we'll release a statement. Until then, our thoughts and prayers are with the men and women who are trapped, their families, and the families of the deceased."

He placed a hand low on Dahlia's spine, and the three walked to the waiting limousine while the reporters yelled more questions at their retreating backs.

In taking ownership of the mining companies, the government also had to take ownership of the tragedy. Safety was always a concern in the mining industry, but accidents did happen. For the first time, an accident resulted in fatalities on Zamibian soil.

No one said a word on the drive to The Grand Palace. Once inside, Kofi stopped in the marble foyer. "I'm going to my office to get more information about what's going on."

"Should I come with you?" Dahlia asked, concern in her eyes.

Kofi shook his head. "Go. I'll be up soon."

She hesitated, as if she wanted to say something else, and he also felt as if words remained on the tip of his tongue—words he didn't get to share because of the interruption from Abdalla less than twenty-four hours ago.

"I'll see you later, then." Dahlia led Noel away by the hand toward the elevator, but the little boy looked back.

Kofi smiled to reassure him. Children were such sensitive creatures, able to pick up on moods from the adults around them. He didn't want the stress of his own thoughts to rub off on his son. Noel smiled back and picked up his steps to keep up with his mother.

Kofi strode toward his office. Inside, he removed the robe and cap to reveal a simple cotton shirt and pants underneath.

Minutes later, his head of security, Oriyeh, arrived. Her light-colored skin was the result of a French father and a Zamibian mother. A few years past forty, she was an unassuming woman who wore her thick hair in an Afro puff at the back of her head. She went into military service after she finished school and was not only an incredible fighting machine, but very intelligent, as well. After completing her service, she enlisted again, and by the time she left the service had earned an engineering degree. She was a brilliant strategist, and he trusted her with his life. The king expressed no reservations when Kofi appointed her head of palace security.

"Your Highness." Clutching her fist to her chest, she gave him the bow of respect.

"Come in, Oriyeh. What do you have for me?" From their brief phone call, he deduced there was more to the story than a simple mine collapse. He sat in the chair behind his desk.

Oriyeh sat across from him. "It's not good, Your Highness."

Kofi's shoulders tensed as he braced for the news.

"I've been in close communication with the local police and the rescue team, and after preliminary investigations, the collapse doesn't appear to be an accident or breach of safety protocol. They believe it was purposefully done, using dynamite or a bomb of some kind."

A rush of heat swamped his body. "Bomb? Why the hell would anyone put a bomb in the mine? What did any of those men and women do to warrant such an attack?"

"The motive is unclear."

Kofi laughed bitterly. "I believe I know the motive."

Oriyeh quirked a brow upward.

Sitting back in the chair, Kofi said, "Before I left on my honeymoon, we turned down Titanium Oil's offer to work with them. This might be a way for them to twist our arm and show we need outside help with the project."

Oriyeh frowned as she mulled the words. "Perhaps, but then how do you explain this?" She removed a sheet of paper encased in plastic from inside her jacket and gave it to him.

Kofi turned the document over in his hand. *You must pay for your sins.* "What is this?"

"King Babatunde found this note on the bench in his private garden when he went for his evening walk."

Kofi shot to his feet. "Are you telling me someone breached the security of the palace grounds?" Outrage was taut and vivid in his voice.

Oriyeh flinched. She stood, too. "I don't know how, but it seems—"

"It *seems*? We have cameras all over this property."

"Yes, Your Highness. But the perpetrator took advantage of a blind spot to deliver the message."

"This is absolutely unacceptable!" Kofi thundered. Oriyeh flinched again and he took a deep breath. "What are you doing to prevent this type of breach from happening again?"

"Another camera is being installed, I've placed more guards around the king, and we've altered his routine."

His father would hate the changes. A man of routine, he ate breakfast at the same time every day and took a walk to meditate in his garden at the same time each evening. But with his safety at stake, he'd have to adjust.

"What else do you know?"

"Nothing. Whoever they are, they're very good."

Kofi paced to the window and back. "Could they be targeting anyone else in the monarchy?"

"I have nothing to confirm it, but that is my belief."

Panic seized his throat when he thought about Noel and Dahlia. "Then we need to make sure my wife and child are protected at all costs. My uncle, his wives, his children. Everyone."

"Including you, Your Highness."

"I will be fine."

"Until we figure out who these people are, all of you should have additional protection and change your schedules."

"Fine. Leave me."

She picked up the threatening note and walked to the door.

"Oriyeh." She faced him. "Not a word of this to anyone."

"Yes, Your Highness."

She quietly left the office.

Kofi sat down and dialed his secretary. He told her to pull together the CVs and every bit of information she could on everyone in charge of safety at the mines. Despite Oriyeh's intel, he wanted to eliminate the possibility of human error in the collapse. He also told his secretary to put together the names and tribal affiliations of the injured and dead. The government would pay for the three-day funerals, and he wanted the Finance Office to estimate the loss in wages to the affected families so compensation packages could be prepared.

When he hung up, Kemal came in and stopped in the middle of the floor.

"What?" Kofi asked irritably.

He arched an eyebrow. "How was your honeymoon?"

"Short."

Kemal came closer. "You won't want to hear this, but I received a call from Alistair Davies. He wants to know if you'll reconsider working with Titanium Oil."

A mirthless laugh left Kofi's throat. "And why would I reconsider?" Kofi set his arms on the armrests of the chair and rested his ankle on his knee.

"I suppose he thinks with the mine collapse, now is a good time to mention their expertise to make sure a similar situation doesn't happen when we drill for oil."

Kofi tapped his fingers on the chair. "Did you keep an eye on them like I asked?"

"Yes."

"And?"

"No unusual behavior or suspicious activity was reported back to me on Ambassador Stephens or Mr. Davies."

Kofi studied the other man. "Well, that's good news, isn't it?"

"Yes, good news."

"What do you think we should do?"

"The decision is yours."

"Yes, it is. Always."

An awkward silence filled the room.

Kofi rubbed a hand across his bearded chin. "For now, we're going to stick to the plan we already have in place. We're going to work with Barrakesch on the offshore drilling."

"Alistair and the Ambassador won't be pleased."

"You're on a first name basis with Davies?" Kofi asked, eyebrows raised.

"I...I've spoken to him a few times, and he insisted I call him by his first name."

"Well, I'm glad you've developed such a good rapport with him." Kofi smiled tightly. "Please let him know I don't give a damn if he's pleased or not. I don't work for his pleasure."

"I'll pass on the message." His face remained neutral, but his voice held an underlying note of...something. Tension, anger? Kofi couldn't be sure.

"By the way, Dahlia told me something I need to ask you about. She said when she found out she was pregnant, she called but didn't reach me. She said she spoke to you. Do you remember that conversation?"

In Tofo, when she mentioned she tried to reach him to let him know she was pregnant, it triggered a memory. Back in Atlanta, Dahlia told him she spoke to Kemal, but anger and a sense of betrayal made him ignore her and he never followed up with his assistant.

The first sign of discomfort appeared when Kemal swallowed. "I remember the conversation," he said in a composed tone.

"Why didn't you tell me she had called?" Kofi became very still.

"You were on your honeymoon."

"And after I returned?"

"I didn't think you wanted to have anything to do with her. This woman stole from the kingdom, and you gave no indication you were still interested in her."

He had a point, except for one small detail. "I no longer believe she stole from us, and furthermore, I confided in you about my feelings for her. So tell me again how I gave no indication I was interested."

Kemal rolled his shoulders. "She wasn't right for you."

Kofi shot up from the chair and marched over to Kemal. He

watched his body tense as they stood eye to eye. "That was not your decision to make."

Kemal's jaw went rigid, and his gaze dropped to the floor.

"Six months after Azireh died, I asked you to find Dahlia. You never told me then that she called, either." Kemal told him he hadn't been able to find a trace of her in New York, which made sense. By then she'd left for Atlanta. But did Kemal put in the necessary effort to find her? When Kofi hired an investigator himself, the man located her within weeks.

"The mourning period had not passed," Kemal said quietly.

"Again, not your decision to make." Kofi slammed a hand against his chest. "*I* determine how long I should mourn. Not tradition. Maybe we should reevaluate your role."

Kemal's head jerked up. "I've been loyal to you for over five years."

"Have you?" The question hung in the air like putrid smoke.

Much of the anger he felt was directed at himself for not believing Dahlia when she told him she had nothing to do with the stolen funds and did try to contact him about Noel. Recognizing her innocence made him feel like a louse when he considered how he'd treated her and the accusations he'd hurled.

Kemal's lips tightened and defiance sparked in his eyes. "You're tired and stressed because of the problem at the mine. I'll call Alistair—Mr. Davies—and let him know nothing has changed." He swung on his heels.

"On second thought, I'll handle Davies from now on."

Kemal paused at the door. "If that's what you prefer."

"That is what I prefer."

"Very well." He exited the office.

Kofi's eyes didn't leave the closed door. After a few minutes, he rounded the desk and sank into the leather chair, mind racing. He needed time to think. His relationship with Kemal was sensitive and complicated, and in all this time he'd never questioned his loyalty. Had he made a mistake in hiring him?

He was starting to think he had.

23

D ahlia awoke with a start and sat up. The image of a familiar figure stood next to the bed.

She pressed a hand to her chest. "Kofi, you scared me. What are you doing?" she whispered. She didn't want to wake Noel, who slept beside her with the stuffed worm sandwiched between the mattress and his leg.

"Thinking."

She peered at him in the near darkness and blinked to adjust her eyes. "Are you okay?"

"Couldn't sleep."

Dahlia pulled back the linens and silently invited him into the bed. He settled behind her, draping an arm across her waist and sliding a knee between her thighs. They fit together like two magnets, lying together for the first time since their return from Mozambique a week ago. Kofi spent every day in meetings and visited the mine where the accident took place, all to get to the bottom of the catastrophe and make sure those affected were adequately compensated.

The news cycle hadn't been kind, questioning whether the Karunzika family had been careless and not hired the right people.

Five people died, and she saw the toll the negative press and the deaths took on Kofi. He appeared distracted most days, and at breakfast this morning, there'd been bags under his eyes.

She did her part to help change the narrative by spending an entire day visiting the injured in the hospital and eating lunch with the doctors and nurses who treated them. The photo ops presented the royal family in a different light and allowed them to appear more compassionate. The visit didn't only affect the patients. She gained personal satisfaction knowing she'd brightened their day and made a small difference.

The very next day, she met with her social secretary and scheduled another visit, this time to the children's hospital, without the cameras. Children suffering from injuries and life-threatening illnesses perked up when she appeared. She and her assistants handed out toys purchased with funds from her budget, and she signed casts and kissed and hugged a lot of children. Her cheeks hurt when she left, but she'd never been so invigorated and decided visiting the children's hospital would be a regular part of her duties.

"Has Oriyeh or the police figured out how the note ended up in King Babatunde's garden?"

Kofi had briefly discussed the threatening note with her. Since then, additional guards had been assigned to travel with her and Noel at all times. She felt crowded by the extra security but didn't have any choice since no one knew who the threatening person or persons were.

"They're no closer to figuring that out than they were before. Oriyeh is working closely with the police and their contacts."

"Is it possible the culprit is someone already in the palace? Not someone from the outside?"

Kofi remained silent.

"I'm not wrong, am I?" Dahlia asked quietly.

"The thought crossed my mind," Kofi admitted.

"Have you discussed your thought with Oriyeh?"

"Yes, among other ideas." He shifted. "What I hate is this waiting, as if we have to wait for them to strike again before we can get another clue to their identity."

Dahlia brushed her knuckles gently over Noel's cheek. He had surprisingly long eyelashes, which he didn't inherit from either her or Kofi. They came from his grandmother, Queen Nahla, who from all the photos that she'd seen, had long, thick, curly lashes.

He slept quietly and peacefully in the bed beside her, with a pillow behind his back to make sure he didn't fall off the bed in the middle of the night. She'd been spending more time with him lately, worried to let him out of her sight. Not knowing from which direction the danger could come filled her with queasy dread, but she didn't share her thoughts with Kofi because she didn't want to burden him more than he already was.

"I won't let anything happen to either of you," Kofi said.

She didn't reply. He'd told her once no one would dare harm them. Now she wondered if he'd been wrong.

∿

"Ow! STOP," Dahlia howled as Kofi pummeled her with a pillow. She collapsed onto her back in a tangle of sheets and a deep belly laugh, the lavender nightgown riding up her thighs.

He dropped on top of her, pinning her arms on either side of her head. "Oh, now you wish to cry stop. How do you think I felt when you ambushed me as soon as I came out of the bathroom? You started this war, and I'm going to end it."

"That was over an hour ago."

"This is my revenge."

"Well, you know what? I got you good. Some great warrior you are. You didn't see that pillow coming."

"You think it's funny to question my skills?" He held her wrists in one hand and tickled her stomach with the other.

Dahlia burst into a fit of giggles. "Stop. Stop."

She looked so delicious writhing beneath him, Kofi kissed her.

He couldn't help himself. Her soft mouth gave under his, but then she retaliated with a nip to his top lip.

His head popped up. "You better behave," he warned.

"*You* behave and let me go," Dahlia said.

His eyes held hers. "Never."

They both stopped laughing and he bit his bottom lip, gazing at her as if she were the most beautiful woman he'd ever seen. A spark of desire lit his eyes, and he kissed her softly on the mouth again.

"No, Baba. Enough." Noel shoved his father's face and then climbed on top of Dahlia, resting his head on her chest.

Dahlia burst out laughing at Kofi's bewildered expression. "You don't want Baba to kiss me?"

Pouting, Noel shook his head.

"He's going to be very disappointed, then," Kofi said with amusement, falling onto his back.

"Let's get him," Dahlia said to Noel in a loud whisper.

Noel jumped on top of his father and landed tiny-fisted punches in Kofi's stomach, and he pretended to be hurt, grunting after each soft blow landed. In the meantime, Dahlia picked up another pillow and raised it over her head to pummel him.

"Excuse me, Your Highnesses."

An attendant brought in the lunch Kofi ordered. The man kept his eyes averted from the three of them roughhousing in their nightclothes.

The servant set the silver platter with drinks and covered dishes on a table in the sitting area. With eyes trained on the floor and his hands crossed before him, he asked, "Will there be anything else?"

"That will be all," Kofi said.

At the closing of the door, Dahlia snorted. "What must he be thinking?"

"That my wife is a bad influence on me."

She tossed the pillow toward the head of the bed. "I'm serious."

"So am I." He smirked. "Come on, we can't stay in bed all day." He sat up and scooped up Noel with him, tossing the toddler over his shoulder. Noel squealed and kicked his feet.

Dahlia groaned and followed him over to the table. They sat down, Noel in his lap.

Kofi thought back over the almost two weeks since the mine collapse. The tragedy had fallen out of heavy rotation in the news cycle, and Dahlia helped initiate the shift. By visiting the injured and their families, she softened the bent of the stories and allowed him more time to work with law enforcement on catching the perpetrators.

And their relationship was blossoming. Most nights she slept in his room, like last night, and this morning Aofa brought in Noel. They'd taken advantage of the weekend day and been lazy, watching television, playing with Noel's building blocks—an entire box of which migrated into Kofi's room somehow—and play fighting. Their cheerful family life was almost too good. A part of him half expected a rhino to come barreling through the front door to disrupt their peace. Or maybe he was being pessimistic.

"What's all this?" Dahlia asked. She inhaled deeply, concentrating her attention on the uncovered plate in front of her.

"I asked the chef to create a South African dish for you. That's peri-peri chicken with basmati rice and vegetables." He lifted the silver dome off another plate. "These are ostrich steaks for you to try." He lifted the dome off his own plate. "Slow-roasted antelope chops in an herb-butter sauce." His meat was served with a healthy serving of mushrooms and other vegetables.

"I ate an ostrich burger once and enjoyed it, so I'll give the steak a shot."

"No antelope for you?"

"A little piece, in case I don't like it."

"Don't worry, it's delicious. Have I led you wrong yet?" She'd been very adventurous in her food choices lately. She was now a biltong convert and most memorably devoured a bowl of peanut stew after wrinkling her nose and declaring she didn't want any.

"Not yet," she admitted.

Kofi cut a small piece of the tender meat and set it on her plate, and then cut off another piece and shared it with Noel.

His son chewed fast and swallowed. "All gone." He opened his mouth wide to show it was empty.

Kofi chuckled. "You like that, eh?"

Noel nodded vigorously.

"Here's another piece, but Baba needs to eat, too." Kofi shared another piece with him and then cut up additional slices. Across the table, Dahlia was looking at them.

"He fits right in, doesn't he?" she said, her voice thick.

"This is home. It's where he belongs," Kofi said. He kissed the top of his son's head.

"More, Baba!"

Kofi and Dahlia laughed.

"All right, all right." Kofi gave him some more food. "What do you say?"

"*Ese-gani,*" Noel said, using the Mbutu word for Thank you.

"*Odi.* Good. You're going to be bilingual soon. Unlike Mommy, who only speaks English." He looked pointedly at Dahlia.

She glared at him. "I'm going to take classes. I couldn't decide between French or Mbutu, but I've already spoken to the language coach, thank you very much. I'm starting with Mbutu."

Her decision to start with his tribal tongue pleased him immensely. "I didn't know that."

"I don't tell you everything, *aremoh mi.*" With a cocky smile, she took a sip of bissap.

He chuckled and gave Noel a mushroom from his plate. "So tell me, what did you buy for my uncle's wife, so I won't be surprised when she opens the gift?" Kofi asked.

Prince Kehinde, his father's younger brother and Imani's father, was throwing a birthday party for his youngest wife tonight, who turned fifty. Initially, they'd planned for a huge celebration, but in light of the recent mine collapse, King Babatunde asked them to tone down the festivities. Instead of throwing a big party at a local hotel, they'd opted to have a small, outdoor event on the grounds of the palace, with family, close friends, and servants.

"Kehinde said she wanted jewelry, and my secretary found a gorgeous diamond bracelet for her. It's with the other gifts."

"We're all set for this evening, then?"

"Yes, and we can be lazy for the rest of the day."

24

With lush green mountains in the distance forming a boundary to the hundreds of acres occupied by the royal family, the grounds in the back of the palace were the perfect place for a birthday party. Servants set up lanterns and poles which suspended strings of light over tables filled with food and presents, creating a festive but charming ambiance.

"I want to thank you all for coming tonight to help me celebrate my wife's birthday. Fifty years is a milestone many people don't achieve, and I am the lucky man who has been fortunate enough to spend the last thirty years with this lovely woman. Thank you for my beautiful children. You've been a blessing to me and my family. Happy birthday, my love."

Dahlia applauded and cheered with everyone else. She watched as Kehinde's wife blew out the candles and everyone cheered and whistled again, including his other two wives.

She may not have understood their type of arrangement before she arrived in this country, but she accepted their relationship now. Theirs wasn't the type of marriage she could see herself in, but they were a happy, close-knit family. The three women lived like sisters, and their children were all close.

Imani gave her mother a hug and a kiss on the cheek. Then the music started, a traditional Zamibian beat that relied heavily on drums and other percussion instruments, which made her want to shake her shoulders and get up and dance. Her eyes searched for Kofi among the small group. He and his father sat beside each other, their heads close together as they apparently discussed something important. She didn't want to interrupt.

"I love your outfit," Imani said.

"Thank you." She'd picked out the dress herself, since she'd given Mariama the day off. The royal blue dress draped over her body in a flattering way. She kept the jewelry to a minimum but added an African flair with colorful balls attached to handmade copper earrings.

"Kofi told me you're going to learn Mbutu," Imani said.

"I'm going to *try*. I'm intimidated because the language is completely foreign to me, but I'm giving it a shot instead of learning French."

Imani nodded. "Even if you learn a few phrases, people will appreciate you for trying. I think you're making the right choice."

She knew she was making the right choice. She was starting to feel closer to the culture of the Zamibian people, less of an outsider and more like a citizen herself. Learning the language would bring her closer to an affinity with them, which she wanted, particularly since she and Kofi were closer now. At times when he looked at her, she saw the reciprocated love in his eyes, and she couldn't imagine losing that or being apart from him again.

Dahlia caught sight of Aofa on the outskirts of the group, sitting with Noel in her lap. She had asked Aofa to come to the party and keep an eye on Noel, allowing Dahlia to spend time with the adults.

Dahlia did a double take. Noel looked odd. Almost lethargic.

She walked toward them, and when she was a few feet away, he leaned over and vomited on the grass. Dahlia rushed the rest of the way and crouched in front of him.

"He hasn't been well since we came to the party," Aofa said.

"He was fine this afternoon." Dahlia rubbed his back.

"Mommy," he moaned, reaching for her. She took him in her arms and used the handkerchief Aofa handed her to wipe his mouth.

"Let me take him upstairs. That way you can stay and enjoy the party," Aofa offered.

"No, you stay and enjoy the party. I'll take him up." The way Noel held onto her, she knew he wouldn't let her go. She stood and hoisted him higher on her hip. He was gaining weight and getting so big.

"I don't mind," Aofa said.

"I insist. You stay here, and I'll go up to the apartment."

"Are you sure, Your Highness? Do you know what to do?" Aofa stood, her arms extended as if to take him.

Dahlia took a step back. "I'm perfectly capable of taking care of my own child."

Aofa dropped her hands. "I'm sorry. Forgive me. I did not mean to imply you could not take care of him."

Aofa spent almost every day with Noel for hours at a time. Of course she'd grown attached to him. Dahlia calmed down. "And I didn't mean to snap. We'll be fine. If I need your help, I'll send someone to get you."

"All right. I have an herbal tea that might help him feel better. It's in the pantry on the third shelf in a glass jar. It's good for nausea and will help him sleep."

"Thank you."

She left the party with Noel in her arms, and a guard drove her to one of the back doors of the palace on a golf cart. Because of the new security rules, the guard stayed with her as she walked through the first floor and joined her in the elevator.

She rubbed Noel's back, and he moaned softly.

"Are you in pain?"

He didn't reply. They'd eaten a heavy lunch earlier. Maybe he was allergic to something the cook served.

"Does your tummy hurt?"

"Yes," he answered, sounding pitiful.

"I'm going to try to make you feel better, okay?"

He nodded and placed his head on her shoulder.

She pressed her thumb to the biometric pad that gave entrance into the part of the east wing where they lived. The door opened silently and she walked down the hall with the guard following behind.

Dahlia stopped, the hairs on the back of her neck rising.

The guard, a stocky man of medium height, stopped, too. "Is there something wrong, Your Highness?"

"I..." Dahlia sensed something, but what? The hall and the alcoves were empty. "Hello? Is somebody here?"

The guard turned in a full circle and then walked a few steps away, peering from one end of the passageway to the next. "Hello?" he called, his voice ricocheting off the walls.

She shook off the jitters. "Ignore me. It's probably my imagination."

She continued to her and Kofi's living quarters and pressed her thumb to another biometric panel, which let her into their private residence. Before closing the door, she smiled at the guard. "You can go back to the party. I'm staying in for the rest of the evening."

He bowed and went back the way they came.

Dahlia placed Noel on her bed and covered him with the blanket. She checked for a fever, but he wasn't hot, which was at least a good sign. He wasn't fighting an infection.

She would make him the tea Aofa suggested since the older woman knew a lot about herbal remedies.

"I'm going to the kitchen to make some tea for you. I'll be right back, okay?" She didn't want to leave him alone, but she'd only be gone a few minutes.

"Mommy, wiggle worm."

"Oh, of course." Dahlia picked up the toy from a chair across the room and handed it to him. "Give me a few minutes, and I'll be back with something nice and warm to make your tummy feel better, okay?" She rubbed his belly.

"Okay," Noel said in a faint voice. If he didn't feel better within an hour after drinking the tea, she'd call a doctor.

Dahlia exited the bedroom, leaving the door open in case he called out to her while she was gone. Just like Aofa said, she found the jar of herbs on the third shelf in the pantry. She set the kettle to warm, and minutes later mixed a little honey in the hot water and dropped a mesh bag filled with tea leaves into the cup.

Dahlia made her way back down the hall. "Okay, here you..."

The room was empty. No Noel, but the wiggle worm remained on the mattress.

"Noel?" Dahlia frowned as she walked around to the other side of the bed. "Noel, honey, where are you?" She went into the dressing room. He wasn't there, either.

The bathroom was also empty. Her fingers went numb, and she dropped the cup of tea on the tiled floor, barely registering the hot spray spattered her ankles.

Rushing out of the bathroom, she yelled, "Noel!"

She dropped to the floor and checked under the bed. Empty.

She recalled her unease outside the apartment and panic set in. Dahlia jumped up and ran into the hall. "Noel!" she screamed. She ran from room to room, screaming his name, shoving open doors.

"Noel!" she screamed from a throat raw with terror.

She ran back down the hallway and heard movement in the bedroom. She pushed the door open, but it wasn't Noel. It was Kofi.

He frowned. "What's going on? Aofa told me Noel was sick and you came up here with him. Where is he?"

The room began to spin and Dahlia reached out to him for balance. He moved swiftly and grabbed her hands to steady her.

"Dahlia, where is he?" he asked again, louder this time.

"I don't know." An uncontrollable shaking overtook her body. "He's not here."

25

When she finally stopped hyperventilating, Dahlia shut down. Time lost all meaning. In her stupor, she heard Abdalla, Kofi, and Oriyeh talking but couldn't understand a word they said. All she could do was imagine her little boy, sick and terrified, without her or his stuffed animal for comfort.

Who would take him? Did they want money? Were they going to hurt him—cut off an ear or a toe to send a message? Nausea bubbled in her stomach and, elbows to knees, she covered her face with her hands.

My baby, my baby. She was so close to cracking.

"How could someone get in here without being seen?" Kofi shouted.

"We don't know for sure, but I have an idea," Oriyeh replied. "I've checked the records for the panel outside your door. No one entered the apartment after Princess Dahlia except you. They must have entered through the escape room behind your bedroom and slipped into the princess's room through the hallway connected to yours."

A hidden room behind a wall in Kofi's bedroom could be used

as an escape route in the event the palace ever came under siege. He and his family could be whisked away to safety through an underground route.

"Very few people know about that," Kofi said.

"I believe that's the only way the kidnapper could have entered undetected, which means he or she knew about it, too. We can only wait to see who claims responsibility for the kidnapping."

"Wait! We need answers and we need answers now. Our son is gone."

"Since the note that was left for King Babatunde, we've been working with the police to identify anyone who might have a grudge against the monarchy. There has been no communication to the palace. No ransom demands. Nothing at all."

"He's a child. Who would do this?" Dahlia asked, surprised at the raspy sound of her voice.

All eyes turned to her.

"Is it possible he wandered off, Princess Dahlia?" Oriyeh asked gently.

"Wandered off? He's sick."

"There are secret passages—"

"Are you suggesting—" Kofi cut in, eyebrows drawn together.

"He didn't go through a secret passage!" Dahlia snapped. "I left him in bed with his stuffed toy. Even if he got up and went somewhere on his own, he wouldn't leave that damn worm. He loves it too much. He's sick and it comforts him. Someone took him." She sniffed and rubbed away the tears that trailed down her cheeks. "I was only gone for a few minutes."

"Don't blame yourself," Kofi said gently.

She sat up straighter. "I am *not* blaming myself. I blame the man who promised me nothing would happen to my child, who promised me he would be safe."

Abdalla and Yasir dropped their eyes to the carpet.

"Dahlia—"

She jumped to her feet and pointed a finger at Kofi. "Don't you say a word to me!"

"We will find him, Princess Dahlia," Oriyeh said in a soft voice.

Dahlia paid no attention to Oriyeh. She kept her eyes on Kofi. "You said no one would dare touch him. You were wrong." Her voice trembled and tears filled her eyes. "I don't care what you do or how you do it. You find him, and you find him safe. Or I'll never forgive you."

She stormed out of the bedroom and slammed the door.

∾

KOFI FOUND Dahlia in the Great Holy Place, a large room in the palace that served as a shrine, where anyone could come and pray to gods, the one true God, their ancestors, or whatever being they believed in. Priests kept incense and candles burning at all times.

He swallowed his own pain and fear and walked over to where Dahlia lay prostrate on a prayer mat, head bent, arms outstretched on the floor. Her thick hair created a shroud around her head. As he neared, he heard her quiet sobs and lowered to the floor next to her.

"We'll find him." She didn't respond and continued crying.

Kofi helped her to her feet without a fight. She rested her tear-stained cheek to his chest and let him lift and carry her all the way back to their apartment. In her bedroom, he removed her clothes and dressed her in a cotton nightshirt and tucked her into bed.

Then he undressed down to his boxers and slipped in beside her, pulling her into his arms.

"Parents are supposed to protect their children," Dahlia whispered. "I shouldn't have brought him here."

Dragging his fingers through her soft hair, Kofi held her until she fell asleep in his arms.

When this nightmare was over, he knew what he had to do.

∾

DAHLIA WOKE UP. Blinking, she stared into the semi-darkness.

She rolled over. The bed was empty and the sheets cool. Kofi had been gone for a while. She winced when she remembered what she said to him. It was terrible to blame him. She needed to tell him they were in this together and let him know how sorry she was for what she said.

She swung her feet off the bed and went through the panel in the wall. His bedroom was empty. Where was he at this time of night?

She went back through the secret panel and pulled on a robe, then she went in search of her husband. Maybe he was in his office on the first floor. She padded quietly through their dimly lit quarters, when she heard raised voices.

Dahlia swung around. Angling her head, she listened. The voices came from the back of the apartment. Hurrying, she went toward a room where a light shone under the door. As she edged closer, one voice became louder.

"Tell us what you know!" Oriyeh yelled.

Dahlia rushed forward and pushed open the door. Five sets of eyes swung in her direction. "What's going on?" she asked, though she saw well enough what was taking place.

Aofa sat with each wrist handcuffed to an arm of a chair, while two members of palace security were stationed nearby, both wearing their blue-on-blue uniform and weaponry.

"Aofa is being questioned," Kofi answered.

"Does she know something about Noel? Does she know where he is?"

Kofi sent a silent message across the room to Oriyeh, and Dahlia swung in the woman's direction. "Tell me! What's going on?"

"My investigation has led me to believe Aofa knows where Prince Noel is. We're trying to get the information and learn who else is involved."

Trying to get the information? Why wouldn't she tell them?

Dahlia opened her mouth to ask that very question and paused when she saw the tears in Aofa's eyes. The woman looked terrified. She definitely knew something.

"Where is Noel?" Dahlia asked.

Aofa averted her eyes.

"Where is my son?" Dahlia asked, a faint tremor inflicting the tone.

"Your Highness, please let us handle this," Oriyeh said gently.

Dahlia's head pounded with tension, worry, and fear. "Is he alive?" she asked.

Surely Aofa would give her something. Anything, to ease her chaotic thoughts.

She didn't say a word. She continued to stare at the wall.

"Answer the question," Oriyeh said.

Nothing. Nothing at all, from the woman who'd bathed and played with her son for weeks, slept in the same room as him, kissed him, fed him, and treated him the way Dahlia imagined she treated her own grandchildren. She'd entrusted Aofa with the most precious thing in her life, and she sat there saying *nothing*.

Dahlia couldn't bear not knowing anymore. Her eyes zoomed in on the dagger hitched to the hip of the nearest guard. In a fit of rage, she yanked the weapon from its holster and charged toward Aofa.

"*Ne touche pas!*" Kofi barked when the guard moved to come after her.

Aofa's eyes widened in panic. Her wrists rattled against the handcuffs.

Dahlia grabbed her by the throat. "Where is my son?"

Aofa babbled in her native tongue, eyes stretched to the size of a fifty-cent Zamibian coin darting back and forth among the other people in the room.

"Tell me!" Dahlia screamed.

"I don't know!"

"Tell me where he is!" Dahlia lifted the dagger above her head.

"Cape Ndugu!" Aofa yelled, letting out a gut-wrenching wail at the end.

Dahlia's hand tightened around the handle of the dagger, and tears flooded her eyes as relief poured through her bloodstream. "Is he alive?"

"Yes. I believe he is alive, Your Highness."

Her son was alive!

"Why was he taken?"

"Revenge. He wanted r-revenge."

"Who wanted revenge?" Oriyeh asked.

"Please, if I tell you, he will slit the throat of my grandchildren."

"If you don't tell us, I'll slit your throat where you sit." Dahlia's hand tightened around the handle of the knife.

Aofa openly wept, her entire body shaking. "Kemal. Kemal has the prince."

Gasps filled the room.

Aofa's head fell forward, and her shoulders shook from the force of her sobs. "I did not want to do this."

Dahlia stared at the woman charged with taking care of her son. Her mind rewound all the times Aofa cradled Noel in her arms. It destroyed her that Aofa could have been involved in this crime.

"You should have come to me," she said.

"Have mercy on me, Princess." Aofa's eyes pleaded for forgiveness.

Firm fingers encircled Dahlia's wrist. She turned to see Kofi standing behind her. Gently, he applied pressure and her fingers slackened. The dagger clattered to the floor.

Dahlia collapsed in his arms, suddenly weak. Exhausted. It felt as if Noel had been missing for weeks instead of hours.

She listened as Kofi's soothing voice gave out commands and Oriyeh replied. After several minutes of the same, the conversation ended and Kofi escorted Dahlia from the room, nestled to his side.

~

Kofi paced with the phone to his ear, carrying on a conversation in Mbutu. Dahlia watched him from her position on the bed, reclining against the pillows.

When he hung up, he heaved out a heavy breath.

"How far away is Cape Ndugu?" she asked. She had a vague sense of the fishing village's location but knew little else, other than most of the villagers there belonged to the Ndenga tribe.

"Far." The solemnity in his voice and eyes disturbed her.

"What aren't you telling me?" she asked. A tennis-ball size of dread blocked her throat.

"He has a head start on us. We'll have to fly there."

"Who's going with you?"

"Abdalla, Yasir, and Oriyeh. We'll meet with the local authorities at the Cape."

Dahlia sat up. "I'm coming with you."

"No." He shook his head.

"Kofi, please."

"It's not a good idea."

"Noel must be terrified. He'll need me."

"No."

"Why not?" She hopped off the bed. "I'll stay out of the way, I—"

"No!"

"Why not!" she screamed.

"Because I can't risk losing you, too!"

She stared at him, aghast. "You don't—you don't think he's coming back," she whispered in a tremulous voice.

Kofi expelled air through his nose. "We don't know if anyone else is working with Kemal or what they'll do if cornered."

She walked over to him and fisted her hands in his shirt. "Kofi, please, let me come with you."

He held onto her wrists. "It's too dangerous."

"But you're going."

"I'm a trained soldier. If I alone go, security will only have to be concerned about my safety and the safety of our son. We shouldn't add you to the mix."

"I need to see him. I need to hold him. Please."

"Dahlia." He closed his eyes.

"Please. I'm begging you."

He sighed and opened his eyes. Speaking very slowly, he said, "You will stay out of the way and do exactly what I say."

Dahlia nodded vigorously. "Yes, I promise."

He shook his head, as if he couldn't believe he was going to say the next words. "Get dressed. You have five minutes."

26

Dahlia had never dressed so quickly before in her life. She dressed in all black and secured her hair in a ponytail. As she exited the dressing room, Kofi hung up the phone.

"Oriyeh confirmed she's at the helicopter now." He glanced at the gold watch on his wrist. "We'll be at the Cape in a couple of hours. Assuming Kemal left as soon as he kidnapped Noel, we should arrive ahead of him, with enough time to pick up the SUV Oriyeh arranged and drive to his house to lie in wait for him."

"Perfect." More hope came alive in her chest.

"Let's go."

Dahlia placed her hand in his, and the two rushed through the apartment on speedy feet.

"Do you have any idea why Kemal did this?" Dahlia asked. Aofa stated revenge was the motive, but revenge for what?

"I have an idea," Kofi said in a grim tone.

He obviously didn't want to say his thoughts out loud, so she said them for him. "I don't think he wanted you to marry me. He hates me, and I've known for a long time."

"You're right, he didn't want us to marry. Three years ago when you called to tell me you were pregnant, he kept the call from me on purpose because he knew how I felt about you. He doesn't hate you. It's me he hates." He opened the front door and they hurried through.

"Why would he hate you?" The door closed behind them as they exited the apartment.

"It's a long, complicated story." He tugged her along behind him, his long strides forcing her into a jog to keep up.

"If he hates you so much, then why take Noel? Why not come directly for you?"

"For the same reason you probably thought he'd taken Noel because of you. He knew taking Noel would hurt me most." His jaw settled into a hard line.

"It was foolish of him to go back to Cape Ndugu. He should have known you'd go looking for him there once we found out he was gone."

Abdalla and Yasir waited at the head of the stairs, and the three of them rushed to the first floor. This time of night, the halls were empty, their footsteps making only a slight sound as they hurried across the marble.

They were making their way to the exit when Kofi, leading the group, suddenly swung around and frowned at Dahlia.

"You're right. He counted on Aofa cracking and sending us in that direction. Or, at the very least, he knew we'd question everyone about Noel's disappearance, including him. If we couldn't find him, he knew the first place we'd look was the village. Which means he didn't go back to Cape Ndugu." His eyes lifted toward the ceiling. "He's in the palace."

"But Your Highness, if he's here, how will we find him? He could be anywhere," Yasir said.

"Not anywhere." Kofi's eyes widened. *"You must pay for your sins.* He's with the king!"

The three men took off running, and Dahlia raced behind them. The king's quarters were on the third floor. The men had longer legs and were in better shape, sprinting up the stairs two at a time, with Kofi leading the way.

On the way up, Abdalla spoke Mbutu into a device attached to his wrist. Dahlia didn't know what he said or to whom, but his voice adequately conveyed a message of urgency to the other party.

Outside his father's apartment, Kofi jammed his thumb to the panel and the door swung open. By the time Dahlia caught up, she was out of breath, but she pushed through and met them outside Babatunde's bedroom suite.

Kofi pounded on the door and wiggled the doorknob.

"Father, it's Kofi. Are you all right?"

He wiggled the knob again.

Not a single sound came from inside.

"I need to get in there." He stepped back and looked at Abdalla. "Open it."

The big man smashed his huge foot into the door. The frame splintered on the inside, and the door slammed against the interior wall. Abdalla stepped back immediately and let Kofi take the lead.

"I have a gun. Don't come in here!" Kemal's voice.

"I'm unarmed." With his arms raised high, Kofi eased forward into the room.

"Kofi, no," Dahlia whispered.

He continued to move, hands up, until he advanced several feet inside the room. Dahlia stood on the outside, both hands covering her mouth, watching the tense scene unfold.

"Baba!"

At the sound of her son's voice, Dahlia charged in after Kofi and skidded to a stop. To her horror, Kemal stood at the foot of the king's bed, a gun pointed at him and Noel. The toddler, huddled at his grandfather's side, lifted his head up and reached out a hand. "Mommy."

"Hold onto him, or I will blow his brains out," Kemal said to the king.

Babatunde tightened his grip on his grandson.

"Mommy." Noel began to cry. Fat tears rolled down his cheeks.

"Kemal, please. Let me comfort him," Dahlia said.

Kemal swung the gun at her. "Shut up." He swung the weapon back to the king. "Move, and I'll kill him."

Dahlia kept her eyes on her son, only feet away but she couldn't touch him. "It's okay, Noel." She put a finger to her lips.

"Shut him up," Kemal said.

Babatunde didn't appear to be the least bit ruffled by the current situation. "He's a child and he's scared. Let his mother comfort him."

Kemal laughed without humor and, using the gun to point, said, "You can't help yourself, can you? You have to be the man in charge. You have to speak out of turn, as if you're in control of this situation. Get this through your head, old man. I am in control right now!"

While Kemal was distracted with the king, Kofi took advantage and eased a few more inches into the room. "Yes, you're in charge. You have our father. You have me. Let Noel and Dahlia go."

Kemal snorted. "Why should I let anyone go? I have the last of the Karunzika male heirs right here. I could end your lineage and alter the line of succession to the throne."

Every muscle in Dahlia's body froze. Surely he wouldn't slaughter them all.

"You would throw the entire kingdom into chaos," Kofi said.

"But when the dust settles, the people will have no choice but to accept their new king."

"That would be Kehinde or the king's other brother."

Kemal laughed so hard the gun shook in his hand. "Come now, you know that's not true. Prince Kehinde is unfit and uninterested in being king. The same goes for Babatunde's other brother, who is too busy chasing women and strong drink around the world. We both know who should rightfully ascend the throne after the old man is dead. The only one qualified and with the right temperament to lead."

What was he talking about? And why did Kofi say *our* father a few seconds ago, instead of *my* father? She gasped when it dawned on her why he chose that specific pronoun and what it meant.

Kemal smirked. "She doesn't know, does she? But something tells me she's starting to understand. Should I tell her, Kofi, or will you? Who will tell the fair princess that her husband's title rightfully belongs to someone else?"

"You have no right to the crown. It doesn't belong to you," Babatunde said.

"I should have been the crown prince after Jafari died," Kemal snarled, face twisting into an ugly mask. "I should be next in line, not Kofi. Tell her. Tell her why I should be next in line and not you."

When Kofi didn't start talking, Kemal pointed the gun and aimed right at his chest. Dahlia took a step back, fear clamping tight around her throat.

Kofi lifted his head to a haughty angle and said, "Kemal believes he should be the crown prince, because my father had an affair with his mother, and as the second oldest son, he believes he should be next in line. But the line of succession goes through the Great Wife, my mother, Queen Nahla."

"I don't *believe* I should be the crown prince. If there were any justice, I would have been. I would have been raised in The Grand Palace, not stuck in a coastal village with my mother, who lived in shame until her death. Why? Because she had the misfortune to fall in love with a man who has no heart and doesn't understand what love is. A man who couldn't stay faithful to his wife—his queen—and refused to take care of the woman he said he cared about. Never bringing her into the palace and making her a legitimate wife."

"I did care about your mother. I built the largest house in the village for her, and I gave her money—" Babatunde said.

"You did not care about my mother!" Kemal wiped spittle from the corner of his mouth with the back of his hand. "You did not care about me, or that I had no father growing up and didn't receive any special treatment, though I have royal blood running through my veins. I was considered a shame and an embarrassment, and hidden like a dirty secret. Well, I'm not a secret anymore. Get up."

Dahlia's hand covered her mouth. What was he going to do? She glanced behind her but saw no sign of Abdalla or Yasir. Where were they?

"I'm an old man. I don't care about myself. Let them go and deal with me the way you want to."

"I said get up," Kemal said slowly.

Noel wasn't making a sound, his face buried in his grandfather's armpit. But when Babatunde grabbed the staff beside his bed and gingerly got to his feet, Noel pressed his face into a pillow, put his hands over the back of his head, and started crying.

"Please let me go to him," Dahlia begged.

Kemal rolled his eyes. "Fine. Go to him and shut him up. Or I will."

Dahlia crossed the floor and climbed onto the bed. She pulled Noel against her breasts, mashing his face into her neck. She gently rocked him and spoke in a hushed voice, encouraging him to be quiet.

"Now, oh great king, you will give me the respect that I deserve."

"Kemal, this isn't the way," Kofi said.

"Shut up. You brought me here after Jafari and your mother died, as if I should be happy to serve you."

"I gave you a job because we're brothers."

Kemal sneered. "How could we possibly be brothers when we aren't on equal footing? You wanted me here because Jafari was gone."

"That's not true. I asked you to come because I wanted a relationship with you."

"Then why didn't you bring me here and try to have a relationship before he died?"

"I couldn't hurt my mother in that way."

"Is that the real reason, or is it because you're as selfish as our wonderful father? As indifferent and uncaring as he is?"

"What do you want?" Babatunde asked.

"What do I want? I know I won't get your love, so I'll settle for your respect. I want you to bow down to me and show me the respect I deserve."

"Bow?" The king repeated the word as if he'd never heard it before.

Rage filled Kemal's eyes, and air blew from his nose in a loud whoosh. "Bow!"

Babatunde lifted his head high and stared his son in the eye. "A king bows to no one but his queen."

Kemal leveled the gun at his father's chest and the room erupted into chaos. A door at the other end of the bedroom crashed open with a bang and fell flat on the floor. Oriyeh rolled in and took cover behind a piece of furniture. Kemal fired off two shots at her before getting slammed to the floor by Kofi, the tackle audibly forcing air from his lungs and sending the gun skidding across the floor out of reach.

Abdalla and Yasir came bounding through the same entrance. As Yasir rushed the king out the door, Abdalla lifted Dahlia with Noel in her arms, from the bed. He swept toward the exit, while a slew of guards descended on the room and swarmed Kemal like an army of ants attacking a hapless insect.

27

The nightmare was over.

Sitting on the bed, Dahlia simultaneously sipped tea and watched over Noel, fast asleep with one arm around his wiggle worm. She smoothed a hand down his back and set the cup on the table. Stretching, she walked over to the window and squinted at the brightness of the sun. Another lovely day outdoors, but in here, a quiet sadness had settled over the palace. Staff smiled and remained polite, but they were watchful. She sensed their eyes on her, and the confrontation with Kemal had sucked the energy out of everyone who resided there.

Kofi came in and stopped in the middle of the room, dressed in a plum-colored suit and striped tie.

"You're going out?" He hid his emotions well. Not once since the incident had she seen him give any indication he'd been affected by Kemal's actions. His father behaved the same way, as though nothing out of the ordinary had happened. Just another day like any other at the palace.

"I have a meeting with Alistair Davies." He shot a glance at Noel. "How is he?"

"Better."

Last night marked the first night he hadn't woken up. Quite a change from the first two nights, when he whimpered while he slept and woke up several times, only going back to sleep after she rocked him and whispered soothing words.

"And you?" he asked.

"I've been better, but I'll be fine."

"You haven't been eating."

Dahlia shrugged.

"You should eat. To keep up your strength."

She hadn't been eating much because she didn't have much of an appetite. "You're right. I'll have Mariama bring me a glass of orange juice and some toast." She shifted from one foot to the other. "Is there some reason you never told me Kemal was your half-brother?"

She remained dumbfounded at Kemal's plot to punish the king and Kofi. He used his knowledge and ability to travel throughout The Grand Palace without suspicion to leave the note for the king and slip undetected into Kofi's bedroom and hers, using the escape room as Oriyeh suggested.

He raised an eyebrow. "You think I kept it from you on purpose?"

"I don't know. Did you?"

"He was sensitive about it." Kofi shrugged. "He never told me so, but I knew he didn't like admitting he was the illegitimate son of a king." He shoved a hand in his pants pocket. "He was bitter, but I had no idea just how much. The fact that we were brothers was an open secret. Everyone knew, but we never discussed it with anyone, or with each other except for once or twice that I can recall. I would have told you eventually, but it simply never came up. When I brought him into the palace, I thought I was doing the right thing by establishing a relationship with him. And the entire time..." His eyes focused outside the window. Clearly, Kemal's hatred for him and his father left Kofi speechless.

"What's going to happen to him?" Dahlia asked.

His jaw and lips tightened. "My father has signed a decree. He'll be hanged."

A cold chill swept down Dahlia's spine. "H-hanged?"

Kofi kept his eyes trained on the mountains in the distance.

"A-and Aofa?" she asked.

Sadness settled over his face. "Justice will be served."

"How?"

"She will be hanged, too."

She rushed over to where he stood, emotionless, unmoving, and grabbed his arm. "No, that doesn't make any sense. Kemal forced her to participate."

"She poisoned our son to get him away from the birthday party and hand him over to Kemal. She was an active participant in the kidnapping of one member of the royal family and the attempted murder of another—the *king*."

"He threatened her grandchildren, Kofi. She would've never participated in his crazy plot otherwise. I agree, she should be punished, but hanged? Even Kemal, what he did was wrong, but we're all still alive."

"He threatened to wipe out our entire line and throw the country into chaos."

"Then lock him up and throw away the key, but you can't kill him. Does the council know? Did they approve the king's decree?" She would speak to them herself if she had to, to convince them to overrule the king's decision.

"We don't need The Most High Council's permission. Zamibia is an absolute monarchy, which means the king has unrestricted power, and anything he says is law. The royal family chooses to include the council in their decision-making, to give the people a voice."

Dahlia blinked. "The council has no power?"

"They are advisors. Nothing more. Their power is limited to duties extended to them by the king."

"All right, fine. Still, he's your brother. He's Babatunde's son."

"A brother and son who wanted no part of the life he was

offered and threatened to murder us. Do you understand what that means? If we don't enforce the law, what do you think will happen? Someone else will try. Our son won't be safe in his own home, or anywhere. None of us will be."

"This...this is barbaric," Dahlia whispered.

Kofi's mouth shifted into a sardonic smile. "You pulled a dagger on Aofa."

Her cheeks flushed. "In the heat of the moment, I made a mistake."

"You didn't make a mistake. There's a bit of barbarian in all of us."

She hated she couldn't change his mind. "I wish there was another way." Her throat became tight with emotion.

"The law must be obeyed."

"Babatunde would listen to you. You have the power to grant Kemal and Aofa mercy."

"Yes, I do. But they did this. Not me, and not my father."

"I'm not going to change your mind, am I?"

"No, you won't."

Quiet descended between them.

She wrapped her arms around her waist, suddenly feeling cold and distant from him. They would never see eye to eye on this matter, and sadness filled her when she recalled Aofa's tear-filled eyes begging her for mercy. Yet there was nothing she could do.

"How long will you be gone?"

"I don't expect my meeting to last long. Why?"

Clasping her hands in front of her, she said, "You and I need to talk, about us, and...things." She owed him an apology for the accusation she'd thrown at him when she panicked over Noel.

For a split second, his expression tightened, and then he dropped his gaze to fiddle with his cuffs. "I agree. We have plenty to talk about." His chest lifted up and down as he breathed in and out deeply. "A lot has taken place over the past few days with the arrest of Aofa and Kemal. We've since confirmed there were no other people involved. During all of this, I've been thinking about you and me and Noel." His gaze shifted to their son asleep on the bed and remained there for a long time. "I've decided to send you and Noel back to America."

Dahlia's hand touched her throat. "Excuse me, *what*? Why?"

Expressionless eyes looked into hers. "I can't risk another incident like what happened this weekend."

"Unless you have another half-brother who'll kidnap Noel and try to murder your father, I think we're safe." Dahlia laughed shakily. "Kofi, where is this coming from?"

"You were right. I told you I could protect you, and I didn't."

"I know what I said, and that's precisely what I wanted to talk to you about. I was wrong. I was emotional when Noel went missing and the things I said...they, they were said in a panicked state. You're not Superman. I don't expect you to have super powers and protect us all the time. We have guards and other measures to keep us safe. Kofi..." Her throat went dry, and she swallowed hard. "I don't want to leave."

"The decision isn't up to you. *I* have made the decision." He glanced at his watch.

"Stop looking at your *damn* watch," Dahlia whispered fiercely.

His gaze flicked up to her. "I didn't make this decision lightly."

"You made it without including me. Don't I get a say? What am I supposed to tell Noel? He loves you. I love you. You told me you love me and now you're sending me away?"

"It's because I love you that I'm sending you away." Kofi grabbed her upper arms. "No one knows who you are in the U.S. You could go back to living a normal life, without the media attention and without the worry of threats."

"You don't want me here."

"I *do*, but—I've lost enough people that I care about. Understand that I'm sending you back because it's in your best interest and Noel's best interest. In America, no one would try to harm you."

"You don't know that for a fact. You don't know we'll be safer in another country. I want to stay here under your protection."

He stepped back, his face resigned. "That's not possible. We can discuss the details when I return."

"You can't do this!"

"Dahlia," he said, speaking to her through gritted teeth, the way a parent would a child. "It's a waste of time to argue. You won't change my mind. We'll talk when I get back."

Kofi swung around and walked out the door.

⁓

KOFI EXITED the limousine and buttoned his jacket as he walked toward the office building where Titanium Oil rented a temporary office, set up to lobby the government. Abdalla and Yasir walked on either side of him, with two more members of his security pulling up the rear.

The Jouba police chief and two of his officers approached when Kofi came within a few feet of the door. "Your Highness, I'm glad you could join us."

"I wouldn't miss this for the world," Kofi said.

Initially, he'd assumed the sabotage at the mine had been connected to the threat against the royal family. Instead, a break in the case made it clear they were two separate issues.

A miner made a drunken confession to his girlfriend one night about his role in the sabotage. He'd been paid to set the bomb in the mine shaft. His girlfriend turned him in, and in exchange for a lesser sentence, he set up a meeting with Alistair and wore a wire. They had the British man on tape admitting to his role in the tragedy. Kofi had listened to the recording, where both men discussed that no one should have been injured.

Not that it mattered. Families had been affected, people hurt, and the dead couldn't speak for themselves. Kofi intended to speak on their behalf.

The chief led the way into the office, and a receptionist at the front greeted them with a friendly smile. "Good day. May I help—"

They walked right by her.

"Excuse me. Excuse me, what are you doing?"

The chief shoved open the door to Alistair's office without knocking. He was on the phone, and when he saw them all enter the room, his mouth fell open.

"What the devil is going on?"

One of the officers snatched the receiver out of his hand and slammed it in its cradle.

"Do you care to tell me what the hell is going on?" Alistair came to his feet and directed an angry stare at Kofi. "Do I need to call Ambassador Stephens to get whatever your problem is with me straightened out? You can't just come in here and take over my office without explanation."

"I would love for you to call Ambassador Stephens and explain your role in the deaths of five innocent people and the injuries of dozens more who worked in the gold mine. Be sure to explain why you thought sabotage was the best way for you to convince us to do business with your company."

"I have no idea what you're talking about," Alistair said, though his pallor had gone decidedly paler. "I'm not interested in the mining industry. We're an oil drilling company."

Kofi walked slowly toward him and stopped. "Remove the desk."

Abdalla, Yasir, and the other two bodyguards each grabbed a corner of the desk and set it out of the way against the wall.

Alistair's eyes widened, and he took two steps back.

Kofi closed in until they stood two feet apart. "I'm the protector of my people. You came here and disrupted our peace because of your greed. Now you must be punished."

"I didn't do anything! I have no idea what you're talking about." Alistair's eyes were wild and jumpy.

"Play the tape," Kofi said, keeping an eye on him.

The chief pressed a button on the recorder he held in his hand, and Alistair's voice filled the room.

"You used too much. It was supposed to look like an accident, and no

one was supposed to get hurt. I can't imagine what would happen if
anyone found out we had anything to do with that bloody mine
caving in."

Alistair had gone as pale as a sheet of paper. "This is some kind
of trick. Because I'm an outsider, you're framing me for these
people's deaths."

Kofi stepped aside and an officer came forward. He spun Alistair toward the wall and slapped handcuffs over his wrists. "Mr.
Alistair Davies, you are under arrest for the sabotage of the Djimah
gold mine and the murders of Samuel Musa, Yaya Appiah,
David..."

"No!" Alistair yelled as the officer continued to list the names
of the victims. "We didn't mean to hurt anyone. Please, I'm so
sorry." He started sobbing. "I only wanted to get your attention, to
make you think about why you needed us."

Kofi stared dispassionately at his reddened, despicable face.
"And now you can spend the rest of your life thinking about why
we don't."

"No!"

And with that, the officer hauled him toward the door.

28

Dahlia entered the room where Kofi sat with his head resting against the back of the sofa. He hadn't come to find her when he came back from his meeting, and it was nighttime and he still hadn't come to her, so she'd come to him.

"Kofi?"

He lifted his head, and the bleakness in his eyes touched a place in her chest. He was hurting. A lot had happened in a short time. With Kemal, he hadn't simply lost an assistant. He hadn't only lost a friend. He'd lost another brother, and he thought he had to give her and Noel up, too.

"I saw on the news that Alistair Davies was arrested today. That's wonderful."

"We have him on tape, but he still denied his role in sabotaging the mine." He lifted a glass half filled with bissap and swallowed a mouthful.

Dahlia sat down beside him. "Do you want to talk about Kemal?"

"There's nothing else to talk about. The threat was contained."

Dahlia looked at Kofi. Really looked at him and thought about everything she'd seen him do since they arrived in Zamibia. Before their arrival, she held her own ideas and admittedly, misconceptions about what it meant to be royalty, thinking for the most part that Kofi lived a life of ease and privilege. While he did possess the type of riches most people would never see in multiple lifetimes, he'd traded in the privacy for the privilege. He lived constantly under a microscope, with the knowledge that every decision not only affected his life, but the lives of every person in the nation.

As the crown prince, the expectations on him were many and varied. Not only was he expected to be an ethical and moral leader who was fair and kind, at the same time he was expected to mete out justice to people who broke the law and pursue solutions for the greater good. It was a complicated balancing act, and though he was immensely popular, every decision and every action was dissected and presented to the people for public consumption.

"Talk to me. I'm not one of our citizens. I'm not the press."

He set the drink on the table and ran a hand down his face. Time dragged by in silence, and she thought she'd wasted her time.

Keeping his eyes on the glass, Kofi finally spoke. "I couldn't bring him to the palace while my mother was alive. It would have been disrespectful and too painful for her. I brought him here as a peace offering, to fix the years of neglect he'd experienced, and establish a relationship. My father wasn't pleased, but he allowed it. Maybe because I'd already lost a brother and he'd lost a son."

"I understand."

"Azireh was pregnant when she died."

"Oh my god, Kofi—"

"It wasn't my child. We never consummated our marriage."

"Your honeymoon...?"

"No. She was withdrawn and acted oddly. To be honest, I left her alone because I didn't want to sleep with her. She was chosen for me. She wasn't the woman I wanted for my wife. The woman I wanted for my wife lived in New York." Their eyes met, and the pain of nostalgia twisted in her chest. "Two months later, she was dead. Killed herself. The note she left contained only two words: *I'm sorry*. No explanation." He took a deep breath. "After the autopsy uncovered her pregnancy, everyone thought the child was mine. They grieved that I'd lost my wife and child—a child that didn't belong to me."

"She was in love with someone else."

He nodded. "She never wanted to marry me, but she did what her father asked. Fulfilled her duty. I believe she was miserable because she couldn't be with the man she loved, and in the end she killed herself to escape the marriage."

"Do you know who the father of the child was?"

Kofi nodded. "We spoke once. He's Ndenga, like she was. He moved to Nigeria not long after she died."

"You never said a word."

"I didn't want to dishonor her name."

Dahlia pulled her bottom lip between her teeth. Kofi was being open and honest, and she needed to do the same.

"My mother used to tell me I was a dreamer. Her polite way of saying I never wanted to face reality. I wanted everything to be perfect, and I'd make up my own reality so I didn't have to face the truth." She swallowed. "My father was a drug addict."

She'd never said the words out loud. Never admitted the truth to anyone, not even Angela. Kofi silently watched her, and Dahlia grimaced as she smiled, embarrassed to reveal the truth and the extent of her lies. She'd crafted such a believable story there were times she believed the tale herself.

"He didn't fall asleep at the wheel and cause the accident that killed my mother and put me in a coma. He was high, in the middle of the day. They traveled around the country doing odd jobs because my father couldn't keep a job, and he was always running from people he owed money to. My mother couldn't, or wouldn't, leave him. She started taking photos so when times got bad, we could look at all the pictures and remember happier times." Thanks to her mother, Dahlia developed a love of photography, too, and they'd discussed displaying her photos of Zamibia so tourists could see them when they visited the palace.

As tears stung her eyes, she ran her tongue along the inside of her upper lip.

"When he was sober, he was the best father. But when he was high, I didn't know him, and I hated that glassy-eyed stare. One night I heard my parents arguing. Whisper-arguing, I used to call it. They thought I was asleep. My mother begged him to get help. She *begged* him. 'I can handle it,' he said. 'Why don't you trust me? Why don't you believe in me? You're stressing me out and making it worse.' The day of the accident, she begged him to let her drive. He didn't. She got in the car and made me get in with them." Pain vibrated in her voice.

Kofi took her hand.

"He didn't protect me. She didn't protect me." Love and hate for her father warred for dominance inside her. She felt sympathy because of his addiction, but also anger that he loved drugs more than he loved them.

Kofi squeezed her hand.

"Don't send me away." Her voice shook. "I don't want to live anywhere else. This is my home. These people have accepted me as one of their own."

Kofi released her and went to stand in front of the window. "It's for the best. For both of you to be safe."

"We *are* safe. Who else would dare try to harm us again? The threat came from within, not without. What happened with Kemal was an unusual occurrence, and security already set new protocols in place to keep us safe."

"That's not good enough for me," he said in a harsh voice. "If you don't want to live in the U.S., we have an apartment in Monaco and a place in London. Not that you're limited to those locations. I can buy you a home in any country you wish." He stopped, his chest heaving as if he were out of breath. As if speaking the words required immense effort and he needed to pull the strength to say them from someplace deep inside him. He bowed his head. "Outside of Zamibia, very few people are familiar with the royal family. You can live a normal life. That's what I want for you. For him."

Dahlia hopped up from the sofa. "And what about my work here? People are depending on me."

"The work will get done."

"By who? Your new wife?"

"You think I want to get married again?"

"Don't you? The option is open to you. What happens when I leave?" Her hands started shaking. "How long am I supposed to be gone? And while I'm gone, what will you do? Who will you spend your time with?"

"I haven't made the decision to send you away so that I can get another wife. I made the decision because I need to keep you and Noel safe."

"Are you listening to yourself? *You* made the decision. We're a team. We're in this marriage together, and we have so much work to do. The stadium needs to be finished, we haven't broken ground on the children's center yet, and expanding substance abuse treatment is a priority for me. I want to do it all." She took a tremulous breath. "You can't get rid of me that easily. You came to find me. You brought me back because you wanted me here, and I've done a lot of thinking since this morning. You didn't need to convince the council to accept Noel as next in line. You allowed me to think you did, but you only needed your father's approval, which he gave. Did we go through all of that for you to turn around a couple of months later and tell me I should leave? No, we didn't. And no, I'm not leaving."

"No?" He stared at her as if she'd sprouted another set of arms. "I am the Prince of Zamibia, and I say you will leave."

"And *I* am the Princess of Zamibia, the Great Wife of Prince Kofi Francois Karunzika of Zamibia. And *I* will remain with my prince. Because we're one. Because I want my son to know his heritage and learn about his ancestors and claim his birthright. I'm not leaving, Kofi. *This is my home.*"

She stared at his hardened features. He could still make her leave, and there was nothing she could do about it. She waited, her stomach in knots.

"This country isn't perfect, Dahlia."

"No country is." She blinked back tears.

Kofi cupped her face in his hands. "You're miserable here."

"I'm not. I wanted to leave at first, but I don't anymore. I told you, I have no regrets about coming here."

He studied her face, a frown wrinkling his brow. "Are you sure? I don't want to extinguish your light."

"You can't. You make me shine brighter."

He pulled her into his arms, and she buried her face in his neck, relieved. She couldn't bear to be apart from him. She couldn't bear to leave the place she'd come to love.

"You are so damn feisty." Kofi locked eyes with her. "*Moni fey-eh.*" A smile stretched across his lips, and she didn't need a translation. *I love you.* She knew, because those were among the first words she'd learned with her Mbutu language tutor.

"*Moni fey-eh,*" she whispered back. Standing on tiptoe, she pressed her mouth to his.

EPILOGUE

Sandwiched between her chief of staff and her social secretary, Dahlia made rapid progress from her office on the way to Kofi's.

She shook her head, dismissing a suggestion from her secretary. "I know I have a full schedule on Monday, but I don't want to cancel my trip to the children's hospital. Move the visit to the substance abuse clinic from the afternoon to the morning, after my breakfast with the Association of Women Entrepreneurs. I can spend a few hours there, grab lunch, and then go to the hospital in the afternoon. That gives me plenty of time to participate in the ribbon-cutting ceremony with the chief's wife and return to the palace in enough time to change clothes and have dinner with the Kenya delegation."

Her secretary wrote the changes as quickly as Dahlia dictated them. "Yes, that works. I'll have the new itinerary typed up and on your desk within the hour. Background information and cultural details for the delegation will be completed by noon tomorrow." She made a U-turn and went back the way they came.

Dahlia stopped outside Kofi's office and accepted a folder of resumes from her chief of staff. She needed to hire a language tutor for Noel. His Mbutu was coming along well, but she and Kofi agreed they wanted to foster his language ability by having him work with a tutor for one hour three times a week. They needed someone with experience working with children and skilled at using playtime to create a learning experience. There weren't a lot of people with those skillsets, but they'd found six so far.

Dahlia scanned the resumes and pulled out two. "Bring in these women for interviews. Take a look at my calendar. Next week I should have a couple of afternoons available to slot them in."

"Yes, Your Highness." Daisy walked away.

Dahlia entered Kofi's office and greeted his secretary. "Is he busy?"

"No. You can go right in."

She walked straight to the door, knocked lightly, and let herself in. Kofi's smile and warm gaze welcomed her.

"Don't you look lovely," he said, rising from the chair.

"Do I?" Dahlia posed with a hand on her hip.

More often these days, she dressed in either a combination of traditional African and Western-style clothing, or wore full African attire. Not only were the clothes comfortable, they were also color-ful, and she liked discovering combinations that worked well together. Today a green and dark yellow head wrap completely covered her hair. She paired the headdress with a dark blue dress that appeared black from a distance, and a chunky silver necklace with a black diamond in the center.

"You don't look so bad yourself." Dahlia tugged the long sleeves of his white shirt. She'd picked this one for him because she liked the gold detailing on the front.

"How are you feeling this morning?" Kofi covered her belly with his hand.

"No morning sickness today." She barely had a baby bump, but at just past twelve weeks, they felt it was safe to announce to the public that they were having another child. "Can I see the announcement?"

Kofi retrieved the paper from his desk and handed it to her.

ANNOUNCEMENT FROM THE OFFICE
OF HIS ROYAL HIGHNESS
KOFI FRANCOIS KARUNZIKA

THEIR ROYAL HIGHNESSES Crown Prince Kofi Francois Karunzika and his Great Wife Princess Dahlia Karunzika, are pleased to announce they are expecting their second child. His Majesty King Babatunde and all the royal family are excited by the news and look forward to the new addition with great anticipation.

"SHORT AND TO THE POINT. PERFECT," she said.

"Good. We can send out the press release later today."

"Ready?"

"Not quite."

Kofi took her by the hand, laced their fingers together, and pulled her in for a kiss. He took his time, leisurely moving his mouth over hers. She enjoyed the interlude, tasting him, and slipped a little tongue between his lips. Kofi reached around and squeezed her bottom before taking a quick nip of her lower lip and pulling back.

"Now I'm ready," he said.

Giggling, Dahlia exited the office on his arm.

One day a month they surprised visitors touring the palace by greeting them when the doors opened at ten, part of a new policy Dahlia suggested, to have the royal family seem more approachable. Security was already at the door and, at the appointed time, they let in the visitors.

With smiles on their faces, she and Kofi greeted each person, looking them squarely in the eye as they shook their hands.

"Oh my goodness, it's Princess Dahlia," a young girl said, her eyes wide. From her accent, Dahlia knew she was from the United States.

While surprised the girl knew who she was on sight, she was excited to see someone from back home.

"*Bahwo*," Dahlia said, by way of greeting. She took the young girl's hand in hers. "I'm Princess Dahlia Karunzika. *Eyeh-kabo*. Welcome to The Grand Palace of Zamibia."

~

ALSO BY DELANEY DIAMOND

Royal Brides

- Princess of Zamibia

Brooks Family series

- Passion Rekindled
- Do Over (coming soon)
- Wild Thoughts (coming soon)

Love Unexpected series

- The Blind Date
- The Wrong Man
- An Unexpected Attraction
- The Right Time
- One of the Guys
- That Time in Venice

Johnson Family series

- Unforgettable
- Perfect
- Just Friends
- The Rules
- Good Behavior

Latin Men series

- The Arrangement

- Fight for Love
- Private Acts
- The Ultimate Merger
- Second Chances
- More Than a Mistress
- Undeniable
- Hot Latin Men: Vol. I (print anthology)
- Hot Latin Men: Vol. II (print anthology)

Hawthorne Family series

- The Temptation of a Good Man
- A Hard Man to Love
- Here Comes Trouble
- For Better or Worse
- Hawthorne Family Series: Vol. I (print anthology)
- Hawthorne Family Series: Vol. II (print anthology)

Bailar series (sweet/clean romance)

- Worth Waiting For

Stand Alones

- A Passionate Love
- Still in Love
- Subordinate Position
- Heartbreak in Rio

Free Stories: www.delaneydiamond.com

DANI, P I

0388

Saturday, July 6, 2019

3126812555515045

ABOUT THE AUTHOR

Delaney Diamond is the USA Today Bestselling Author of sweet, sensual, passionate romance novels. Originally from the U.S. Virgin Islands, she now lives in Atlanta, Georgia. She reads romance novels, mysteries, thrillers, and a fair amount of nonfiction. When she's not busy reading or writing, she's in the kitchen trying out new recipes, dining at one of her favorite restaurants, or traveling to an interesting locale.

Enjoy free reads and the first chapter of all her novels on her website. Join her mailing list to get sneak peeks, notices of sale prices, and find out about new releases.

CPSIA information can be obtained
at www.ICGtesting.com
Printed in the USA
LVHW081340160419
614362LV00032B/641/P

COURAGEOUS LIVING

BIBLE STUDY

Michael Catt   Stephen Kendrick   Alex Kendrick

as developed with

Nic Allen

B&H Publishing Group
Nashville, TN

ISBN: 9781415871195 • Item: 005422891

Dewey Decimal Classification: 248.642
Subject Heading: Courage\Men\Leadership\Family Life

Courageous Living Bible Study is a resource for credit in the Christian Growth Study Plan.
Visit *www.lifeway.com/CGSP* for more information.

Photo credits: page 13, United States Marine Corps; pages 20 and 30, Todd Stone; page 23,
Truro Daily News; page 33, Billy Graham Evangelistic Association; page 43, EthnoGraphic Media

Unless otherwise noted, Scripture quotations are taken from the Holman Christian Standard
Bible®, copyright © 1999, 2000, 2002, 2003 by Holman Bible Publishers. Used by permission.
Scripture quotations marked NIV are taken from the Holy Bible, New International Version, copy-
right © 1973, 1978, 1984 by International Bible Society.

To order additional copies of this resource: Write LifeWay Church Resources Customer Service,
One LifeWay Plaza; Nashville, TN 37234-0113; Fax order to 615.251-5933; Phone
1.800.458.2772; E-mail to *orderentry@lifeway.com;* Order online at *www.lifeway.com;* or Visit the
LifeWay Christian Store serving you.

Printed in the United States of America

Leadership and Adult Publishing, LifeWay Christian Resources,
One LifeWay Plaza, Nashville, TN 37234-0175

Contents

It takes courage to fight for my family.

It takes courage to value what matters most.

It takes courage to impact future generations.

It takes courage to stand with Christ.

About the Authors

Alex, Stephen, and Michael with Jim McBride (center back), the fourth member of Sherwood Pictures' leadership team.

Michael Catt is a husband, father of two grown daughters, and, since 1989, he has served as senior pastor of Sherwood Baptist Church, Albany, Georgia (*www.MichaelCatt.com*). With Jim McBride, Michael is also executive producer of Sherwood Pictures. The church's mission is "to touch the whole world with the whole Word, motivated by a passion for Christ and compassion for all people."

Stephen Kendrick is a husband, father of four, and associate pastor for Sherwood Baptist Church. Stephen oversees the church's prayer ministry and produces all Sherwood movies. In addition to this study, Stephen and Alex co-wrote the *The Love Dare* best seller, *The Love Dare Bible Study*, and the movie-release curriculum *Honor Begins at Home: The COURAGEOUS Bible Study* (fall 2011).

Alex Kendrick is a husband, father of six, and associate pastor for Sherwood Baptist Church. He is a speaker, actor, writer, and the director of all Sherwood movies. Alex acted as Grant Taylor in *FACING THE GIANTS* and as Adam Mitchell in *COURAGEOUS*.

Nic Allen is a husband, father of two girls, and pastor. After 10 years in student ministry at Rolling Hills Community Church in Franklin, Tennessee, he transitioned to family and children's ministry to focus on parents, specifically fathers.

Honor Begins at Home
About the Movie

Four men, one calling: to serve and protect. As law enforcement officers, Adam Mitchell, Nathan Hayes, and their partners in the sheriff's department, David Thomson and Shane Fuller, are confident and focused. They willingly stand up to the worst the streets have to offer.

While Adam is winning at work, he struggles to connect at home. He and his teenage son are running in different directions. Between Dylan's video games and late-night training runs, there seems to be little common ground between father and son. And while his young daughter is his pride and joy, Adam definitely doesn't share Emily's zest for life.

Nathan, who grew up not knowing his dad, has done all he can to break the cycle of fatherlessness in his family. Nathan's young sons look up to him, but his teenage daughter is turning away as she begins to attract the attentions of young men.

Shane struggles as a divorced father attempting to stay involved in his son's life and to get ahead financially. Young officer David is single, with a well-hidden past.

Spending time together is a value of these men who eagerly welcome a new friend, Javier, into their circle. Javier finds humor in life as he works diligently to make ends meet. Focused on God, Javier lovingly strives to provide for his wife and two young children.

When tragedy strikes, these men are left actively wrestling with their hopes, fears, faith, and fathering. Can a newfound urgency help these dads draw closer to God and to their children? How will their stories impact your family?

"But as for me and my household, we will serve the Lord" (Josh. 24:15, NIV).

IN THEATERS SEPTEMBER 30, 2011
www.Courageousthemovie.com • *www.LifeWay.com/Courageous*

Introduction
Live a Courageous Life

The word *pandemic* describes a disease outbreak that is larger in scale than expected and covers a large geographical area, often crossing international borders. It is broader in scope than an epidemic and often more threatening. The influenza outbreak of 1918 claimed in excess of 20 million lives worldwide and could easily be described as pandemic.[1]

Studies today prove that children living without fathers are more likely to be poor and to endure significant emotional, educational, medical, and psychological problems. Similar studies reveal that more than 24 million American children currently live without their biological fathers. That statistic is in excess of 36 percent of American children, making fatherlessness a problem of pandemic proportions.[2]

The only solution to this widespread problem is a return to biblical fatherhood: men of courage taking a powerful stand in their homes and communities to love, lead, and protect their children and thereby eliminating the problems associated with fatherlessness. In the *COURAGEOUS* movie, four men recognize this need and boldly answer the call to be better fathers.

While Adam Mitchell and fellow law-enforcement officers Nathan Hayes, David Thomson, and Shane Fuller consistently give their best on their job, "good enough" seems to be all they can muster as dads. But they're quickly discovering that their standard is missing the mark. They know that God desires to turn the hearts of fathers to their children, but their children are beginning to drift further and further away from them.

Will they be able to find a way to serve and protect those who are most dear to them?

As is the case with these four dads, taking the principles outlined in this Bible study and applying them to your life as a believer will take courage.

The *COURAGEOUS* movie and this Bible study sound the call for the:

- father who is always working and feels somewhat disconnected at home
- soldier who has been deployed for months and can't wait to engage with his wife and kids
- dad who is home on weekends but flies out every Monday morning to work out of town
- young guy whose relationship went too far too quickly and who became a dad too young
- divorced dad who becomes a full-time dad every other weekend and one month during the summer
- stepdad who lives full time with stepkids
- single mom raising three children while wearing both parent hats every day
- young man with a new wife waiting for the arrival of their first child
- mature father who looks back on his life with regrets and wants to now impact his grandkids
- dad who never knew his father and longs to discover how to lead his family well

This is a call for believers to take a courageous stand for the sake of their children and their future. This study is for you!

1. Martin I. Meltzer, Nancy J. Cox, and Keiji Fukuda, "The Economic Impact of Pandemic Influenza in the United States: Priorities for Intervention" [online] 2005 [cited 5 January 2011]. Available from the Internet: *http://www.cdc.gov/ncidod/eid/vol5no5/meltzer.htm*
2. "The Extent of Fatherlessness" [online] 2007 [cited 5 January 2011]. Available from the Internet: *http://www.fathers.com/content/index.php?option=com_content&task=view&id=336*

How to Use This Study

Courageous Living Bible Study is organized into sections and can be used for small-group or personal study. Allow 45 to 60 minutes for group sessions.

 The introductory section of each study contains the story of a modern-day hero whose life exemplifies or grapples with the day's topic. Learners should read the excerpt and be prepared to note and apply transferable principles when prompted by questions during group discussion.

 The Bible study DVD contains clips from the film *COURAGEOUS* to accompany each of the four sessions. Each clip is 1:30–4:00 minutes in length and is supported by discussion questions based on the principle illustrated.

 This section is the primary focus of each session. Learners will read a portion of Scripture and be prompted by a summary section to discuss questions related to the Bible passage.

LIVE Finally, a lesson summary and a challenge to live courageously complete the session. A personal application point for all believers (Everyone) as well as one for parents (Dads and Moms), is followed by a closing prayer experience. The group facilitator should be sensitive to any nonbelievers in the group.

Ideally, LIVE is processed as a small group that has experienced all other parts of the session together. Yet, if your group prefers, some application can be done during the week (there is no designated homework). Some activities, such as the courage commitment scale in session 1, may be better done privately at home. However you do it, commit to make meaningful application within your context to courageous living and to building courageous families.

A Letter to Leaders

Thank you for answering the call to lead this small-group Bible study. Know that as we prepared this study, we were lifting you up and considering the incredible role you will play.

While this Bible study targets dads and a return to biblical fatherhood, the material is for all learners in your church whether or not they have children. Even without kids of their own, everyone has a physical father, and the relationship we have with our dads has powerful implications on how we operate as believers in Christ. This study is also important for the women in your group.

Perhaps you are doing this study as part of a larger churchwide campaign anticipating the release of *COURAGEOUS*. Perhaps your group has already seen the movie and is engaging this four-week study as a follow-up. Regardless of the timing of your study or the format of your class, this study has enormous potential to help reshape families in your church and community.

The words on these pages are not powerful nor are they part of a secret formula guaranteed to improve family relationships and to grow your church. But combined with the life-changing, living Word of God, this message can be an incredible tool that inspires dramatic revival in the hearts of believers and offers a solid gospel tool for nonbelievers.

You may be experiencing some fear about leading this study. Be courageous! You have not been called by God to facilitate this study because you are the perfect parent or have raised perfect children. You may not even be a parent. You are leading this study because God equips His people to do His work. Our prayer for you is that as you guide this study you'll see God working in your life in mighty ways and sense real Holy-Spirit power sustaining you.

The best way for you to prepare each week is to complete the study yourself. Be open and transparent with your group, honestly revealing areas in which you also struggle. Pray that God will direct your conversation and empower you to lead well, and He will! Thank you for answering this courageous call.

A Special Note to Women

Undoubtedly you entertained the question, "What's in this for me?" as a wife, mother, or woman of faith engaged in this study. You are not alone. The movie *COURAGEOUS* is first targeted at men. There is an unmistakable void of biblical fatherhood in this country and its effects are far-reaching. As a mom, you have a direct hand in raising sons who will one day be fathers as well as in raising daughters who will one day choose a man to marry who will serve as father to her children.

You have an incredible responsibility before you. Even if you don't have children, you have a father, and you know the effect that either his presence or his absence has had in your life. This study is not only an opportunity for you to unpack the relationship you have with your own dad but also an opportunity for you to draw closer to your Heavenly Father.

While we desperately need men to step up and be the fathers that God has called and equipped them to be, we also need women to understand that call and to provide the necessary support and daily encouragement to make it a reality for our families. Thank you for recognizing the value of this study and for engaging it with an open heart and open mind. There is a specific application portion in each session just for you.

Our prayer for you as you engage in this study is that you will be drawn closer to the heart of God and His call on your life to be a courageous believer!

Guidelines for Small Groups

The following keys will help ensure that your group Bible study experience is as meaningful and impactful as possible. *Leader:* During the first meeting go over all four and ask each participant to commit to the guidelines.

Confidentiality

As you dive into small-group Bible study, members will be prompted to share thoughts and feelings related to the family they were raised in as well as the family they are forging now. All of these expressions are made out of trust and should be kept with the strictest confidence by the group.

Respect

As trust forms and participants begin to open up about their personal and family struggles, it often becomes easy to offer advice. Scripture teaches us to be quick to listen and slow to speak (Jas. 1:19). Listening is a key to respect. Even well-meaning advice can be ill-received if it is shared too quickly or before someone has full understanding.

It is important that participants commit to respecting one another's thoughts and opinions and to providing a safe place for those thoughts and opinions to be shared without fear of judgment.

Preparation

To get the most out of this Bible study, each group member should attend group meetings having read through the study and answered questions, ready to discuss the material. Each participant can respect the contribution of other members by taking the time to prepare for each session.

Accountability

The goal of the small-group experience is transformation. Each session helps learners identify aspects that need attention in their walk with Christ and their life as a believer, spouse, parent, and friend. Each week participants will be asked to consider courageous next steps. As a group, commit together to the accountability that is necessary to stay the course and live a courageous life.

COURAGEOUS CALL

It takes
COURAGE
to fight for
my FAMILY.

Do you know the name Rafael Peralta? Corporal Adam Morrison of the United States Marine Corps certainly does. On November 15, 2004, Rafael Peralta—a member of Morrison's unit—saved his life and "every Marine in that room."

Their unit had been cleansing Fallujah, Iraq, of terrorists "house by house" for seven days straight. That morning they entered a home and cleared the front rooms only to find a locked door on the left side. Sergeant Peralta opened the door to be met with gunfire from three terrorists with AK-47s. Peralta, alive but severely injured and lying on the floor in the doorway, noticed a grenade rolling into toward him. He grabbed the grenade and tucked it under his abdomen. When it exploded, he died, but the rest of his troop survived.

Peralta was a 25-year-old Mexican immigrant who enlisted in the Marines the day he received his green card. Leaving his parents for Iraq, he signed up to serve on the front lines. His bedroom at home contained three items on its walls: a copy of the Constitution, the Bill of Rights, and Peralta's certificate of graduation from boot camp.

SERGEANT PERALTA
April 7, 1979–November 15, 2004

His heroic act was foreshadowed by a note he wrote his younger brother, saying, "Be proud of me, bro. … and be proud of being an American." Those who know of Rafael Peralta can indeed be proud.[1]

It takes courage to enlist and sign up for frontline duty in an ongoing war. It takes courage to risk and voluntarily end your life for others and the perseverance of the mission. On the military battlefield, freedom is at stake. On the spiritual battlefield, our families are at stake and in danger. Our homes are under intense pressure and will become casualties unless we each answer the call to stand and fight for them.

Watch

MOVIE CLIP

View Clip 1, "Carjacking" (2:23), from the small-group DVD, and then use the discussion to start your study.

SUMMARY

In this scene, a man named Nathan Hayes pulls into a service station and begins pumping gas. Deciding to clean the dirt from his windshield, he steps away from the pump for a moment and a gang member steals his car. Much more concerned with the truck's contents than the truck itself, the action begins when Nathan risks everything to stop the thief. He is willing to lay down his life for what matters most to him, and the best thing he can do is keep his hands on the wheel.

OPEN DISCUSSION

As a group, do some basic introductions. Refresh everyone on the names and ages of your kids.

Danger and *fear* are words often associated with the word *courageous*. It takes courage to respond to a threatening situation. According to one popular description,

"COURAGE *is not the absence of fear, but rather the judgment that something else is more important than fear."* [2]

---

1 Before you realized Nathan's objective, did you find yourself agreeing with his actions, or were you hoping he would give up? How did you feel once you realized what Nathan was fighting for?

 Would you call his actions courageous and heroic? Why or why not?

2 Describe the most dangerous situation in which you ever found yourself. Would you react the same way now as you did then? Or, looking back, do you wish you had responded differently? Was your safety all that was at stake, or was someone else involved?

3 What scares you most about the life stages of your children? If you don't have kids, what concerns do you have about the possibility of one day being a parent?

4 What three things do you think most threaten families today? What sacrifices are you willing to make so these threats don't harm or destroy your family? How does courage help us make changes?

It's not unusual to be fearful about important people and important responsibilities. Yet Scripture teaches us that a better way is available on the path of life and parenting.

Study

The Book of Joshua begins with Moses' death and Joshua being named the newly appointed leader of God's people. Formerly, under Moses' leadership, Joshua led a victorious battle against the Amalekites (Ex. 17). Along with 11 others, Joshua spied the land of Canaan (Num. 13–14). Only he and Caleb came back with a favorable outlook toward the impending battle. Joshua's name means "The Lord is salvation" and corresponds with the New Testament name Jesus. Joshua was filled with the spirit, and now God was commissioning him for even greater service.

JOSHUA 1:1-9

1 After the death of Moses the LORD's servant, the LORD spoke to Joshua son of Nun, who had served Moses:

2 "Moses My servant is dead. Now you and all the people prepare to cross over the Jordan to the land I am giving the Israelites.

3 I have given you every place where the sole of your foot treads, just as I promised Moses.

4 Your territory will be from the wilderness and Lebanon to the great Euphrates River—all the land of the Hittites—and west to the Mediterranean Sea.

5 No one will be able to stand against you as long as you live. I will be with you, just as I was with Moses. I will not leave you or forsake you.

6 Be strong and courageous, for you will distribute the land I swore to their fathers to give them as an inheritance.

7 Above all, be strong and very courageous to carefully observe the whole instruction My servant Moses commanded you. Do not turn from it to the right or the left, so that you will have success wherever you go.

8 This book of instruction must not depart from your mouth; you are to recite it day and night so that you may carefully observe everything written in it. For then you will prosper and succeed in whatever you do.

9 Haven't I commanded you: be strong and courageous? Do not be afraid or discouraged, for the LORD your God is with you wherever you go."

Note the number of times God instructed Joshua to be "strong and courageous." Why might Joshua have been afraid? Why is courage a key to being a good leader?

What did God *promise* Joshua in this passage (vv. 3,7,9)?

God promises to bless us and give us true success. He is faithful to keep His promises. Most of all, He promises us His presence wherever we go.

What did God *require* of Joshua in this passage (vv. 6-9)?
What did God say is the key to success (v. 8)?

If you knew God was commanding you to do something, was going to bless you if you did it, and would always be with you helping you succeed, would you be more courageous?

Is there something God has already told you to do for which you need to take courage, trust Him, and obey?

Read Deuteronomy 31:23.

What was Moses telling Joshua before he (Moses) died?

Give examples of modern-day commissions. Do we have a parallel for Christian leadership today? for fathers or mothers?

Specifically, what have you as a man been commissioned by God to do?

Read Joshua 1:16-18.

How did the response of the people toward Joshua confirm God's call in his life?

What did the people promise to do? How did the requirements of God in Joshua's leadership translate to the lives of the people?

Compare Joshua 1:7-8 with Joshua 1:16-18. What connections do you see?

First, God commanded Joshua to be obedient to the book of the Law and to the Word of God. Then the people who were under Joshua's care committed to the same. Although Joshua made mistakes as a leader, he continued to seek the Lord and to get back on track as a strong example to those he led.

As men and women of faith, *the* **COMMITMENT** *of the people God entrusts to us will only be as strong as our own.* This is true of other believers we lead and disciple. It is also true for the children we are charged to raise.

Everyone

We are a people who value measurements in life. We get grades as children and seek merit raises as adults. Measurements are useful tools.

God's call to leadership for Joshua was also a call for him to commit to read and to dwell on God's Word (Josh. 1:8). In this study you will be considering your personal commitment to God's Word. Rate yourself on a scale of 1 to 10 with 10 being *completely committed* and 1 being *walking far from God*, and answer, "Why did I give myself that rating?" This is for your own understanding, not to share.

Courage to Follow God's Word

1   2   3   4   5   6   7   8   9   10

What factors influenced this rating?

Obedience to God's Word

1   2   3   4   5   6   7   8   9   10

What factors influenced this rating?

Meditation on Scripture

1   2   3   4   5   6   7   8   9   10

What factors influenced this rating?

Success as a Christ Follower

1   2   3   4   5   6   7   8   9   10

What factors influenced this rating?

What kind of commitment to Christ do your children see in you?
What kind of sacrifices are you making to help your family obey God?

Summary

We can all stand to improve in consistently reading God's Word and obeying His voice. Like Joshua, you may need reminders to be strong and courageous. You may need to recall that God will help you lead your family and will never leave you as you obey Him. You may need His reminder that He is calling you to spiritually lead, guide, and protect those under your care. Your success in spiritual leadership of your family is directly tied to your commitment to the Word of God.

Write three steps you will take this week to better read God's Word and obey His voice.

1

2

3

Dads and Moms
Consider how God wants you to sacrifice your life for the sake of your family.

Consider how He wants you to be a hero in your home. Consider the threats that war at the doors of your children's hearts and lives every day. Sometimes they can be physical threats (yellow grenades and carjacks), but often they are spiritual ones.

For example, boys often face bullying or peer pressure at school. Starting very young, girls may face issues of body image and a sexually pervasive culture. Even a toddler faces threats. Identify threats you think of in this space.

Other dangers to your family are not as easily spotted. What about attitudes of bitterness toward your spouse or children (Heb. 12:15)? How could unresolved marriage issues hurt your children? Do you allow harmful Internet, TV, or movie content into your home? What about friends who pull your children away from God? Do hobbies or other activities keep you or your kids away from church involvement?

Many godly parents have been where you have yet to go. You can benefit from their wisdom and friendship. They can encourage and support you.

Constantly pray for courage to address in a godly way the threats to your children. Pray for each child as he or she faces these challenges. Intentionally spend more time with your kids, learning their day-to-day routines. Like Nathan, hang on tightly to the wheel!

Pray for the wisdom and boldness to step up and be the dad you need to be—to serve, lead, and protect your family. God is calling men and women to courageously follow Christ and His Word. He is calling us to make the sacrifices needed to fight for our faith, for our families, and for future generations.

IT IS TIME TO ANSWER THE CALL.

1. Oliver North, "Hero in Fallujah: Marine Laid Himself on Top of Grenade to Save Rest of Squad." [online] 16 December 2004 [cited 5 January 2011]. Available from the Internet: *http://www.humanevents.com/article.php?id=6062*
2. "Ambrose Redmoon Quotes" [online] 1999-2010 [cited 5 January 2011]. Available from the Internet: *http://thinkexist.com/quotes/ambrose_redmoon*

COURAGEOUS PRIORITIES

It takes
COURAGE
to value what
matters most.

Living Large has a new meaning as of July 2010. While entering a lottery is not advised, Allen and Violet Large of Nova Scotia, Canada, won 11.3 million dollars in one and gave all their winnings away to local churches, charities, hospitals, and even the local fire station. After taking care of family and friends, the couple set out to give away the remainder of the money. They told the *Toronto Star,* "What you've never had, you never miss."

Violet, who was suffering from cancer at the time and undergoing chemotherapy, felt compelled to give generously to local hospitals and to cancer research. Allen told the *Star* that the money meant nothing and that it was much more important that the two had each other.

ALLEN AND VIOLET LARGE Truro Daily News

The Larges spoke openly about how the winnings had complicated their lives and had been as much a burden as a blessing.[1] Their generosity easily begs the question, "What is really important in life?"

Keeping up with the Joneses is a challenge for anyone. Comparison can lead to one of two things: aggression or depression. It can either lead you to aggressively pursue what you don't have in order to achieve status that in the end won't satisfy or will cause overwhelming depression as you shift your focus from life's blessings to unmet wants and desires.

What makes the Larges' generosity so newsworthy is that it is so uncommon. When we find people who understand what matters most, they stand out. It takes courage to be that different and to have your life set apart according to a different (higher) standard.

Watch

MOVIE CLIP
View Clip 2, "Javier Suit Scene" (1:28), from the small-group DVD, and use the discussion to start your study.

SUMMARY

In this scene Javier is trying on a brand-new suit. His wife and children are excited about how nice he looks. Money is tight so the suit is an obvious stretch for the family budget; Javier expresses misgivings about the cost. Carmen insists it was the right thing to do for this special occasion—the time Javier will commit to spiritually lead his family. Javier tells her that he feels like a very rich man, and Carmen confirms that he should. When it comes to the things that matter, Javier is indeed wealthy.

Javier and Carmen are a couple who understand what matters in life. They are much richer than one might suppose.

OPEN DISCUSSION

Jesus reminds us, "For where your treasure is, there your heart will be also" (Matt. 6:21). If you consider what you talk about, think about, and spend your time and money on, you will discover where your heart is right now. You will also discover what you treasure most.

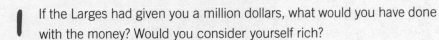

1 If the Larges had given you a million dollars, what would you have done with the money? Would you consider yourself rich?

2 How do our financial decisions reveal our values—what we think is most important?

3 What three things did Carmen identify in Javier's life that made him a true rich man?

4 In the space below, list five things in your life that matter most to you.

When we stop to consider what matters most in life, relationships usually make their way to the top of the list. Javier's relationships with God, his wife, and his children—those things that last—are what make him a rich man.

5 Why do you think we invest so much time and energy on things that do not last?

How would your life be different if you began prioritizing and living for the things that matter most to you?

Study God's Word vividly illustrates the principle of wrong priorities. The city of Jericho had been burned (Josh. 6). God commanded that no one should take and keep the precious metals and ores of Jericho, but instead place them in the treasury of the Lord's house. If they obeyed, it would reveal that pleasing God was more important to them than possessing worldly treasures.

God was with Joshua and Israel just as He had promised. His specific instructions spread. Then it happened. Joshua 7:1 tells the story of Achan and the anger of the Lord imposed on the Israelites as the result of his sin.

JOSHUA 7:1

The Israelites, however, were unfaithful regarding the things set apart for destruction. Achan son of Carmi, son of Zabdi, son of Zerah, of the tribe of Judah, took some of what was set apart, and the LORD's anger burned against the Israelites.

What did Achan do that was so terrible?

What did God do in response to Achan's sin?

Read Joshua 7:2-12.

How did Joshua respond to God right after the battle of Ai (vv. 7-9)?

Read Joshua 7:19-21.

Why did Achan take from the articles consecrated to the Lord?

Why do you think Achan's sin stood out enough for God to teach the people such a strong lesson?

God judged the nation based on the sins of just one individual. He removed His hand of blessing because Achan, without the knowledge of all Israel or their senior leader, acted in disobedience to God. There was sin in the camp, and it had to be removed.

One failing grade is enough to bring down an entire GPA. One act of infidelity is enough to break apart a family. One single sin of omission or commission can have effects on your life and the life of your family for generations. In the case of Achan, it was a sin of value. He was tempted by the treasures of the world and chose them over obedience to the Lord.

JESUS SAID IT BEST:
"But collect for yourselves treasures in heaven, where neither moth nor rust destroys, and where thieves don't break in and steal. For where your treasure is, there your heart will be also."
Matthew 6:20-21

One misplaced value can be all the sin needed in the life of your family for Satan to grab a foothold. Achan coveted the things of the world more than the richness of God's promise. In reality, the things he coveted did not satisfy him. He couldn't even enjoy the spoils of the treasure; he had to hide them in order to have them. That certainly isn't satisfaction.

How does the world tempt you to place value on material wealth more than on Christ?

Share a time when something you thought was very satisfying turned out not to satisfy at all. What things other than God do you look to for satisfaction?

Does the philosophy of "keeping up with the Joneses" ever take hold of your family?

How does the current economic climate have you wanting more or fearfully holding on to what you have?

Read Joshua 7:24-26.

Achan's entire family suffered and died because of what he had done to Israel. This death sentence was legal under God's law and not only established justice but warned the entire nation to not make the same mistake and instead always to keep God first.

Are we allowing hidden sin in our lives? Do we really think it will *not* affect our families?

How can we literally stamp sin out of our lives today?

Achan confessed his sin, but Scripture does not state that he repented of it. Look at the actions of Joshua when he heard of the sin in Joshua 7:6 and contrast that with the attitude of Achan who merely stated the facts (7:20).

How is repentance from sin like putting it to death in our lives?

Anytime our selfish desires take priority over God's Word in our lives, we sin. That sin has powerful implications for our spiritual health as well as the condition of our family's spiritual health.

When we desire the things of this world more than the things of God, we open up our lives and our family to dissatisfaction and ultimately to the consequences of our actions. Misplaced values mean displaced lives.

"Do not love the world or the things that belong to the world.

If anyone loves the world, love for the Father is not in him.

For everything that belongs to the world—the lust of the flesh,

the lust of the eyes, and the pride in one's lifestyle—is not from

the Father, but is from the world. And the world with its lust is

passing away, but the one who does God's will remains forever."

1 John 2:15-17

LIVE

Everyone

With the favor of God renewed among His people, the armies of Israel went on to defeat Ai in dramatic fashion. In response to their success, Joshua erected an altar and the people worshiped God through the reading and hearing of God's Word. Continue evaluating your commitment to God's Word as you read (or write out, if you prefer) the following verses of Scripture.

Joshua 1:7

Psalm 1:1-2

John 14:21

Summary

God commands us to keep His words. It is the key to success and the source of our happiness and delight. It is an indication of our love for Him and a direct link to further revelation from Him. It is the road of being blessed.

Write a sentence of renewed commitment to God. Remember, obedience to God is of the greatest value in life. What we value indicates our level of love and obedience to God.

Dads and Moms

Consider how God wants you to reprioritize your family's values. Discern how He wants you to lead and help script what matters to your sons and daughters.

1. Evaluate the world's attempts to entice your children with material things and Satan's ploys to create "sin in your camp" at home.

How has a misplaced focus on self kept you from freely giving from what God has given you? How have priorities regarding time kept you from serving?

How can you lead your family to desire the things of God?

Take a moment to identify misplaced values in your family. For example, how does the way you observe birthdays, Easter, and Christmas reinforce materialism rather than gratefulness to God for what He has done for you?

2. Remember what Carmen said to Javier. She spoke of three things that described great value and made Javier a very rich man.

How can you help reshape what your family views as true wealth?

On a separate piece of paper if needed, try to script three new values for yourself and your family. For example: "Turn off the TV and spend time as a family." "Get rid of things in our home that are weakening our spiritual lives." "Volunteer as a family to serve others."

Lastly, pray that God will give you the courage to value and prioritize what really matters.

1. "What you've never had, you never miss" [online] 5 November 2010 [cited 5 January 2011]. Available from the Internet: *http://www.dailymail.co.uk/news/article-1326473/Canadian-couple-Allen-Violet-Large-away-entire-11-2m-lottery-win.html*

COURAGEOUS LEGACY

It takes COURAGE to impact future generations.

President George H. W. Bush → President George W. Bush

Reverend Billy Graham → Reverend Franklin Graham

Archie Manning → Peyton, Eli Manning

The expression "Like father, like son" has many famous examples. The fathers mentioned have many reasons to be proud of their footstep-walking sons. While many children take roads completely different from their parents, we probably all know some who sadly have mirrored harmful ways and examples left by their parents as well.

Think for a moment about your own father and the patterns you hope to repeat—and those you hope to leave behind. Many of us, whether we like it or not, when it comes to raising kids of our own, we seem destined to repeat the same patterns of our own parents. In many cases, that's great. In other cases, it is not. As we parent children, a good question to ask is what personal characteristics we would be excited to see being instilled in our future grand-children. If there are things we think/believe/do that we would be alarmed by our kids' repeating, we would do well to reconsider our courses.

Perhaps the problems lie in waiting for those patterns to emerge naturally, as if fate has something to say rather than intentionally following Christ and modeling Him in our homes. Leaving a legacy starts with looking back and then setting a clear plan for going forward.

Billy Graham holding his young son, Franklin

What we learn very naturally growing up can easily translate to healthy or unhealthy patterns of behavior in our adult lives. It takes courage to walk a different path. It takes courage to break cycles. It takes courage to choose and to leave a legacy that will still matter for many generations to come.

Watch

MOVIE CLIP
View Clip 3, "Grill out/What was your dad like?" (2:40), from the small-group DVD, and use the discussion to start your study.

SUMMARY

In this scene, Adam and the guys are doing what guys do—grilling out! Adam is dealing with very specific challenges as a father and seeking wisdom about how to be a better dad. The lazy afternoon conversation takes a serious turn when the guys all share about the relationships they had with their own fathers.

OPEN DISCUSSION

Dad stories ... we all have them, both good and bad. The men in the clip articulated theirs in just a few sentences. Take a few moments to express your own dad story.

1 What impact has your father's presence or absence had on you? How has he influenced your faith, your family, and your choices in life?

(Nathan mentions the profound effect his father's absence had in his life and also the positive influence of another man who stepped into the gap for him. If you lost your dad at a young age, describe the effects of the loss but also feel free to talk/write about the stepdad or father figure in your life.)

2 As part of your dad-story exercise, identify which of the four men in the clip you relate to most (circle or check). Was it—

Nathan, with the absentee father but positive mentor?
Shane, with the dad who didn't practice what he preached?
David, whose dad left after infidelity and the home was never the same?
Adam, who had a good dad, leaving no failures worth mentioning?

3 As a group, take time to share your dad stories with each other. How have your father's decisions impacted your life? Try to be as open and transparent as possible.

4 What are the positive elements of your family of origin that you are trying to keep strong in your own family?

5 With what negative elements from your family of origin do you struggle to break the chains?

Study

Much of the Book of Joshua is about tribal territories. Each of the clans, named for the sons of Jacob, was given portions of the promised land as an inheritance. Violent nations filled with pagan idolatry, child sacrifice, and endless immorality had been driven out and replaced by God's people. The promises God made as far back as Genesis 12 were being fulfilled in the life of Joshua's Israel. For Old Testament Israel, the legacy of their forefathers came packaged in the promise of land.

In Joshua 23, an aging Joshua gives a final address to the people of God. His life and leadership left a powerful legacy, and the words in his final farewell add intentionality to the mark he made. Carefully read this account.

JOSHUA 23:1-10

1 A long time after the Lord had given Israel rest from all the enemies around them, Joshua was old, getting on in years.

2 So Joshua summoned all Israel, including its elders, leaders, judges, and officers, and said to them, "I am old, getting on in years,

3 and you have seen for yourselves everything the Lord your God did to all these nations on your account, because it was the Lord your God who was fighting for you.

4 See, I have allotted these remaining nations to you as an inheritance for your tribes, including all the nations I have destroyed, from the Jordan westward to the Mediterranean Sea.

5 The Lord your God will force them back on your account and drive them out before you so that you can take possession of their land, as the Lord your God promised you.

6 Be very strong and continue obeying all that is written in the book of the law of Moses, so that you do not turn from it to the right or left

7 and so that you do not associate with these nations remaining among you. Do not call on the names of their gods or make an oath to them; do not worship them or bow down to them.

8 Instead, remain faithful to the LORD your God, as you have done to this day.

9 The LORD has driven out great and powerful nations before you, and no one is able to stand against you to this day.

10 One of you routed a thousand because the LORD your God was fighting for you, as He promised."

What words in this passage seem familiar to you? (Reference Josh. 1.)

How had God accomplished for Israel what He promised (v. 10)?

Read Joshua 23:11-13.

How had this warning already been reality for the people of God? (Reference Josh. 7.) Continue with Joshua's farewell speech.

JOSHUA 23:14-16

14 "I am now going the way of all the earth, and you know with all your heart and all your soul that none of the good promises the LORD your God made to you has failed. Everything was fulfilled for you; not one promise has failed.

15 Since every good thing the LORD your God promised you has come about, so He will bring on you every bad thing until He has annihilated you from this good land the LORD your God has given you.

16 If you break the covenant of the LORD your God, which He commanded you, and go and worship other gods, and bow down to them, the LORD's anger will burn against you, and you will quickly disappear from this good land He has given you."

What did Joshua *remind* the people of in verse 14?

What did Joshua *warn* the people about in verses 15-16?

Everyone

Joshua used his legacy speech to remind the people of God's faithfulness and to warn the people of God's response to their unfaithfulness. A good legacy of faith both reminds and warns future generations. Whether it is a good example with rewards or a bad example with consequences, we can learn a lot from those who have gone before us.

Based on these terms, who has left the best legacy of faith in your life?

How did this person's life and words include both a *reminder* and a *warning* for you and your faith?

Consider the impact your biological dad has had on your life. Whether by his absence or his presence, he has left a considerable mark.

Before you can actively take part in leaving a positive legacy for the next generation of your family, you have to unpack and deal with the legacy left in your life.

While none of our earthly fathers are perfect, many of them have made much of Christ with their words and actions and made incredible spiritual investments in our lives. However, many suffer significant scars from a father who left or a dad who was around but whose actions brought hurt and unrest.

If your father's legacy was largely positive, continue with Part A before going to the Summary section. If your father's legacy was largely negative, skip to Part B and then conclude with the Summary section. First, watch a clip highlighting some contemporary experiences related to legacy building.

View Clip 4, "Sherwood Dads Share Parenting Experiences" (6:15), before moving into your time of application.

THE SHERWOOD DADS
Jim McBride, Stephen Kendrick, Michael Catt, Alex Kendrick

PART A: If your father left a worthwhile spiritual legacy in your life, write down the most important lessons and warnings he spoke into your life. These are offerings you will strive for in your own legacy.

Commit this week to contacting your dad and expressing your gratitude for his faithful legacy. Offer to him the specifics of his investments in your life, and tell how each one continues to impact your walk with Christ and leadership in your family.

If your dad is no longer with you, consider writing a prayer of thanks to God for your dad. Keep it in your Bible as a reminder of God's favor in your life and to invest the same in the lives of others.

PART B: If your father left a wealth of pain in his wake, moving forward will require healing and health. Both require forgiveness.

In *COURAGEOUS*, Nathan learns to work through the hurts from his father and forgive him. This is a vital step in breaking past chains and moving forward. Healing does not begin until forgiveness takes place (Mark 11:25). Forgiveness allows us to turn all the anger and hurt over to God so He can be the Judge and deal with those who have wounded us (Rom. 12:17-19).

If you are ready to be free from any bitterness with your father, write down a statement of pain caused by his past actions. Then follow it with a declaration of your choice to be like Jesus and grant your dad complete forgiveness. Pray and tell God of your choice to forgive your father. Ask Him to break the chains in your heart. Write FORGIVEN across this page.

Finally, if you feel ready to do so, consider contacting your dad and expressing your desire to begin rebuilding your relationship. Apologize if you have also hurt him in the past. If your dad is no longer with you, consider writing a letter of forgiveness to him. Keep it with you as a reminder of God's healing power in your life and to break the cycles of sin in your future family.

Summary

Before we can choose the legacy we leave to others, we have to fully consider the ones left in us. By forgiving and learning from their lives, we can move forward with strength. Perhaps you have started out on shaky ground with your spiritual investment. As long as you have life and breath, you can change the impact you make. Even if you had a lousy legacy from your earthly father, you can cling to a perfect legacy of faith from your Heavenly Father who has, according to Joshua 23:14, fulfilled every promise He has ever made.

Dads and Moms

Consider the legacy you want to leave for your kids. Consider the legacy your life is already leaving by the things you say and do and the way you represent God in word and deed. Ask God to help you identify those things you are doing well and those areas in which you need to improve—for your sake and for the sake of future generations.

My positive legacy:

1.

2.

3.

My commitment to change:

1.

2.

3.

Pray now for courage to boldly leave a legacy of faith in your family. The greatest impact you have on your children will be how you love God and love your spouse.

The direction of your kids' *dating, marriage, career, service, leadership, faithfulness* to God and His church, and ultimately their *parenting* will be a direct reflection of you and the marks you leave in their lives.

If that sounds frightening, that's because it is. It is an incredible responsibility, and doing it with success will take courage! Be strong and courageous!

COURAGEOUS FAITH

It takes
COURAGE
to stand
WITH CHRIST.

Only in recent years has the name Steve Saint rung any bells. Steve was the five-year-old son of Nate Saint, the missionary pilot who died alongside Jim Elliot and three other missionaries in 1956 at the hands of the Waodani (whoa-DONNY) tribe in Ecuador. At age nine, Steve returned to the Waodani

Steve Saint with Mincaye

territory for the first time. As a young man, Saint began a long-lasting friendship with Mincaye (min-KY-yee), one of the men who killed his father. "What the Waodani meant for evil, God used for good," says Steve.[1]

The stories of Elisabeth Elliot and Rachel Saint have long been associated with forgiveness. What better picture of grace and mercy than that of a missionary widow and sister to return and share good news with the very people who murdered their family members? Perhaps there is no greater illustration of forgiveness than the forged relationship between a son and the tribal murderer who took his dad. Here we see vividly illustrated the life-changing gospel of Jesus that Jim, Nate, and the other missionaries set out to share in the first place.

Jim Elliot wrote in his journal, "He is no fool who gives what he cannot keep to gain that which he cannot lose."[2]

The apostle Paul wrote in his Letter to the Philippians, "My eager expectation and hope is that I will not be ashamed about anything, but that now as always, with all boldness, Christ will be highly honored in my body, whether by life or by death. For me, living is Christ and dying is gain" (Phil. 1:20-21).

When choosing to stand with Jesus, the stakes are always high. The question is not what you lose by standing with Him but what you will lose if you do not.

Watch

MOVIE CLIP
View Clip 5, "Gospel Presentation at Gun Range" (3:40), from the small-group DVD, and use the discussion to start your study.

SUMMARY

In this scene Nathan seizes an opportunity to share his faith with his rookie partner, David. When David asks Nathan about the importance of fathers. Nathan realizes that David's concerns go much deeper than the question indicates. Nathan shares an allegory that helps the young officer understand Christ's saving grace. Recognizing his own sin and guilt, David admits that he is tired of feeling guilty.

Nathan speaks the gospel, and David responds. What will David do with his new understanding?

OPEN DISCUSSION

Whether related to fear of death, fear of controversy, fear of failing, or some other fear, we consider courage a prerequisite when it comes to actively sharing the gospel.

1 As a group, take time to briefly share your own faith story. Who introduced you to Jesus?

2 Now consider those with whom you have never shared how to have a relationship with Christ. What is at stake if they never hear the gospel?

3 What was your first reaction to hearing how Nathan opened the door and shared Christ with David? What seemed natural to you? What seemed difficult?

4 Nathan didn't create an opportunity to share Christ as much as he seized one. How did Nathan balance truth with kindness in how he shared with David?

What day-to-day opportunities do you have to begin sharing Christ?

5 How actively are you seeking to share Christ with your children (age appropriately)? Or are you trusting the church to do it for you?

6 God's Word commands parents to lead and teach their children spiritually (Deut. 6:1-7). How openly do you discuss spiritual matters in your own home?

"Honor the Messiah as Lord in your hearts. Always be ready to give a defense to anyone who asks you for a reason for the hope that is in you."
1 Peter 3:15

Study

The final chapter of Joshua is a continuation of the leader's address that began in chapter 23. It contains one of the most frequently referenced verses about the family (Josh. 24:15) and sets up Israel's continued story as told in the Book of Judges.

Whereas Moses, by God's power, led the people out of Egypt, Joshua led them into Canaan. Both leaders endured hard seasons of wilderness wanderings, and in the end Joshua courageously claimed the prize that was promised to Abraham, Isaac, and Jacob.

JOSHUA 24:1-13

1 Joshua assembled all the tribes of Israel at Shechem and summoned Israel's elders, leaders, judges, and officers, and they presented themselves before God.

2 Joshua said to all the people, "This is what the LORD, the God of Israel, says: 'Long ago your ancestors, including Terah, the father of Abraham and Nahor, lived beyond the Euphrates River and worshiped other gods.

3 But I took your father Abraham from the region beyond the Euphrates River, led him throughout the land of Canaan, and multiplied his descendants. I gave him Isaac,

4 and to Isaac I gave Jacob and Esau. I gave the hill country of Seir to Esau as a possession, but Jacob and his sons went down to Egypt.

5 'Then I sent Moses and Aaron; I plagued Egypt by what I did there and afterward I brought you out.

6 When I brought your fathers out of Egypt and you reached the Red Sea, the Egyptians pursued your fathers with chariots and horsemen as far as the sea.

7 Your fathers cried out to the LORD, so He put darkness between you and the Egyptians, and brought the sea over them, engulfing them. Your own eyes saw what I did to Egypt. After that, you lived in the wilderness a long time.

8 'Later, I brought you to the land of the Amorites who lived beyond the Jordan. They fought against you, but I handed them over to you. You possessed their land, and I annihilated them before you.

9 Balak son of Zippor, king of Moab, set out to fight against Israel. He sent for Balaam son of Beor to curse you,

10 but I would not listen to Balaam. Instead, he repeatedly blessed you, and I delivered you from his hand.

11 'You then crossed the Jordan and came to Jericho. The people of Jericho—as well as the Amorites, Perizzites, Canaanites, Hittites, Girgashites, Hivites, and Jebusites—fought against you, but I handed them over to you.

12 I sent the hornet ahead of you, and it drove out the two Amorite kings before you. It was not by your sword or bow.

13 I gave you a land you did not labor for, and cities you did not build, though you live in them; you are eating from vineyards and olive groves you did not plant.'"

What did God say about Himself to His people in this passage?

Why is it important to periodically be reminded of an historical account of God's work in our lives?

What specific activity of God in the life of His people from Abraham to Joshua do you find particularly exciting? What part of the Israelite story speaks most to you and why?

JOSHUA 24:14-15, NIV

14 "Now fear the LORD and serve him with all faithfulness. Throw away
   the gods your forefathers worshiped beyond the River and in
   Egypt, and serve the LORD.

15 But if serving the LORD seems undesirable to you, then choose for
   yourselves this day whom you will serve, whether the gods your
   forefathers served beyond the River, or the gods of the Amorites,
   in whose land you are living. But as for me and my household,
   we will serve the LORD."

What do Joshua's final words say about his own leadership of his home?

Why was it important that Joshua speak for his entire house?

Knowing what you know about Joshua, do you think he would have carried
out his commitment even if he were the only one? What about you?

JOSHUA 24:16-18

16 The people replied, "We will certainly not abandon the LORD
   to worship other gods!

17 For the LORD our God brought us and our fathers out of the land
   of Egypt, out of the place of slavery, and performed these great
   signs before our eyes. He also protected us all along the way we
   went and among all the peoples whose lands we traveled through.

18 The LORD drove out before us all the peoples, including the
   Amorites who lived in the land. We too will worship the LORD,
   because He is our God."

How did the people respond to Joshua's call?

How did Joshua's narrative retelling of God's faithfulness affect how the people thought and responded?

Hundreds of years later, in his address to the Hellenistic Jews in Acts 7, Stephen used the same method to share his faith by recounting the history of Israel from Abraham to Solomon. He challenged their belief in the earthly temple for the sake of Christ's temple and proclaimed Jesus as the fulfillment of God's promise. Stephen laid down his life for Christ and was stoned for his courageous faith, becoming the first Christian martyr. The gospel he shared not only impacted those in his day but also spread around the world.

By recounting God's faithfulness throughout history and our own lives, we can create a strong "apologetic" argument of the gospel for the lost to hear. *Apologetics* refers to a branch of theological study aimed at providing a defense for God and for one's faith in Christ. It comes from the Greek word a*pologia,* which means to give a verbal defense for one's opinion against an attack. It is the word translated "defense" in 1 Peter 3:15 (p. 45).

Our response to Jesus Christ being Lord of our lives is to share who He is and what He has done. The apologetic argument often involves a narrative approach to faith sharing. The apostle Paul used this approach by recounting the complete story of how Christ changed his life and called him to salvation.

What was the significance of Joshua's or Stephen's historical recounting of God's faithfulness dating back to Abraham?

How is the entire faith story important when it comes to boldly sharing one's faith?

What advantages do you see in using a narrative approach in sharing Christ?

Look back at the first part of 1 Peter 3:15. How is honoring Christ as Lord in your heart good preparation for God to make you a witness for His name?

LIVE

Everyone

Consider the God of the universe and His pronounced judgment on sin. Consider His love, that He would create an alternative to such punishment by the death of His own Son, Jesus.

Joshua contended the same. The people were slaves in Egypt, and God sent a savior. God blessed the Old Testament Israelites by giving them the land He promised. And He blesses us by offering us the promise of eternal life if we will repent of our sins and place our total faith in His Son, Jesus.

If you have not settled this today, in the words of Nathan, "What is holding you back?" Make the choice to trust Christ today. Page 53 walks you through simple steps to trusting Christ. Turn there now.

If you have trusted Christ for eternity, what is holding you back from boldly seizing opportunities to share the hope you have with others?

Summary

It takes the fullness of the Holy Spirit working in our lives for us to see the opportunities to share Christ that present themselves every day. It also takes courage to act and seize those opportunities as they come.

Christ is best shared in the context of relationship. Nathan and David were already friends. They were partners at work. After David's decision, they would be brothers in Christ for life.

Write the names of three people with whom you already have a relationship and can share your hope in Christ this week.

1.

2.

3.

As you await the right moment, pray: "Heavenly Father, I thank You for those You sent into my life to share how I could have a relationship with You through Christ. Please make me an effective soul winner and equip me with the gospel of peace so I can boldly share the good news as well. In Jesus' name, amen."

Be prepared, in season and out, to share Christ. Confidently pray, asking God to open doors; conduct yourself with wisdom when you are with nonbelievers; and tailor your speech to the situation (Col. 4:2-3).

Dads and Moms

It took courage for Joshua to stand with God despite the wickedness of the people, and it takes courage to stand with Christ today. There are many faiths and religions out there, and Jesus said that if we stand for Him we will be rejected by the world. But our strong witness for Christ will not only honor God but also draw the lost to salvation.

In what ways does your family need to unapologetically take a stand for Christ? It may be as simple as making church participation a priority over sports. It may be as deep and difficult as openly sharing Christ with a neighborhood family who is antagonistic to faith.

If you are a mom or dad of older children, ask yourself if you have been a strong example of keeping Christ first before your children. If not, isn't it time to step up and stand firm with Christ in your conversations? This may mean owning up to your part in allowing other things to prevent Christ from being first place in your home. Pray for courage as you boldly share with your children the hope you have found in Jesus.

Perhaps as a mom or dad of young children you are working to lay a foundation for faith so that one day your kids will choose Christ. Satan does not want you to be successful. You likely are already experiencing the attacks of a world that would deter your resolve. Courageously renew your commitment today. As for you and your house, determine to worship and serve the Lord.

Perhaps your family needs to actively share Christ with other family members and close friends. Identify those today who need to see and hear the gospel narrative from you and your family. Specify those individuals you will invite to church with you this week. Be willing to help your children do the same, even if it means driving out of your way to pick up their friends.

Take time this week to lead your family in a discussion about faith sharing. Talk about it daily. Decide as a family the people you would like to share with, and pray as a family for each person. Write down names and pray for opportunities for each member of your family to courageously stand with and share Jesus.

In the *COURAGEOUS* clip we viewed, Nathan made his case and asked David, "What's holding you back from settling this today?" Scripture tells us how Joshua made his case for God and called the people to choose, based on the reputation of God, whom they would worship. Then Joshua pronounced that he and his house would worship the Lord.

After all that Christ did for us, who would choose otherwise?

1. "Steve Saint: The Legacy of the Martyrs" [online] n.d. [cited 5 January 2011]. Available from the Internet: *http://www.cbn.com/700club/Guests/Bios/steve_saint010305.aspx*
2. "Jim Elliot Quote" [online] 2008 [cited 5 January 2011]. Available from the Internet: *http://www.wheaton.edu/bgc/archives/faq/20.htm*

Appendices
A New Life

The Bible tells us that our hearts tend to run from God and rebel against Him. The Bible calls this "sin." *Romans 3:23 says, "For all have sinned and fall short of the glory of God."* Every lie, bitter response, selfish attitude, and lustful thought separates us from God. We all deserve His judgment.

Even though you deserve judgment, God loves you and wants to save you from sin and offer you a new life of hope. *John 10:10 says, "I [Jesus] have come that they may have life and have it in abundance."*

To give you this gift of salvation, God made a way by sending His Son, Jesus Christ. *Romans 5:8 tells us, "But God proves His own love for us in that while we were still sinners, Christ died for us!"*

You receive this gift by faith alone. *Ephesians 2:8 says, "For you are saved by grace through faith, and this is not from yourselves; it is God's gift."*

Faith is a decision of your heart demonstrated by the actions of your life. *Romans 10:9 says, "If you confess with your mouth, 'Jesus is Lord,' and believe in your heart that God raised Him from the dead, you will be saved."* The Bible commands everyone to repent and to believe on the Lord Jesus Christ to be saved. If you choose right now to believe Jesus died for your sins and to receive new life through Him, consider praying a prayer like this:

> "Dear God, I confess that I am a sinner and that my sin separates me from You. I believe Jesus died to forgive me of my sins. I accept Your offer of eternal life. Thank You for forgiving me of all my sin and giving me my new life. From this day forward, I will choose to follow You."

If you prayed such a prayer, share your decision with a Christian friend or pastor. If you are not already attending church, find one that preaches the Bible and will help you worship and grow in your faith. Following Christ's example, ask to be baptized by immersion as a public expression of your faith.

The What, Who, How, and Why of Accountability

Nic Allen

Google™ the word *accountability*. The top 10 hits (after Wikipedia® and Merriam-Webster®) will likely include articles or sites dealing with fiscal responsibility, corporate integrity, and product reliability. The personal accountability of the Christ follower is something similar yet different altogether.

While Scripture doesn't explicitly mention accountability, its urgency is implicit particularly in passages describing successful Christian community. So what exactly is accountability? How do we do it? To whom should we be accountable and why?

The What

One day we all will stand before God to give an account for who we are and how we have lived. Scripture references the judgment seat of God in numerous passages. Trusting Christ for salvation will be all that matters when we meet our Maker.

Becoming a Christian by believing in Christ is very easy. But when it comes to following Him, we often flounder. Accountability is a discipleship tool that operates in the context of relationships. It is one friend helping another to live for Christ and holding another to a standard of faith and vice versa.

The Who

Several essentials can be identified for successful accountability relationships.

1. Faith. Both parties must be people of expressed faith in Christ. While it is important to develop influential relationships with nonbelievers, accountability is best in a relationship yoked by Jesus.

2. Homogeny. Both parties must be of the same gender. There is a world of difference between how men and women communicate and relate to the world. Men and women deal with different temptations and pressures.

Entering into an accountability relationship with a member of the opposite sex (other than the one to whom you are married) could lead to a level of intimacy that births physical attraction. That is an unhealthy temptation. While there is certainly a call for accountability in a marriage relationship, each spouse should also seek the accountability of a friend of the same sex to walk with them through life's challenges and maintain fidelity in their marriage.

3. Shared struggle. Perhaps it makes sense to find someone to hold you accountable in areas in which you struggle but they do not. But who better to help you toe the line than someone who needs the same encouragement? When your accountability partner struggles in the same area you do, he likely understands the temptation and knows intimately the signs of weakness and the weight of consequences. The shared struggle can be a shared incentive.

The success of 12-step programs is due in part to sponsorship relationships. Sponsors may be people further down the road of recovery, but they always understand the struggle firsthand. Who better to hold you accountable in daily Bible reading than someone who also needs to be asked about his personal time with God? Who better to hold someone accountable in struggles with morality than someone else who knows firsthand the dangers of the sin?

The Why

Dozens of biblical mandates and illustrations come to mind when considering our need for accountable relationships. None are quite as obvious as the wisdom of Solomon in Ecclesiastes and of James in the New Testament.

"Two are better than one because they have a good reward for their efforts. For if either falls, his companion can lift him up; but pity the one who falls without another to lift him up. Also, if two lie down together, they can keep warm; but how can one person alone keep warm? And if somebody overpowers one person, two can resist him. A cord of three strands is not easily broken."—**Ecclesiastes 4:9-12**

"Therefore, confess your sins to one another and pray for one another, so that you may be healed. The urgent request of a righteous person is very powerful in its effect."—**James 5:16**

The How

So how do you do accountability? Here are some steps to get you started on a successful road to healthy accountability.

1. Identify an accountability partner. Both parties must agree to be honest about struggles and to sharing the load of carrying another brother.

2. Select the frequency and methodology of your accountability relationship. Decide whether to meet weekly face to face or have several phone check-in times. Determine a method for outside communication.

3. Agree on honesty and confidentiality. Both parties must agree to be honest and to keep what is shared completely confidential in order to build and maintain trust.

4. Pray for one another. James said that confession is only part of the process. The other half is prayer, the most powerful medium for the faithful Christian.

5. Spur one another on toward Christ. The writer of Hebrews discouraged us from abandoning our gatherings with other believers (Heb. 10:25) but to instead encourage one another toward love and good deeds. Accountability shouldn't ever be just about that from which we abstain. It should also be about the values we work to incorporate into daily Christlike living.

Done right and given the proper place in our lives, accountability can prove to be the most mutually beneficial relationship in our lives. Any covenant relationship where people are honest about sin and committed to prayer is bound to enjoy the favor of God and the success of following Christ better every day.

Courage to Keep Commitments

A movie-release curriculum *Honor Begins at Home: The COURAGEOUS Bible Study* (item 005371686, fall 2011) can take men or couples deeper into concepts of this Bible study. Through this follow-up, men can grow in courage to keep commitments to God, their spouses, and their children as they walk "doubly accountable" to God and other believers. *The Resolution for Men* and *The Resolution for Women* are accompanying resources.

Leader Notes
Small-Group Quick Tips

1. Distribute the responsibility.
As a leader, the temptation is always to do everything personally; that quickly leads to frustration. Your main focus is to prepare the lesson in advance and prioritize the most important aspects during class discussion. Divvy maintenance tasks such as keeping track of attendance, prayer request follow-up, and refreshment sign-ups. In group meetings, ask different learners to read Scripture and sections of content and to lead out in group discussion.

2. Make the group a safe place.
Remind your group weekly as you engage in open discussion about the sensitivity of things people may share. Keep confidentiality and respect in focus.

3. Set the pace.
As a leader, you set the pace for your group. Your willingness to share and be transparent will have a direct impact on others' willingness to do the same. Your advance preparation and commitment to start and end on time will influence the group's direction. Your desire to stay on task and not chase rabbits will indicate what is appropriate and inappropriate in terms of group dynamics.

4. Be comfortable with silent moments and unanswered questions.
Often silence creates discomfort for a leader who may feel pressure to fill the awkwardness by talking more. As a leader, be OK with long pauses. Sometimes this is just an indication that the question has warranted more thought.

Some people may present difficult life challenges. Often they aren't looking for answers as much as a listening ear. Be sensitive but guide conversations to stay focused. Sometimes you may only recognize the difficulty of the situation and acknowledge the need to seek the Lord when answers are not clear.

5. Pray for your group members.
Oswald Chambers has said, "Prayer does not fit us for the greater work; prayer is the greater work."[1] How you commit to praying for your group is much more

valuable than how well you lead your group. In fact, how well you lead will be a direct reflection of how well you pray for the people in your group.

Commit to pray for the people God has entrusted to you, that they will:
- have eyes that are open to see God move
- have ears that hear the Word and commit to doing what it says
- genuinely repent of sin as the Holy Spirit convicts them through God's Word
- grow spiritually and begin to develop a daily intimate walk with the Lord
- make wise choices
- be committed to the group study
- live lives of integrity in their homes, communities, and places of work
- lead their children well
- be committed to their spouses
- trust Christ in any and all circumstances of life
- be free from temptation and the attacks of the enemy
- take on the full armor of God as both their defense and offense in the spiritual battles they face
- love God supremely and love others well

Optional Group Icebreakers

My Story

Ask learners to recount a significant moment in their lives using ideas from the following list. If you have couples in your group, you may want to ask them to share together the story of how they met and married.

To whom are you married? How did you meet?
What do you do? How did you choose that career?
What are your kids' names? How and why did you choose those names?
Where are you from? How and why did you or your family move here?
Who are your parents? What do or did they do in life?
Who are your siblings? Where do you fall in birth order? Who were you closest to growing up? Who are you closest to now?[2]

Snapshots

Help people get a glimpse of who you really are by writing or drawing snap-shots of yourself and telling your group the most interesting one(s). Depending on time and the number of people, complete one or more statements.

A time:
I was really happy ...
I took a big chance and it paid off ...
I toughed it out and accomplished a big goal ...
I was really embarrassed ...
I really chickened out ...
I was in a rut ...

My Stock Market

How many people hold stock in your life? How many invest in you? Who would suffer most if the "company of your life" filed for bankruptcy? Who would benefit most if your stock soared?

You have been given 1,000 shares. Indicate how this stock is currently distrib-uted and who owns how many shares of you:[3]

Spouse	_____	Shares
Children	_____	Shares
Parents	_____	Shares
Friends	_____	Shares
Workplace	_____	Shares
Other	_____	Shares

1. Taken from *My Utmost for His Highest* by Oswald Chambers. © 1935 by Dodd Mead & Co., renewed © 1963 by the Oswald Chambers Publications Assn., Ltd., and is used by permis-sion of Discovery House Publishers, Box 3566, Grand Rapids MI 49501. All rights reserved. Available from the Internet: *http://www.myutmost.org/10/1017.html*
2. Adapted from *Icebreakers and Heartwarmers: 101 Ways to Kick Off and End Meetings* by Steve Sheely (Nashville, TN: Serenity House Publishers, 1998), 67.
3. Ibid., 77.

Follow-Up Resources

COURAGEOUS

- *Honor Begins at Home: The COURAGEOUS Bible Study* (fall 2011 release, member, item 005371686; DVD leader kit, item 005325609) Eight-week study can serve as impetus for starting men's accountability groups and be used with movie
- *Courageous Living; The Resolution for Men/The Resolution for Women* (pp. 61,64)
- *http://www.LifeWay.com/Courageous, http://www.courageousthemovie.com*
- Also visit *www.dayspring.com/courageous* for additional resources.

PARENTING

- Life Truths Small Group Curriculum
  http://www.lifeway.com/article/165133/; http://parent2parent.ning.com/
- All Pro Dad: *http://www.allprodad.com/*
- *The Parent Adventure: Preparing Your Children for a Lifetime with God* (7 sessions: member: item 005181385; DVD leader kit, item 005126524)
- *Raising Girls and Boys: The Art of Understanding Their Differences* (October 2011 release; 6 sessions: member, item 005260397; DVD leader kit, item 005324579)
- *HomeLife* magazine See monthly "Wise Guys" section just for men. To interact with other parents, go to the blog *http://homelifemagazine.ning.com/*
- *ParentLife* magazine (available monthly; also quarterly bundles and subscriptions) To interact with other parents, go to the blog *http://blogs.lifeway.com/blog/parentlife/*

MEN'S MINISTRY

- *Game Plan for Life* (Vols. 1 and 2)
  http://www.lifeway.com/product/005259409; www.gameplanforlife.com
  (Vol. 1: 6 sessions; member, item 005259409; DVD leader kit, item 005269065;
  Vol. 2: 6 sessions; member, item 005371575; DVD leader kit, item 005371574)
- Every Man Ministries: *http://www.everymanministries.com/*
- Iron Sharpens Iron: *http://www.ironsharpensiron.net/*
- *Stand Firm* magazine, a Christian devotional magazine for men

Dare to Live Courageously

Be strong and courageous, all you who put your hope in the LORD. —Psalm 31:24 (HCSB)

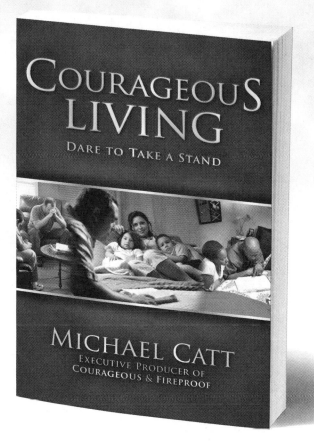

Available Sept. 2011
LifeWay.com/Courageous

If you like the changes in your home now,

imagine what could happen if you go even deeper.

The 8-week *Honor Begins at Home: The COURAGEOUS Bible Study* will take individuals and small groups deeper into biblical truths for a godly family, exploring topics such as redeeming your history, walking with integrity, winning and blessing the hearts of your children, and more.

Each session uses movie clips to engage people in discussion. And daily readings from *The Resolution for Men* and *The Resolution for Women* will help you connect with God and His best plan for your family.

This study will be available exclusively at LifeWay Christian Stores on October 1, 2011. Or you can visit www.lifeway.com/courageous or call 800.458.2772 to order.

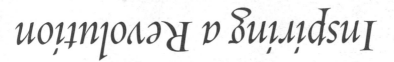

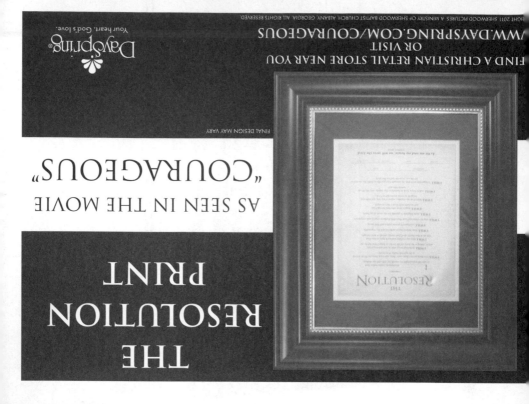